All six of the Tribunal members cleared their throats again, but only one spoke.

"We, uhm, we made a mistake," the one who looked like she was close to two-hundred years old said. "A mistake regarding how we handled your case forty years ago."

Endora barely locked her jaw before it fell open. She stared at each and every witch in turn before snarling, "That's the understatement of the last four decades."

The spokeswitch continued as if Endora hadn't interrupted, "An error of potentially catastrophic proportions."

"This sounds like a bad episode of *Mission Impossible*," Endora cracked.

"Ms. Bast," the tall, thin old witch intoned, "we are deadly serious. The situation is perilous...You *must* help us."

"Why risk my life for you?" Endora shook her head in amazement.

"We are on the cusp of Armageddon," said the Head Magistrate. "And you're only one of two who can do anything about it."

At his words, Endora flinched as if she'd been shot. Her legs turned rubbery.

"That one of two part," she managed to say weakly, "can you elaborate on who the other one is?"

"Marcus Morion," the group's mouthpiece supplied.

"I was afraid you'd say that." Endora had to suffer the indignity of fainting for the very first time in her life.

Right in front of half the Tribunal.

To the citizens of New Orleans and the Gulf Coast.
May you rise from the devastation of the hurricanes like a
phoenix from the ashes—strong, and again ready to
celebrate life as only you can.

Acknowledgments

In order to write this book, I consulted many sources, especially for particular horoscopes, and specific spells and incantations. These sources are: Saffi Crawford and Geraldine Sullivan's *The Power of Birthdays, Stars, & Numbers;* Marguerite Elsbeth's *Crystal Medicine*; Diana Ferguson's *The Magickal Year*; Rosemary Ellen Guiley's *The Encyclopedia of Witches & Witchcraft*, 2nd edition; Carol K. Mack and Dinah Mack's *A Field Guide to Demons;* Richard Alan Miller's *The Magical and Ritual Use of Herbs*; Ellen Cannon Reed's *The Witches Qabala*; Marian Singer's *The Everything Wicca and Witchcraft Book*; and *The Witches' Almanac,* Spring 2005 to Spring 2006 edition.

Any liberties taken with the information these books contain is strictly the fault of this author.

Other Books by Laurie C. Kuna

Some Practical Magic

Writing as Laurie Carroll

A War of Hearts
Fate's Fortune (Coming in 2006)

"Tex" —

That Old Black Magic

You're the best!!

***

Laurie C. Kuna

ImaJinn
Books

Love + Magic (and
contracts!)

Laurie

02/06

That Old Black Magic
Published by ImaJinn Books

ISBN: 1-933417-76-5

10 9 8 7 6 5 4 3 2 1

PUBLISHER'S NOTE:
This book is a work of fiction. Names, characters, places and incidents are products of the author's imagination or are used fictitiously. Any resemblance to actual events or locales or persons, living or dead, is entirely coincidental.

Books are available at quantity discounts when used to promote products or services. For information please write to: Marketing Division, ImaJinn Books, P.O. Box 545, Canon City, CO 81212, or call toll free 1-877-625-3592.

Cover design by Patricia Lazarus

ImaJinn Books, a division of ImaJinn
P.O. Box 545, Canon City, CO 81212
Toll Free: 1-877-625-3592
http://www.imajinnbooks.com

Prologue

She'd been in his dreams every night for forty years.

Actually, if he was brutally honest, and he had been of late, he'd admit she'd crossed his mind at least once every day of that time, too.

Seeking answers, he shuffled an intricate deck of tarot cards and laid several out in a Celtic Cross spread. The first card he placed in the middle of the table, putting the second card sideways across the first. The third went directly above the two-card cross, the fourth directly below. To the left of the cross he placed the fifth card. The sixth went to the right. The seventh card he positioned to the right of the entire six-card cross, level with the number four card. Cards eight, nine and ten were lined up in ascending order above the seventh card.

Then he studied the spread intently.

The King of Wands was upright in the first position. His current circumstance. So, he was handling the people around him with strength and compassion. *True,* he thought wryly. *I'm just a compassionate sort of guy.*

His light mood was instantly engulfed by resignation when he considered the card lying crosswise over the King of Wands. The Queen of Swords. That fit her completely. Amazing wit, inventiveness and grace. A strong ally. But the disturbing aspect of the Queen of Swords was her ultimate need to put her own interests first. He had no doubt this would be true, and he wasn't certain he was ready for that.

Finding the Two of Swords in position three made his wry smile return. The best he could do at present was balance all the aspects of his life as skillfully as he could manage. *Guess that's going to take some doing, given what's coming up.*

The next two cards changed the tone of the reading. The Wheel of Fortune and The Tower. A negative situation over which he had no control, and the harbinger of bad luck, respectively.

Cards six through nine continued on the theme of unrest, danger and change. *Very little to misinterpret here,* he concluded. *Cut and dried.*

In the tenth and final position lay the Death card, reversed.

It represented major changes for which he was ill-prepared but which were nonetheless entirely necessary. Change. Renewal. Possibly in a real sense death itself. Yet the latter really held little fear for him. Being what he was, he was philosophical about all aspects of the spectral universe. Physical death was just a shifting of energy on the metaphysical plane. Of course he was now fifty-nine, not twenty, and even though witches aged at about a third of the speed that humans did, he'd matured tremendously over those years. He liked the body he now occupied, yet he knew eventually it would break down and his light, the core of his being, would take some other form.

Right now, he had a bigger problem to worry about than dying, though.

She was coming.

And that scared the hades out of him.

One

"You've got to be kidding me!"

Scowling, Endora Bast studied the directions the on-line map service had produced for her. 142 Rowan Boulevard, New Orleans, Louisiana. The corner of Rowan and Rood. This was the place.

But, even in her most outrageous imaginings, it wasn't what she expected.

Conveniently, there was an open parking space on Rowan right across from the address. She pulled in, letting her vintage '65 Plymouth Satellite idle while she assessed the situation.

"Suicide Prevention Salon," read the garishly painted sign stretching across the entire shopfront. "No One Dyes by Her Own Hand Here."

She snorted a half-laugh. *Only in the Big Easy,* she thought wryly.

That was likely the last humorous thing she'd get to enjoy for a while, though. And, since she had been summoned to this address and the sign said "Walk-ins Welcome," Endora shut off the engine and got out.

But as she approached the door, the hair on her nape rose.

The corner shop's bizarre name notwithstanding, something wasn't right. The building fairly hummed with paranormal energy, at an unusually high level even for a city as haunted as New Orleans. Her hand halfway to the doorknob, she froze, quickly reviewing her options.

Zero. I have zero options.

A subpoena of sorts had arrived two days before at her home in Salem, Massachusetts, her most recent stop in a nomadic four-decade stretch. During most of those years she had worked as business manager and familiar to Cassandra Hathorne, known to a world of fans as The Kitchen Witch. But known to Endora as a truly good witch and her best friend.

Endora prayed to every supernatural entity she knew that what was about to happen wouldn't destroy that relationship. Or everything she knew and loved. Including herself.

She had been summoned to present herself in two days' time at this address. Nothing more had been written, but she knew the meaning behind what few words there were. Time was almost up for her.

Curiosity supposedly killed the cat, she thought glumly.

And since I've little choice, I might as well test that theory.

With a hand that barely shook, she reached for the handle of the shop's front door, opened it, and stepped inside.

The beauty parlor looked fairly typical, except that she was literally engulfed by enough paranormal energy to power the entire Eastern Seaboard nonstop for a month. Her whole body tingled from the charged air, and she wondered exactly what that energy had done to her stylish coif. After all, she had meticulously put herself together for this command performance, and her look always started with outstanding hair. Hair that, at this time, was completely outstanding, as every strand of it had risen from its normal neat position on her head and was trying to see how far it could stretch before coming out at the roots. It was all Endora could do not to turn around and dive right through the plate-glass window on the way to her car, which she would then drive like a bat out of hell as far away from this place as possible.

She throttled that impulse, refusing to be intimidated by this staged display of authority, especially since she detested every one of its authoritative sources. No one here meant anything to her. And threats had to have relevance to have power.

The moment she decided on fight rather than flight, her hair settled to its original stylishness. And she was grateful to realize she hadn't lost bladder control during her first moments of panic, either. Thank the goddess for small favors.

Deliberately, she raised a brow for her favorite haughty look, then scanned the room with a gaze calculated to project the trademark bored aloofness of her feline species. It would have worked completely on any other assembled group. However, since her audience today was six of the thirteen witches of the Tribunal, it fell a bit short. Not totally, though, as her open defiance caused them all a bit of discomfort, if the drop in paranormal energy levels and the increase in feet shuffling and throat clearing was any indication. And that was gratifying.

Score one for the underdog. Or, in my case, the undercat.

The half-dozen Tribunal members stood directly in front of a huge display of hair products, and Endora recognized several she used herself. She briefly wondered how the elders would react if she walked over and took some samples from the shelves. They'd probably vaporize her where she stood, which would solve the problem of her summons. But since she was not suicidal at this point in her life, she quelled the impulse. Knowing the fine art of pushing insubordination as far as she could without consequences, she made a calculated retreat. Strolling over to a salon chair, she sat and draped her legs over one chair arm. Then, fixing her best cat stare on the group, waited for them to make the next move.

All six of the witches cleared their throats again, but only one spoke.

"We, uhm, we made a mistake," the one who looked like she was close to two hundred years old said.

This time, Endora's brow shot up in genuine surprise. An admission of culpability from the Tribunal? Unheard of. "I'm confused."

"A mistake regarding how we handled your case forty years ago."

Completely blind-sided by that declaration, Endora barely locked her jaw before it fell open. She stared at each and every witch in turn before snarling, "That's the understatement of the last four decades."

The spokeswitch continued as if Endora hadn't interrupted, "An error of potentially catastrophic proportions."

"Fire whoever writes your dialogue," Endora cracked. Sarcasm saved her from succumbing to the undignified urge to pace. And to tear out clumps of her hair. "This sounds like a bad episode of *Mission Impossible*."

"Ms. Bast," the tall, thin old witch intoned, "we are deadly serious. The situation is perilous, and the Tribunal is prepared to reinstate all your powers and remove the sanctions from your name if you succeed."

Endora's gaze snapped to the speaker. "*If* I succeed, I get my powers back? I'm supposed to fix this *perilous situation* without full powers?" She laughed incredulously.

"We're afraid so," the spokeswitch replied gravely.

Pacing was now the only option. Endora rose from the salon chair, but the confined space and the need to negotiate among workstations kept her from putting much distance between herself and the Tribunal. "Have you taken to smoking henbane at coven get-togethers? Because that is the most idiotic, drug-induced proposal I've ever heard."

A short, squat witch who reminded her of a troll said condescendingly, "You've no need to be insulting, Miss Bast."

Endora stopped her restless stalking, turned toward him,

and ramped up her vaunted cat stare. "Pardon me, but I can't help thinking that, with thirteen half-wits on this tribunal, the governing body of the entire witch community has only six and a half brains among them. Three of which are in this room, and apparently having seizures."

Face nearly purple with rage, troll-witch invaded Endora's personal space. "Now see here, that's insubordination!"

Although only five-five, she towered over him. And increased her advantage by stepping even closer, forcing him to look up at her. "Buddy, you haven't even seen what I consider insubordinate."

"Enough." With a flick of her finger, the eldest witch sent a burst of energy between the two combatants that knocked them each back a step. "We have no choice but to ask you, Miss Bast. And you *must* help us."

"Why risk my life for you?" Endora shook her head in amazement before turning her stare on the spokeswitch. "You convicted me of sabotaging a Tribunal operation. As a result, you reduced my powers by three-quarters, ordered me into forty years of servitude as a familiar, and removed my name from every witches' registry in the world. One third of my life has been spent in limbo, and now you think admitting your error justifies asking for my help? What happened to me was not a *mistake*. It was a complete miscarriage of justice."

She felt her face flush, knew she was ranting, but didn't rein in her temper. "And, to get my full powers back, I have to succeed at this mission? I don't give a fat rat's ass if we're on the cusp of Armageddon. I'm not helping you with your little crisis-of-the-week project."

"Ironic you should put it that way, Ms. Bast," the Head Magistrate stated soberly. Apparently, he had finally found his voice. "We are indeed on the cusp of Armageddon. And you're only one of two who can do anything about it."

At his words, Endora flinched as if she'd been shot. Her legs turned rubbery, and she found herself sitting abruptly in the nearest styling chair. That said chair was occupied by a member of the Tribunal meant nothing to her. After all, she was a cat. Cats sat in whatever lap they wanted to. Or not.

"That one of two part," she managed to say weakly, "can you elaborate on who the other one is?"

"Marcus Morion," the group's mouthpiece supplied.

"I was afraid you'd say that." Endora had to suffer the indignity of fainting for the very first time in her life.

Right in front of half the Tribunal.

* * *

Marcus Morion subtly scratched beneath the colorful gypsy scarf covering most of his hair. Sweat trickled down toward his collar, adding to his inexplicable irritation and setting off alarms in his already aching head.

Take it easy, buddy, he reminded himself. *This, too, shall pass…As soon as I get away from this goddess-forsaken city.*

Although it was the last week in October, the weather was sticky in Dallas. Not for the first time, Marcus cursed being there. The only thing he liked about the city was that it hosted his current employer, Medieval Festivals, Incorporated. For which he played Marco the Magnificent, King of the Gypsies. This latest persona, made more believable by his dark hair, black eyes and olive complexion, was a variation on the theme of his life for the past forty years. Moving from town to town, changing identities with every new location. He had knocked around Europe for over fifteen years, but finally succumbed to a bone-deep longing and returned to America. To circus sideshows, state fairs, and now renaissance and medieval festivals. Just a higher-class version of the con he'd run for two-thirds of his life.

A sweet looking middle-aged woman approached his booth, followed closely by a Stetson-wearing cowboy who appeared to be years older. Marcus knew personally that looks could completely deceive. He'd bet his next paycheck the cowboy had gotten his leathery skin from hours in the brutal Texas sun, giving a mistaken impression of well-advanced age.

"I've heard tell y'all do fortunes," the woman said in a soft drawl.

He was seated behind the ticket counter of his booth; nevertheless, Marcus put his right hand over his heart and executed a half bow. "Marco the Magnificent, at your service, Madame," he said in his best fake gypsy accent. "How may I be of service to such a lovely lady as yourself?"

Obviously delighted, the woman tittered softly, then indicated the cowboy with a tilt of her head. "My husband, Daryl, doesn't believe this seeing the future stuff."

"Waste of money, ya ask me," Daryl growled. He leveled a glare at Marcus that would have bored through titanium. "But seein' as how it's Lorena's birthday, I said I'd bring her here."

As Lorena glanced adoringly at Daryl, Marcus shot him a conspiratorial wink. "And we men must do all we can to please our ladies, no?" He looked to Lorena, whose attention he again had, then gestured to the brightly-colored placards decorating the booth. According to their pictures and words, Marco the Magnificent could predict the future via crystal ball, tarot cards, astrology, numerology, tea leaves, palmistry and runes.

"So, my lady Lorena, how do you wish to have your fortune told?"

"Don't y'all do that ooo-wee-gee-ah board thing?" Lorena asked.

High rollers in every gambling establishment in the world would have killed for the poker face Marcus had, so he was confident his revulsion did not show on his face. "Actually, the Ouija board is more for contacting loose spirits," he said in as offhand a manner as he could manage. "Something I don't recommend any amateur do." *Or any honest practitioner of the magickal arts, for that matter,* Marcus thought grimly. *Dangerous black magic, that.*

Lorena's face fell momentarily until her eyes lit on another placard. "What are runes?"

Just the next step up from a Ouija board for me. He glanced at Lorena and Daryl. She looked totally fascinated and he completely uninterested. "Well, let me explain. Runes are an ancient form of forecasting, Germanic in origin. In a reading, the order in which the runes are cast is important, as is the symbol on each one that is cast and the position it's in when revealed."

Lorena turned to Daryl. "What do ya think, darlin'?"

"Yer birthday, yer choice."

Eyes dancing with anticipation, Lorena turned to Marcus. "The runes, please."

Marcus felt his heart sink. He was already sweaty, irritable, out of sorts. Now this. Surprisingly bitter thoughts filled his head. *Why couldn't you just stick to form, Lorena, and pick a common method? Tea leaves...crystal ball...palm reading...Oh no, you're a risk taker. Want to live on the edge, have a fortune told the way none of your bridge club members would ever think of.*

"Runes it is," he said with fake cheerfulness. Smiling at the couple, he gestured to the small room attached to the booth. "Step into my reading room." He winked at Lorena. "Your husband is welcome to sit in with us. Sometimes, having a skeptic as a witness increases the satisfaction of saying 'I told you so.'"

Daryl grunted but followed his wife into the permanent wooden structure and pulled out a chair to seat her before taking the chair at her left.

Marcus turned to the wall behind his seat and opened the black-lacquered cabinet containing all of his props. Reaching inside, he discreetly flipped a switch to start the ankle-level cooling system. It blew a cool mist across the floor, lending an air of eerie authenticity to the proceedings. Next, he switched on a light that centered directly over the table, casting everything else in shadow. Once seated across from his customers, he spread out his black rune cloth and smoothed it over the tabletop.

"What's that circle on the middle of the cloth for?"

Marcus smiled at Lorena. "It's a target, of sorts. Every set of runes has at least twenty-five pieces. Mine has twenty-eight because I prefer to use runes many others don't. To do a reading, I pour them all onto this cloth, and then choose only from the ones that fall inside the circle."

Eyes twinkling, she turned to her husband. "Isn't this excitin', darlin'?"

"If you say so."

Lorena swatted Daryl playfully on the arm before turning her full attention to the runes.

"Now, Lorena," Marcus intoned in his most mysterious gypsy voice, "concentrate on a question you want answered. Ready?"

When she nodded eagerly, Marcus opened the drawstring closure on a black velvet bag and spilled the contents onto the table. Choosing a stone within the circle, he placed it facedown on the cloth. The second stone went beside it on the right. The third to the right of the second. He drew the fourth stone and placed it directly above the second, now middle, stone. The fifth stone went directly below the second, establishing a cross pattern.

"Still visualizing it?" Marcus was amused to note Lorena's eyes were closed tight in concentration. She said nothing, just nodded emphatically. "I start the reading by turning over the center stone. It represents the present, and the problem or issue as well."

He revealed the first rune, then turned over the second.

"Hades!" The epithet escaped his mouth before he even

realized it. Both Lorena and Daryl jumped as if they'd been shot, but Marcus quickly recovered and smiled his most charming, reassuring smile. "Beg pardon. It's just that this is an excellent starting rune, and I'm frankly surprised."

"Ain't that hell?"

Marcus looked directly at Daryl. "Certainly, sir. However, it's customary to invoke that location when reading runes." *And if you believe that, I've got potions guaranteed to assure world peace. And I'll sell them to you for a song.*

Marcus turned over each rune in turn, deliberately leaving the one in the fifth position face down. And he deliberately didn't look at the stones. This was not a casting for Lorena. It was for him. Concentrating hard, he let his paranormal senses envelop the couple across the table. And then he saw it, or rather read it in Daryl's thoughts. He smiled in relief and looked up at Lorena, glad he had an excuse not to look at the rune stones.

"You're going on a trip," he said brightly. Then he winced for effect and turned to Daryl. "Um, she didn't know this, did she?" The cowboy shook his head. "Do you want me to spoil the surprise?"

Daryl snorted a laugh, then leaned back in the chair and crossed his arms over his chest. "Take a crack at it."

With a nod, Marcus continued. Pretending to stare at the runes, he tuned his senses to Daryl. "I see a cruise ship. To Mexico. A week's resort stay, then the cruise ends in San Diego. You fly back to Dallas from there." He glanced at the dumbfounded Lorena, but it was Daryl's expression that made him want to laugh aloud. The cowboy's mouth was hanging open. Marcus allowed himself a polite smile. "How'd I do, Daryl?"

"I'll be damned," Daryl muttered, shaking his head. "I'll be damned."

Marcus turned to Lorena. "Apparently, I was close."

He was still smiling minutes later when he walked the couple out and wished them a safe and happy trip. He hadn't cast into the future to see whether it would go smoothly, but he wouldn't have told them the outcome unless going would endanger their lives.

His smile faltered when he turned back to the table. The slight shaking of his hand as he reached to turn over the last rune had him cursing inventively in several languages. But there was no stopping Fate. He read all five stones, then sighed heavily.

Endora Bast would charge back into his life very soon. In fact, within the next few days. He knew without looking at the rune in the first position–which indicated a past event causing a present situation–that their misadventure of forty years before was the reason she sought him out. He had thought by ignoring the Tribunal's summons to go to New Orleans, he could avoid revisiting that painful time. Clearly, that wasn't the case. The woman he had loved and lost all those years ago was about to reopen deep, unhealed wounds. Just by showing up. He had no idea how he was going to deal with her, but there was absolutely nothing he could do to prevent her arrival.

The runes didn't lie.

* * *

"Cassie, I need your help."

The tall, dark-haired object of Endora's plea jumped nearly a foot, throwing her hands up in a gesture of protection. The bowl of orange Halloween frosting she'd been holding went flying in one direction, the spatula to apply the icing went the other way. In a split-second it looked like a balloon containing shredded pumpkins had burst in the kitchen. Orange frosting was splattered everywhere.

Face a pasty white, Cassandra Hathorne-Sandor spun to face her familiar, sitting in cat form on her kitchen table. "By the goddess, Dora! You should know better than to sneak up on a pregnant woman. You scared me half to death."

"I'm so sorry, Cassie." Guilt swamped Endora. "I didn't stop to think about—"

"My water broke!"

"Oh sweet, unholy hades!" Sudden panic completely replaced guilt. Endora shape-shifted from feline form back into her mortal body so fast she got dizzy. "What should I do? Where's Mick? How far's the hospital?" She couldn't breathe. The hair on the back of her neck stood straight up, and she looked frantically around as if Cassie's husband was there and she just couldn't see him. Then she reached for Cassie's arm. "Shouldn't you lie down?"

"Not *that* water, nitwit." The witch's dark eyes sparkled with suppressed mirth. "I must have shot off some stray energy when I jumped. Burned a hole completely through that jug beside the sink."

"Oh. I knew that." Endora's gaze swung to the counter. On it sat a plastic gallon jug, water streaming out both sides via

two neat holes through its center. Abruptly, the puddles and
spatters covering counter and floor contracted into a stream
that reversed back into the jug. The holes closed up behind the
stream.

"Neat, Cass," Endora approved enthusiastically, panic gone
and hair starting to lie back down. "A year ago, you wouldn't
have even thought to try that spell."

Cassandra Hathorne, also known as the domestic diva the
Kitchen Witch, laughed. "A year ago, I probably *couldn't* have
done it."

"Been practicing?"

"Sure." Cassie flicked her wrist. The bowl, spatula and
globs of scattered icing all returned to their prelaunch places—
icing in bowl, bowl and spatula in Cassie's hands. She set them
on the table and reached two-handed to rub her lower back.
"But I had to accept myself for what I am before all the practice
started paying off."

"Guess that's what love, marriage, and impending
motherhood will do." Sensing her friend was tired beyond what
showed on her face, Endora plopped into a kitchen chair, happy
when Cassie followed her lead. "So how are the twins doing?
Decided on names yet?"

A snap of Cassie's fingers produced two glasses of milk,
one of which she pushed across the table to Endora. She took
a big gulp from her own. "Mick wants Bubba and Louie, but
I'm holding out for Cruella and Maleficent."

When Cassie laughed uproariously, Endora knew her eyes
must have popped wide open over that declaration.

"Gotcha, Familiar," she gloated. "Hooked like a fish.
Cruella...Bubba and Louie. Ha!"

Although she loved her dearly, Endora hated having Cassie
put one over on her. But she supposed pregnant friends should
be allowed some fun, so she merely said truthfully, "My game's
not at its best right now."

Cassie had raised her glass to drink, but lowered it
immediately. "I seem to recall, milliseconds before I tried to
launch myself into orbit, your asking me for help." She studied
her friend through intense, caramel-colored eyes. "Your
summons to New Orleans?"

Although Endora dreaded revealing the lurid details,
withholding information from her best friend and employer of
nearly forty years wasn't even the choice behind Door Number
Fifty.

"I've got until the Winter Solstice to fix a bit of a problem."

Cassie cocked her head. "Define 'problem.' And keep in mind I know you're the mistress of understatement, so don't downplay this."

Endora sighed, wondering how to start. The situation was complex and desperate. And intensely personal. "I...ah...Well, it's a little bit..." She stuttered to a halt.

And was spared the embarrassment of continued floundering when lightning cracked and smoke billowed through the kitchen.

When the pyrotechnics subsided, Medusa Morlock stood in the middle of the room. Her flowing black robe was covered in random blotches of color, so that the burnt-oranges, yellows, reds and browns seemed to form a pattern that actually moved on the material like swirling autumn leaves.

"Mom!" Cassie rose to kiss her mother. "You always know how to make an entrance."

Medusa returned the embrace, then shot the sleeves of her robe and said imperiously. "Yes, I do, don't I?" She turned to hug Endora, who had also risen to greet her. "So, Cassandra, how are my grandbabies, Huey and Louie?"

"Mom, we've decided on Lewis and Clark."

Medusa winked at Endora. "Why not Jekyll and Hyde?"

"Only if one is born a doctor." Cassie gestured to the table. "Have a seat, Mom. Your timing couldn't be better. Endora needs some help."

"Some help is an understatement." Endora shook her head. "I need a miracle."

Medusa took a seat. "Well, let's see what we can do."

With a snap of her fingers, Cassie produced a huge plate of cookies, glasses, a gallon of milk, and a half gallon of apple cider. Plates and napkins arranged themselves in front of the three of them. "I vote for some snacks while we discuss Dora's problem."

"Snacks are good." Endora forced a cheerful tone as she flopped back into her chair. Her stomach felt like it had lead donuts in it.

"No need to put on a brave face, dear." Medusa patted Endora's shoulder. "If you weren't worried, you wouldn't be here seeking aid. Tell us what you need."

With a helpless shrug, Endora swallowed so hard that if she'd had an Adam's apple, it would have popped out like a goiter. "Get comfortable, preggo-witch and grandma-witch-to be. It's a long story." Endora propped her elbows on the table and leaned on them. "Remember that black magic circle back in sixty-five? In Colorado?"

"Didn't the circle leader kill all of the members?" Cassie asked. "A rogue witch named Ash something or other."

"Obsidian Ashmedai." Medusa practically hissed the name. "An evil practitioner of the darkest arts. I always thought he was the spawn of Hecate."

"You knew him, Mom?"

Grimacing, Medusa looked at Cassie. "I never had the displeasure of actually meeting him, but knew of him. I served the customary fifty-year term on the Tribunal and had left it only a few years before he came on the scene." Her daughter's look turned blank and then embarrassed, and she patted Cassie's hand. "That was during your rebellious period, dear, when you didn't associate much with your family."

"I never realized." Cassie blushed furiously. "I'm so ashamed of myself."

Medusa waved away her discomfort. "Children must seek their own paths. At the time, you were traveling in a different direction." But her expression hardened when she said to Endora, "I knew from the start, as did many former Magistrates, that he was trouble. In Hebrew lore, Ashmedai is the undisputed king of demons. The name literally translates as evil spirit. In Christian lore, he's known as Sammael. Coincidentally, that's his middle name. Obsidian Sammael Ashmedai. The most evil witch I've ever known."

Endora and Cassie shared a startled look.

Cassie switched from drinking milk to drinking cider. Then she sat back in her chair and asked her mother, "Why didn't anyone do something to stop him?"

Medusa gave a frustrated snort. "I and several former Tribunal members tried to have Ashmedai's magic severely restricted. But we were blocked by three very powerful Magistrates on the Tribunal at the time."

"But aren't they supposed to protect *all* of witchkind?" Endora's anger at the witches' governing body neared boiling. "If he was so sinister, why didn't they act against him?"

"I was just about to ask the same question, Mom."

"Witches, like all mortals, are susceptible to pettiness," Medusa said quietly. "Pride, greed, hatred. Whatever motivated those three Magistrates to abandon both common sense and caution is anyone's guess." With a snap of her fingers, she sent her plate and silverware floating toward the dishwasher, which opened to accept them.

Something niggled in the back of Endora's mind. "Are those obstructionists still around?"

"Only one. The other two died a number of years back. Separate incidents, and over a decade apart, but both were under mysterious circumstances."

The hair on Endora's nape stood on end. "Is the living one still a magistrate?"

"Unfortunately, Old Troll Face has five more years to serve." Medusa's gaze sharpened. "Endora, you're suddenly very pale."

It felt like a huge hairball was lodged in her throat. Clearing it, Endora forced a casual tone. "One of the magistrates I met in New Orleans looks like a troll. We didn't hit it off."

"Bald, several inches shorter than you? Beady black eyes?" Too stunned to speak, Endora merely nodded. Medusa appeared to be chewing a mouthful of lemons. "Arthur Morass, emphasis on the last three letters of his surname. A sufferer of 'little witch' syndrome if ever I've known one. Completely repulsive."

"For sure. He's like a Chihuahua," Endora said to Cassie, "a rat with attitude."

"I think I'll ask some discreet questions about dear old Arthur," Medusa stated. "He always championed Ashmedai."

"You said yourself this guy hadn't done anything suspicious up to the point he formed the circle," Cassie pointed out. "How did you know beforehand he was so evil?"

"Actions were not the issue." The elder witch leaned forward in her chair. "It was attitude. Deportment. He exudes an unctuous charisma." She sighed. "But that is long since in the past. The present is our critical concern right now. Endora, continue your story."

Two

"Hey, baby, I'm home!" Marcus opened the front door of the duplex he rented from Medieval Festivals, Inc. and braced for collision.

It was quick to come, as his housemate barreled down on him with the speed of a closing linebacker and leaped for his chest. Prepared, Marcus waited until contact was imminent, then turned sideways and met the flying mass of fur and muscle shoulder to shoulder.

The dog spun completely around in midair, landed four-footed in the entryway, and leaped again. This time, a well-placed hip to her shoulder spun her halfway in the other direction. Again grounded, she began her dance of welcome, which included thumping his legs with her enthusiastically wagging, bruise-inducing tail.

"Glenna, sit."

Immediately, the dog dropped to her haunches and offered a paw for shaking. Marcus accepted, then rubbed her muzzle and gave her a good scratching behind the ears.

"How's my best girl this afternoon?"

"She was terrorizing the neighborhood children again."

The fact that he never heard his neighbor's approach didn't surprise Marcus. "Hey, Mav. What's the story?"

Eripmav Alucard was a half-foot taller than Marcus, which made him about six-foot ten. Although he had broad shoulders and a narrow waist, he was so painfully thin he looked like the frame medieval knights had hung their chain mail on. A festival patron once described Mav as so skinny "he could sit in the shade of a barb-wire fence." Marcus considered that a fairly apt description of his friend and co-worker.

"Define 'terrorizing,'" Marcus said.

"She approached them with her normal friend-to-all enthusiasm and frightened them half to death," Mav answered slowly, in his customarily precise diction. "They ran away screaming."

Marcus glanced down at the dog. She hung her head. "Screaming, eh?"

"People are prejudiced against her because she's a pit bull," Mav stated. His black eyes sad, he looked at Glenna. "They see her and believe she'll attack them. Few think to look at her good qualities."

Marcus reached down to stroke the dog's dark-chocolate head. "Seems like all three of us are misunderstood around here, doesn't it, girl?"

Glenna licked his hand and stared at him in adoration, tail thumping slowly on the floor.

She had come a long way since Marcus had found her, half-starved and obviously abused, in a back alley in Texarkana, Texas eighteen months earlier. It had taken him several weeks and numerous mesmerism sessions to get the dog to calm down and settle in. Finally she adopted him as her own, although the strangest things spooked her. And she still slunk cautiously around any stocky, fair-haired man, especially if he was wearing a cowboy hat. Marcus figured if he ever ran into the guy—and he'd know who he was by his dark aura—he'd take him out. Getting off on hurting animals was beyond sick.

"I know pit bulls have a horrible rep," he said, giving Glenna's head a final pat before he straightened, "but she's the nicest dog I've ever had."

"Children tend to fear large dogs regardless of breed," Mav stated philosophically. "Especially when the dog is exuberant."

"You've got that right. I'd better make sure she's inside the fence in the back yard at all times." Marcus moved down the hallway to the kitchen, going straight to the refrigerator. He pulled out a longneck, then glanced at Mav, who'd sat down at the table. "Need a drink?"

"No. I have already quenched my thirst."

Marcus twisted off the cap, leaned back against the serving bar and took a long pull on his beer. He sighed in short-lived satisfaction before leveling a no-nonsense look at his neighbor. Voice low and serious, he stated, "Mav, my friend, we've got more critical things to worry about than kids who are irrationally scared of a dog. Trouble's coming, buddy. I've read it in every method of divination I know. It's going to arrive within seventy-two hours."

Surprise lit Mav's pale face. "In what form?"

"In the only form that's totally unpredictable. The female form." Marcus tipped back the bottle and drained it.

* * *

Medusa, a former Magistrate? Endora's hope grew stronger. This knowledge somehow made telling her story easier. "For his crimes against witchkind, Ashmedai should have lost his life. But the Tribunal screwed up, big time. All they did was strip him of his magic."

"But he killed every member of the cult. In cold blood." When Endora looked down at her plate, Cassie shot a startled glance at Medusa before whispering, "Oh Dora. He didn't kill them all. You're not just a shape-shifter, you're a witch. And you were there."

Under the others' intense scrutiny, Endora felt her face flame. "That's why I've got a problem."

Stunned silence greeted that statement. After a long pause, Medusa said firmly, "Leave nothing out, Dora."

Endora nodded, fighting back sudden tears as horrible memories resurfaced. White-knuckled, she squeezed her glass between both hands. "My dearest friend, Josephine Morris, was obsessed with Ashmedai. She joined his circle six months before the slaughter. I tried to talk her out of it, but we were both immature twenty-year-olds. Foolishly, stupidly romantic. She wouldn't listen. It was a total, fatal attraction.

"Five months after Josie joined, word leaked out that Ashmedai was brainwashing every member of the circle, eight covens of thirteen witches. Turning them to the black arts."

Cassie's expression held horrified fascination. "What did you do?"

"Contacted Josie telepathically. Warned her." Endora's sigh actually hurt her chest. "She made it clear she wouldn't leave voluntarily. So, I went to rescue her."

"But you couldn't get her out before that black-hearted bastard killed them all." Medusa's low tone was nonetheless fierce.

Endora stared at the wall and hardened her heart. To have any chance at success, she had to bury her grief until this challenge was over. Cassie and Medusa would respect that decision. And they would understand Endora's vendetta against the witch who'd killed Josie and one hundred and one other witches.

Smiling gently, Cassie covered Endora's hands with her own. "Keep squeezing, and you'll shatter my exclusive glassware. Then I won't have a full set until K-Mart has another sale."

That brought Endora a brief smile. She hated emotional displays, and Cassie knew that. Endora relaxed her grip. "What was I thinking?"

Cassie squeezed Endora's hands, then withdrew her own.

"How did you escape the slaughter?" Medusa asked.

Cheeks that flamed from embarrassment actually did feel hot, Endora concluded. But she couldn't hold back. "I was...occupied the night of the murders." One of Cassie's brows winged up. Medusa's mouth quirked in a slight grin. "Another cult member, a witch named Marcus Morion, and I sort of hit it off."

Cassie's brow rose even higher as Medusa's expression changed to a knowing smile. Neither of them said a word, just gazed directly at Endora.

She sighed. "You're going to make me spell it out for you, aren't you?"

"Well, confession is good for the soul." Cassie piously folded her hands as if in prayer.

"But since we're about as far from Catholic as anyone can get, you're just saying that to wring the lurid details out of me."

Cassie chuckled. Wickedly, Endora thought. "I'm enormously pregnant. Listening to my friends' prurient stories is as close as I'm getting to sex for quite a while. So have pity on me and spill your guts."

Endora took a huge gulp of milk before obliging. "Ever heard of cosmic twins?"

"Two people born at exactly the same time," Medusa supplied promptly.

"Marcus and I are cosmic twins." To head off the questions she saw in the other two's eyes, Endora continued quickly. "He's an expert in all types of divination. Tarot, runes, astrology—" She saw Cassie roll her eyes. "What?"

"Don't tell me you fell for that old 'What's your sign' pickup line?"

Endora's mouth went dry. "Not exactly."

"Then how'd he know you were twins?"

"He recognized the intense attraction between us," Endora muttered. Cassie's expression indicated no understanding of the meaning of this fact, although Medusa's obvious amusement said the elder witch understood perfectly. "We compared birthdays and found they're exactly the same." Cassie still showed no glimmer of comprehension. Endora cleared her throat. "Opposite-sex cosmic twins automatically lust after each other, and most often become soul mates. Emphasis on *mates*. Put the two of them together, and the outcome is—"

Cassie's face lit up. "Mind-blowing sex?"

Her desperate need for help had Endora swallowing her humiliation. "We were, well, exploring the soul-mate relationship when Ashmedai killed everyone else in his circle."

Suddenly restless, she rose and went to Cassie's liquor cabinet, poured herself a generous portion of Kahlua in a water glass, added an equal amount of milk and knocked back half the drink. "The moment we opened the cabin door the next morning, the sense of death nearly smothered us." Her entire body started shaking so badly she could barely raise the glass to her mouth to gulp the rest of the drink. The alcohol barely slowed her tremors.

For someone pregnant with twins, Cassie was amazingly agile. In a moment, she had left her chair and was at Endora's side, arm around her friend's shaking shoulders. "Stop. You don't have to tell us this."

Usually, Endora didn't like being touched, but just then Cassie's arm steadied her. "I've never spoken of it to anyone. And forty years is too long to keep such horror inside." She took a deep, steadying breath. "He'd mutilated them all in the most hideous ways. I found Josie's body. He'd done unspeakable things to her, I think in part because he knew we were friends."

"By the goddess, that soulless bastard should have been eviscerated." Fury lit Medusa's eyes, and it was obvious she was struggling to control her outrage.

Endora tried to shrug off the sympathy, but couldn't quite manage it. Truth was, she needed it. "When we left the hall, Tribunal officers arrested us for murdering the cult members."

Cassie's jaw dropped. "They didn't arrest Ashmedai?"

"Actually, they did." Endora's laugh was bitter. "He'd underestimated how much cosmic energy murder requires. Especially since he hadn't just killed those witches. He was lying, semiconscious, behind the hall where he'd slaughtered everyone. They picked him up off the ground." Endora fixed herself another drink and took a hefty swallow of it before saying matter-of-factly, "As they hauled him away, he insisted that we'd helped him."

"They convicted you of murder?" Horror rang in Cassie's voice, showed on her face.

"No. The Tribunal had sent Marcus into the circle to investigate Ashmedai. Once they convened and discussed the case, they dropped the murder charges against us."

Cassie gave an unladylike snort. "I'll bet those old codgers on the Tribunal got some real jollies questioning you both about your activities the night of the murders."

"The phrase total humiliation doesn't even come close." Endora set her empty glass in the sink, then returned to her chair. "I wanted to kill myself."

Both Cassie and Medusa gasped audibly.

Endora's look was fierce. "You know I despise sentiment, so if you tell anyone what I said, even Mick, I'll call you a liar...Becoming your familiar saved my life."

Still leaning against the sink, Cassie burst into tears.

"Bat guano!" Endora moved to hug her friend close. "Don't cry, Cass. Stop, please." She looked helplessly at Medusa. "Hex it, I should never have said that."

Cassie clasped Endora's arm with one hand while she snapped her fingers and produced a box of tissue with the other. "No, Dora, I'm glad you did."

"As am I." Medusa rose to rub her daughter's arm and then pat Endora's shoulder.

Cassie sniffed, wiped her eyes. "I'm totally hormonal, so bear with me." After another sniff, a sneeze, and a nose-blowing that rivaled the Cape Hatteras fog horn, Cassie smiled. "Realizing our friendship means as much to you as it does to me got me in the heart."

Endora wanted to respond in kind, but kept her own counsel. She'd spilled enough of her guts for a while. Still, she hugged her best friend tight and held on for a long moment.

Cassie pulled gently away and returned to her chair. "Working for me can't be the only reason you didn't go the suicide route. Tell us the rest of it."

Endora had to consciously stop grinding her teeth. Unable to remain still, she started prowling the kitchen. "Ashmedai destroyed so many lives. I realized if I killed myself, I couldn't get revenge on him for Josie and the others. Or for Marcus and me."

Cassie cocked her head. "What was the official charge against you?"

"Obstruction of a Tribunal mission." Endora stopped moving, grimaced. "For failing to complete his mission, Marcus got the same punishment I did, nearly total restriction of magic for forty years. And we were ordered not to see each other for that whole time."

"A complete miscarriage of justice," Medusa snorted.

The laugh that came from Endora's throat was rusty with irony. "At the time, I thought it was fair punishment for not stopping the murders."

"What did Ashmedai get?" Cassie asked.

"I'd assumed death, but the Tribunal told me yesterday that his punishment was losing his magic for forty years." Endora almost choked on her next words. "The kicker is that his punishment expires on his birthday, All Hallow's Eve. Actually, on November first because his birth day must run its course."

"The *Tribunal* sanctioned this?" At Endora's nod, Medusa's eyes narrowed. "Why?"

"They figured he'd be rehabbed, but have known for a decade he hasn't changed. Still, until a week ago, they ignored the danger." Endora shook her head as if clearing a bad memory. "The problem is, once Ashmedai regains his magic, he's free to use it as he wants."

"Goddess!" Cassie swore, face suddenly drained of color.

"It gets worse." Endora flopped into her chair. "Only Marcus and I can take him and, for reasons only the Tribunal knows, we regain our powers on our birthday December twenty-first."

"The Winter Solstice." Medusa's expression grew thoughtful. "Why not give your powers back on the fortieth anniversary of the day you lost them?"

"It's almost as if the Tribunal planned it this way." Cassie had visibly paled.

"That would certainly explain why they took so long to act against Ashmedai," Endora replied.

"Could they have deliberately left it so late?" Agitated, Medusa twisted the ring on her left index finger. "I can hardly believe they'd be so calculatingly negligent."

"The point remains that he gets his powers back in under a week, and Marcus and I don't until seven weeks later." Despair clogged Endora's voice. "And if Ashmedai's not stopped before then, he'll add Marcus's and my magic to his own."

At that statement, Medusa's look changed from contemplative to horrified. "But that will make him the most powerful witch on Earth."

"Idiots!" In a flash, Cassie was at the counter, whisk in hand, beating a dozen eggs like she'd been ordered to put on a brunch for Satan. "They're sending you after a madman with only part of your powers? That's suicidal!"

That's probably why I met the magistrates at the Suicide Prevention Salon. Endora gestured to Cassie's chair. "Come on, Cass, sit down. Your baking jag is probably upsetting Laurel and Hardy."

"If they're fraternal, we're naming them Fred and Wilma," Cassie retorted almost grimly. She added flour to the mix and began the beating process again.

"This situation is very desperate," Medusa stated. "Now is the time for serious thinking. Cassie, sit down."

Cassie shot a frustrated look over her shoulder at Medusa. "All right. For now, my anger at those Tribunal morons is on hold." She covered the batter with a dishtowel and rejoined her mother and Endora. "Sorry I freaked. How can we help you defeat Ashmedai?"

"Actually, no one but Marcus can help me." When Endora saw Cassie reaching for her whisk, she quickly added, "Not directly, anyway."

"Hades and damnation!" Medusa's eyes flashed pure fury. "If we can't augment your magic, how can we tip the odds in your favor?"

Endora looked at her two friends, bit back an oath, and kept her bitter fear in check. "By casting a spell on me." Suddenly, explaining became very embarrassing, and she felt her face start to flame. "Since Marcus and I have to work together to defeat Ashmedai, I need an anti-love spell strong enough to overcome the attraction between cosmic twins."

Medusa and Cassie exchanged astute looks.

Endora sighed unhappily. "Pretty much all I can think about when he's nearby is, well, you know…"

"And it's the 'you know' you want us to shield you from," Medusa stated, not unkindly.

Endora nodded to the elder, knew her cheeks were still burning. "I won't be able to concentrate on the job if all I want to do is hit the sheets with Marcus."

"Excellent thinking, Endora." Medusa smiled. "An ounce of prevention, so to speak." She studied the shape-shifter. "Tell me, were you and Marcus born anywhere near each other?"

The question seemed odd, but Endora answered without

thought. "Actually, yes. His coven was about a hundred miles straight north of where I was born and raised."

"Is that important, Mom?"

"Very. While cosmic twins are extremely rare, the complete matches—those born in the same time zone as well—come along only once every three or four centuries. The bonds such twins share are breakable only by death."

Endora's heart rate accelerated until she feared the other two witches could hear it crashing into her ribs. "Is that good or bad?"

Medusa shrugged. "It makes you a formidable opponent for Ashmedai. However, you must ignore your potent desire for Marcus in order to defeat a dangerously evil foe." She snapped her fingers and floated three steaming cups of tea gently to the table. "Answer one question before we start the protection spell, Endora. Why did you and Marcus survive?"

For Endora, trying to speak was like swallowing broken glass. "I think Ashmedai suspected a traitor, but he couldn't get to us because of the protection spell, so he killed all the others. Marcus, after all, was there working for the Tribunal. I never thought to ask if he'd gotten an insider's tip."

"If Ashmedai didn't know the traitor's name, he might have decided that by eliminating everyone he could eliminate his problem." Medusa nodded as if in agreement with herself. "He was an amazingly paranoid despot. And, he could turn the blame on you and Marcus."

"Possibly." Endora chewed her knuckle. "But I can't get past the idea that someone tipped him off about Marcus being undercover."

"Only that one time, according to you, though."

Endora groaned, but Cassie's humor steadied her. "Bad one, Cass. Wisecracks are my department."

"Sorry." But Cassie didn't look at all repentant. "I'll keep my jokes to myself now."

Medusa looked like the banter was annoying her. "Before you went to rescue your friend, Endora, did you know Marcus was there on Tribunal business?"

"Not until just before we made love. He had arrived two months earlier and was nearly inside Ashmedai's inner circle. But our mutual lust distracted him from his mission." She hung her head. "If I'd just been able to resist the urge to make love with him…"

Cassie reached across the table to again grasp her friend's hands.

"Impossible." Medusa's statement brought Endora's gaze up to hers. "Cosmic twins cannot resist each other. Obsidian Ashmedai is a depraved monster who killed one hundred and two witches. You and Marcus did not cause their deaths. Never forget those facts."

Endora slowly nodded, then glanced at Cassie. "Can I have my hands back now?"

"Of course." Cassie sat back. "Now, walk us through that last night."

Intense, Endora gripped the table. "Everyone lived in the main hall, but Ashmedai had a cabin near the woods where he initiated the females. Marcus and I snuck out and met up there." She sipped tea. "We risked severe consequences, but would have spontaneously combusted if we hadn't gotten together. We cast a protection spell that surrounded the cabin with an impenetrable shield. Then we made love." Blushing, she looked at the table. "The entire night."

Cassie whistled through her teeth.

"Amazingly, we were both virgins."

"Why amazing?" Cassie rotated her shoulders and stretched before answering her own question. "I'd think cosmic twins would save themselves for their soul mates."

"My conclusion exactly, Daughter." Medusa saluted Cassie with her teacup.

Endora had to know, but almost lost her nerve before asking, "Is it important that Marcus wasn't just my first, he was practically my only?"

Medusa gave Endora a speculative look. "It certainly does."

"You lost me completely here, pal," Cassie stated. "You're saying you're not a player?"

"Hard as it is to believe," Endora said quietly, "I've never been."

"But you've had more dates than a hundred-year calendar." Cassie's matter-of-fact tone was not at all accusatory. "The postdate details you constantly regaled me with?"

"A cover."

"Ah, the lady doth protest too much?" Medusa interjected, still studying Endora.

"Good old Will Shakespeare got that right," Endora replied. "As usual."

Cassie shook her head. "I still don't get why you felt the need to pretend to be, uhm—"

"Catting around?"

Cassie stifled a groan. "You said that, I didn't."

Endora's wit didn't raise her own spirits for long. "I loved Marcus so much, I couldn't bear being apart. But the Tribunal said they'd terminate our magic if we saw each other after the trial. So, I went far away, fast, and quickly took a lover. Then another when that fizzled two months later. Each relationship was worse and shorter than the previous one. After three, I gave up. The vast majority of men I've been linked to since then are gay. And just good friends."

"Oh, Dora." Cassie moved over to rub her friend's shoulders. "Why didn't you tell me?"

"And ruin my image?" Endora snorted. "I couldn't admit to hopelessly loving a witch I couldn't have. So I pretended a love-em-and-leave-em-no-regrets attitude." She was suddenly glad Cassie stood behind her, as her eyes filled with tears.

"Don't cry, honey. We'll help you." Cassie hugged Endora around the shoulders.

"Of course we will," Medusa confirmed.

In a blink, Cassie was back in her chair. "So, what else do we need to know?"

"Marcus and I only have this week to defeat Ashmedai before he regains his magic." Endora swallowed hard before she looked directly at her friends. "We have to stop him, but I'm not sure if we can."

"You'll find a way, Endora." Cassie gave her a confident smile before turning to Medusa. "Think we can pull off this spell, Mom?"

"Naturally," Medusa stated with conviction.

Coming as it did from the most skilled practitioner of the magickal arts Endora had ever known, that statement reassured tremendously. She dared to hope for a good outcome to this mess she'd gotten herself into with very little effort.

Medusa stood and beckoned the other two witches. "Come, this spell will have to be incredibly powerful, so we need all three of us in the circle."

* * *

After Mav left the duplex, Marcus found he couldn't settle. So, he put on jogging gear and took Glenna for a long run. But all he could think of as he pounded out the miles in the humid

Texas heat was what to do when Endora Bast came back into his life. Pushing himself to a higher pace, he felt his heart kick. His increased pulse wasn't just from the physical effort, though.

Since he'd read the runes, every time he thought of Endora, his heart rate accelerated. They had known each other not quite two weeks before they'd made love, something neither of them could have resisted given that their sexual attraction was fated by birth. But Ashmedai's murderous rampage had destroyed their chance at a life together.

Although he suspected it was true, he didn't know if the Tribunal's punishment had devastated Endora as it had him. He was a cosmic twin and a witch. Separation from his mate had torn out his heart, and the loss of nearly all his magic had rent his soul. Forty years before, he'd in essence lost all but his physical life.

Now, Endora was coming to find him, and he couldn't decide how he felt. Of course he wanted to see her. Longed to with all his being. But his longing was tempered by more than a little dread. Before, they'd had no chance to discover if their feelings went deeper than birth-induced lust. He feared if what they'd shared was only physical attraction, he wouldn't survive.

Three

"Will the twins upset the symmetry of the spell?" Cassie asked before standing to join Medusa and Endora. "If so, I can sit this one out."

Medusa moved to the exact center of the kitchen and, pointing with her finger, drew a pentagram of light on the floor. Then she extended her hands to Cassie and Medusa. "You and the twins make a trio, Cassandra, which strengthens your contribution. And we'll need that contribution to make an effective spell. Love, after all, is the most powerful emotion we have."

"I'm thinking lust is," Endora muttered.

"Concentrate," Medusa ordered quietly, eyes closed and head tilted slightly back. "This spell must be impenetrable."

"Unlike my virginity."

Medusa opened her eyes and speared Endora with an intense look. "Finished with the levity? If so, we have a very serious and complex spell to perform."

"Sorry." Endora swallowed hard. "It's just that, when I'm scared I get sarcastic. I can't stop making smart-ass remarks that serve to relieve my tension but don't do much to—"

"Endora," Cassie said calmly. "Shut it."

"All right. All right." Endora rubbed her hands across her face. Then she sighed. "I know how important this is. It's just that I'm completely off kilter."

Medusa smiled sympathetically. "You see your love for Marcus as irrationally uncontrollable."

"I've managed to throttle it for the past four decades, but we've been apart." Endora lowered her gaze as she whispered, "Now, I have to deal with him face to face. And that frankly terrifies me." Panic welled up, but when Cassie hugged her around the shoulders, Endora forced it back. "If my mission fails because I can't block my love for him, there will literally be hell to pay."

"No need to panic," Medusa said mildly. "Nervousness inhibits a clear head."

"And a blank mind is better than no mind at all." Cassie winked at her familiar.

Despite her tension, Endora flashed a brief grin. "You have no idea what your help means to me." She tried to shrug nonchalantly, but couldn't pull it off. "After the episode with the Tribunal, my family disowned me."

When Cassie winced, Medusa calmly stated, "Which allowed us to exploit your talents as a familiar. And from a mother's viewpoint, you were the best thing for Cassandra."

Seeing Cassie's eyes well with tears, Endora gently warned, "You know I hate sentiment, Cass."

"Raging hormones have made me a total softie."

"You were a softie before Chip and Dale enraged your hormones." Putting on her game face, Endora took a deep breath, let it out slowly. "I don't want to let you down."

"You won't." Medusa's tone was grave. "But the importance of keeping your powers from being taken cannot be overemphasized. Very few of our kind are shape-shifters as well. When you regain your magic, you can become a very formidable practitioner of the magickal arts."

"And that's why you can't let Ashmedai take those powers," Cassie added.

Knowing she might have to die to keep her magic from being taken by Ashmedai, that she might die before she had a chance to possibly build a relationship with Marcus, Endora set her jaw. "I'm ready to get this done."

"Good." To close the circle, Medusa took Cassie's right hand in her left. Endora's left hand in her right. Again, she tilted her head and closed her eyes. "Concentrate on visualizing Marcus Morion. Now, focus your every sense on that vision."

A low hum started in the air.

"I call upon the Element of Water to cool the Element of Fire burning in the veins of Marcus Morion and Endora Bast," Medusa intoned.

The hum began a slow crescendo.

"Insulate Endora from the need for her kindred spirit. Mute her passion and keep her composed in the face of an undeniable attraction."

The crescendo built.

"Give her a clear mind, uncluttered by lust and need, to perceive and counteract the dark force that will be brought against her. Within this double circle, three within three, as I ask, so make it be."

The hum increased to a vortex of sound which engulfed them. For several moments, it seemed they stood inside a tornado. Then the swirling power lifted to the ceiling and dissipated like a spent whirlwind.

Medusa slowly opened her eyes. Endora and Cassie did the same.

"Well," the elder witch stated, "that should hold you for a while, Dora."

"Here's hoping 'a while' is long enough." Endora poured herself another Kahlua and cream. She took a long drink, tipped her head back and, closing her eyes, savored the taste a moment before swallowing. "I'm praying to the goddess that it is."

When she opened her eyes, Medusa was facing her squarely. "One important thing."

Here it comes, Endora thought.

Give Mom a chance, Cassie encouraged telepathically. *She knows what she's doing.*

"I appreciate the endorsement, dear." Medusa took Endora's face in both hands and tilted it up slightly. Then she whispered urgently in her ear and let her go. "Don't forget what I just told you, Endora. Your life, perhaps all our lives, depends upon it."

"No pressure though," Cassie added.

"Who said I felt any pressure?" Her situation was still dire, but with the anti-love spell cast, a huge burden had lifted off Endora's shoulders. Now, she just had to take advantage of the magic they'd made and get this mission over with in five days.

And remember Medusa's words.

* * *

He didn't need a crystal ball to know she was there. Marcus would have sensed her presence if he'd been comatose.

As it was, he'd just sat down to a very late lunch when he heard the rumble of a well-tuned engine. He knew without looking that a fire-engine red Plymouth Satellite sat in his driveway. A '65, white ragtop, eight-cylinder muscle car. Fast as lightning and built when gas was around a quarter a gallon. Today, the car was worth over forty grand. He'd seen it in his readings.

But in his dreams he'd seen only Endora. As he'd seen her every day for forty years.

Glenna jumped up from her pallet to race to the door, a deep-throated growl rumbling in her broad chest. When the car's door slammed, that growl turned to an even deeper, more ominous bark. The volume increased as Marcus's fantasy witch approached his duplex.

He had followed Glenna and now found himself rooted in the doorway. Barely able to hear the dog's barking for the blood rushing in his ears, he watched his soul mate stride up the sidewalk toward him. Despite the heat, she wore black leather pants and a short, black leather jacket. Although they'd been separated what seemed like a lifetime, she was still the most alluring female he'd ever known.

Her blouse, silk no doubt, was emerald green. Unlike when he'd last seen her, her black hair was in a short, stylish bob. She wore sunglasses, but he knew her eyes were the color of lush summer grass. The same color as her blouse. Despite the fact that he'd foreseen her arrival, he felt totally off-guard, as if he'd been caught peeping through a hole in the wall of the girls' shower. His heart rioted in his chest, and his only clear thought was that she looked ten times more beautiful than when he'd seen her last. And that was saying something.

He wanted to haul her into bed and not let her out until they'd made up for forty years of missed opportunities, and the one part of his body not currently numb was vital for what he had in mind. But since he stood there like a man facing a firing squad, that one active body part wasn't going to do him much good. He needed blood in his brain, not below his belt.

Everything around him receded into some misty alternate universe. The dog's fierce bark had turned to a whine, but Marcus didn't register that. He couldn't breathe. Couldn't swallow. Couldn't remember how he managed to open the door with paralyzed hands. He was just about to die from lack of oxygen, and not a little shame at his total lack of wit, when she stepped onto the porch. Casually, she removed her sunglasses as she did so, and Marcus got the first up-close look at her eyes he'd had in forty years. That didn't help his oxygen intake.

She raised her elegant brow in the haughty way he remembered so well, and her mouth curved in a half-smile that had brought more than one male to his knees. But the look she gave him could have frozen molten lead.

"Hello, Marcus." Her voice was as cold as her eyes. "Going to leave me standing out here forever?"

Hearing her voice again, even though it chilled, jolted him out of a near stupor. "Yes. No. Of course not." He mentally cursed himself for wanting a happy reunion. Maybe she didn't fondly remember the night they'd spent together. Maybe she'd found someone else in the years they'd been apart. Doubtful, given their relationship, but possible. The tarot cards had foretold she'd come, but not willingly. So, why was she here, although she obviously didn't want to be? He put on his poker face and met her cool expression with one of his own. "Endora. Come in. Please."

She stepped past him into the entryway, positioning her sunglasses on her forehead.

"I was just eating." He motioned toward the back of the duplex. "Hungry?"

"No." But she followed him to the kitchen.

"Have a seat."

"Thanks, but I drove from New England." She leaned against the cooking island. "I need to stand a while."

"Can I get you anything to drink?" When she shook her head, he gestured to his plate. "Mind if I finish?"

"Not at all."

Her aloofness stung. If her posture, her expressions and the extent of their conversation so far were any indication, she couldn't have cared less what he did. She definitely was not happy to see him, and he had no idea how to deal with that. Opening his mouth, with no clue as to what would come out, he started to blurt some inane platitude likely to only make things more awkward between them.

Fortunately, Glenna chose that exact moment to make her presence known. She had followed them, parking herself between Endora and him, her customary post when strangers entered the house. But she acted differently this time. Marcus vaguely registered that the dog's tail had started thumping the floor in an increasingly enthusiastic rhythm. He glanced at Endora.

She glanced down. At once, her aloofness turned to genuine delight. It startled Marcus to realize that she wasn't the least bit frightened. To his complete amazement, she bent over and clapped her hands, bringing Glenna to all fours and into a fit of ecstatic welcoming.

"Aren't you a beautiful girl," Endora crooned as the dog danced in front of her, wriggling in a full-body tail wag. When Glenna dropped to her haunches, Endora reached down to grasp the large proffered paw. "And so formal. Nice to meet you,

Miss Glenna."

Marcus was just about to ask how in hades she knew his dog's name, when memory hit him, preventing self-humiliation. Shape-shifters could communicate telepathically with animals.

Slightly angry that the dog was getting a far warmer welcome than he had, he said tightly, "Glenna, down."

Endora raised her gaze and then her eyebrow. When she straightened, Glenna quickly returned to Marcus's side. Guilt swamped him when he saw the chastised slump of the dog's shoulders, but he was put out enough that he didn't care at that point.

"You're a pit bull, for cryin' out loud," he admonished her in a low voice. "Have you no pride?" The dog's head lowered, and she looked up at him with soulful brown eyes. "She's a *cat!* Couldn't weigh four pounds soaking wet." He glanced at Endora, again leaning back against the counter but now with her arms crossed over her chest and that damned eyebrow just about up to her hairline. *Well, four pounds in cat form*, he admitted silently. But he pushed on. "Forty pounds of the sixty-five you weigh are your teeth. Go bite her or something."

The dog lowered herself to the floor and put her head on her forepaws, completely reprimanded.

Marcus shook his head. "I might call the pit bull breeders' association and tell them they lied. I thought when pits yawned, the theme from *Jaws* played. You're a pushover."

Resigned, Glenna sighed.

"Done taking your anger out on the dog instead of on me?"

The acidic sound of Endora's voice snapped his attention back to her. "I'm not angry."

"Marcus, if what you're radiating was electricity, you could light this duplex for a year."

He found himself gripping his knife and fork so tightly, they were starting to bend. He set them down with a snap. Instead of admitting that the energy was purely lust…all right, and a very healthy dose of frustrated anger…he forced an incredulous tone. "How can you bond with a dog? Cats and dogs are deadly enemies."

Endora snorted. "As even you can tell, I'm in mortal form right now. Besides, we're both *female*, Marcus. And that bond trumps interspecies rivalry any day."

"Just my luck," he muttered.

"And, you're changing the subject."

He was about to make a comment he knew he'd regret when Mav glided in unannounced, and Endora came instantly alert. Marcus saw her nostrils flare slightly, saw her feral nature take over.

Mav looked at Endora, then at Marcus. "Is she the trouble you said would arrive soon?"

He was going to have to speak to Mav about the art of subtlety. Too late this time, though. He swallowed an exasperated growl. "Endora, this amazingly pale beanstalk is my friend Eripmav Alucard. Mav, Endora Bast."

This time, both of Endora's eyebrows cocked, and she went from high alert to highly amused. "Eripmav Alucard? As in *Dracula Vampire* spelled backward?" At Marcus's nod, she laughed. "I'm calling the Bram Stoker estate and telling them you've ripped him off."

Confusion showed in Mav's black eyes. He turned to Marcus. "What does she mean?"

"Nothing. She's making a joke." He patted Mav on the back, shooting a fulminating look at Endora over his shoulder as he steered his neighbor to the back door. "I need to talk to Endora alone for a bit, Mav. I'll fill you in later, all right?"

"If you insist, Marcus."

"'Fraid I have to this time, buddy." He closed the door and, hand still on the knob, turned back to Endora. "All right. Let's cut to the reason you're here and get it out of the way. My shift starts in an hour."

Endora looked momentarily startled. Then her stunning green eyes shuttered, and she was again coolly aloof. "It seems the two of us have to go save the universe."

"I got the memo." His lunch looked totally unappetizing, but probably out of pure spite, he sat down anyway, picked up his fork and started shoving the food around on the plate.

Endora took the chair opposite him, turned its back toward the table, and straddled it. "Then why didn't you come to New Orleans?"

"I read the runes. They told me you'd come here."

"The 'trouble' your friend Mav referred to?"

Marcus shrugged, finding himself slightly embarrassed. "You're hard to explain to anyone."

"I don't know if I should be flattered or insulted." Endora's eyes glittered like emeralds. Flaming emeralds.

He shrugged again. Forty years ago, he'd have rushed to

assure her it was a compliment. But forty yeas ago, he'd been young, gifted and half in love. A cocky, confident witch whose star was rising with meteoric brilliance. Now, the only gift he had was prognostication. And he was just irritated enough with Endora to keep her wondering about his feelings. "Take it any way you want."

"I'm taking it that you're extremely angry I'm here." She sat forward. Intense. "Well, I'm not too crazy about this myself. But, dammit, Marcus, we don't have much choice in this."

He slammed his fork down on the table then rose and moved to the back door. Staring out at the yard, he found himself clenching his fists until they hurt. His shoulders felt bunched up around his ears, although they weren't. He wanted her to show him something besides the cool indifference she displayed, some sign that she loved him as much as he still loved her. But he knew that wouldn't be forthcoming any time soon. If ever.

Deliberately, he unclenched his hands and extended his fingers, beating down his emotions as he did. When he could finally speak steadily, he said, "We can choose to tell the Tribunal to go to hell."

"Which is where we'll all end up if we don't stop Ashmedai."

That declaration brought him up short, but to prevent Endora's knowing she'd disturbed him, he kept his back to her. "For the past four decades, I haven't much cared what happened to that bastard. Or where I end up. Why start caring now?"

There was a long, tense pause before she asked quietly, "Traded in your white hat for a black one, Marcus? Is it one for one and all for none now?"

That barb stung because it came from her. But he'd lost so much as a result of his idealism that his own cynical attitude bothered him very little anymore.

He shot her a glare over his shoulder. "I have no magic, Dora. The Tribunal stripped me of it. I can't even cast the simplest of spells." Her eyes flickered, but her expression didn't change, and seeing it, he cursed silently. Either she'd misunderstood his meaning, or she'd chosen to ignore it. He'd bet the farm on the latter, and for some reason that angered him. Hardening his tone, he spat, "Besides, you're the last witch on the planet who should be giving me the 'Greater Good' speech, especially considering your history."

As he turned to fully face her, he schooled his voice to be as cold as hers had been earlier. "You charged into Ashmedai's circle, no training, no plan, no goal but getting your friend out of there, right into the middle of something I'd taken months to set up. You totally…" He couldn't finish, but her expression told him she knew exactly what he'd been about to say. Her face blanched white, eyes glittering with what looked like tears. In light of the icy façade she'd maintained since her arrival, this look of total devastation twisted his heart. "Endora, I didn't—"

With a look that could have melted steel, she leaped to her feet as if she'd been scalded. Body rigid, fists clenched, she stepped toward him. "Don't you dare, you son of a poxed old crone," she hissed in fury. "Don't you dare say you didn't mean those words."

Guilt made him defensive. "I didn't say anything. I—"

"Stop!"

She shook so hard he didn't know if she was about to break down in tears or physically attack him. In their time together at the circle, he'd seen the depth of her passion— fury at Ashmedai, terror for Josie, ardor for him. She rarely held back. But he'd never seen her this close to the edge of what looked to be a total loss of control. He secretly hoped she attacked him. He could deal with a physical reaction, but tears scared the hades out of him. Cautiously, he raised his hands in a gesture of peace.

"Endora, please listen—"

"No, *you* listen."

He could almost see her rein her emotions in to a manageable level. Admiration filled him, but he didn't blurt out how much he respected her self-control. Or her in general. Instead, he crossed his arms loosely over his chest and assumed a posture of feigned nonchalance. "All right. Talk."

When he saw her swallow hard before speaking, his own facade almost crumbled. At her unexpected vulnerability, every atom in his body wanted to close the space between them, gather her in his arms and just hold her until she was her cocky self again. But that was as bad an idea as telling her he admired her for not bashing his head in with the nearest chair. The "Don't Touch" sign couldn't have been more visible if it was in ten-foot high neon lights. Ruthlessly, he crushed his need to comfort. There would be another time. He'd make sure of that.

"I want my life back." Her look dared him to contradict her.

No vulnerability existed in that statement, or in her expression. Clear, firm, and inarguable. He thanked the goddess for restoring his brassy female and found himself relaxing slightly at Endora's return to sanity. Then it flashed in his mind that she hadn't included him in the life she wanted back. Would she deliberately exclude him?

Before he went down that path, she said, "For forty years, I've lived with the belief that Josie and the others in Ashmedai's circle died because of me." When he started to protest, her sharp look cut him off. "As you so succinctly pointed out, I had no training, no plan. Just an obsessive goal of saving a friend's life. As it was, I got her killed."

"Endora, you don't know—"

Again, her eyes flashed. "Every day for forty decades I've asked myself the same question. If I hadn't joined the circle, hadn't interfered, would you have stopped Obsidian Ashmedai before he killed all those witches? Or did he kill them because I was there and made love with you, and in doing so, ruined your plan?"

"There were two of us in that cabin that night, Dora. We both snuck away. We both risked discovery to be together. We made love together. You didn't ruin my plans by yourself."

If he'd shouted or raged—blamed her completely for his failure, as she'd blamed herself—his words wouldn't have been so wrenching. She'd halfway expected him to do that. But he hadn't. Love for him welled up inside her. Fortunately, the spell was working, and she thanked the goddess her feelings wouldn't get past it. Otherwise, she'd have thrown herself into Marcus's arms and kissed him. She turned away, running her hand across the top of the chair back while she gathered herself to face him again.

"In spite of believing that fate put me in Ashmedai's circle, I'll never stop wondering if I caused my best friend's death. But I've got more critical issues." She took a slow, deep breath and held it for ten seconds before releasing it. "I really need your help, Marcus. I don't care if it's not magic. But I'm here to say that, regardless of your answer, I'm going after Ashmedai. I'll get my life back or die trying."

He almost blurted out that he'd sacrifice anything to be with her, but she'd made it crystal clear her business with him was only because Ashmedai threatened them all. And to gain redemption for her perceived transgressions. Since he wasn't about to let her crush his heart, even unintentionally, he bit his tongue and locked down his feelings. In their place, he summoned his blandest expression.

"Give me the details." He thought he heard her let out a sigh, but wasn't sure.

"Just before midnight on All-Hallow's Eve, Ashmedai will get his full powers back."

Shocked, he swore creatively. "That's five days from now!"

Her look turned grim. "It gets better. We're the only two who can take him on, and if we don't capture or kill him before the Winter Solstice, he gets all the powers we had before our precipitous fall from grace."

Marcus found he had to sit back down. "But we don't get any help?"

"We can't get our powers augmented, if that's what you're asking." Her laugh was bitter when she added, "But the Tribunal was kind enough to tell us where they think Ashmedai is, and to provide a safe house in the same city."

"Big of them." Her bleak gaze gave him the sudden need to play it light. "So, do we get to go to Hawaii or something?"

She sat down across from him. "Denver."

"Better than Transylvania." His smile was calculated to reassure. "Or the Arctic."

"I doubt Ashmedai would go so far north. Too much white snow and bright light. That bastard was made for darkness."

Marcus nodded. "And there aren't enough creatures to torment up there during the Arctic winter." Despite the fact she'd likely take a chunk out of him, and that he had almost nothing to contribute to her desperate quest, he reached across the table to grasp her hand. "I don't know how much help I can be, Endora."

She didn't pull away, but he could feel her instant tension. He released her, admiring the fact that her hand remained resting in the same position a moment before she casually withdrew it. Once again, she was in cool command.

"You can't cast a single spell?"

He shook his head. "Not a one."

"No telepathy?"

"Nope. All I can do is predict the future." At her bleak look, he added, "If it's any consolation, I'm one hundred percent accurate."

"Can you predict the future about yourself?" She abruptly stood again and started pacing. "I mean, if you tried to see how this will turn out—"

"No. I can't do that. And, I probably can't be accurate on this for you, either, since we're cosmic twins."

She surprised him by smiling. "Actually, that's a relief. I don't want to know how this will end."

"Not knowing leaves room for hope."

"It does." With a slight shake of her head, she regained her poker face. "So much for that Kodak moment. We need to get on the road right now. My bags are in the car. I figure we can be at the safe house in Denver in about eight hours."

He smiled genuinely for the first time in what seemed like days. "Denver's almost nine hundred miles from Dallas."

She gave him one of her patented looks. "What's the good of having a prime piece of driving machinery if you're never going to show it off?"

Her statement reassured him that she had, indeed, regained her emotional balance. Mentally, he sighed in relief. "You'll be showing it off to every law enforcement officer in four states."

"And your point would be?"

"Oh, nothing." He shook his head. "I guess we'll see if the Texas Rangers are all they're cracked up to be."

"Guess so." She looked at the dog. "We'll have to leave Glenna here."

Marcus rose to put his dishes in the sink before turning to fix her with a stare. "Absolutely not. Mav's coming, too."

"Neither of them can help," she warned.

"That's beside the point. The dog goes where I go. And I saved Mav from being killed by a slayer a while back. So, like in the Asian cultures, I'm responsible for his life."

Endora frowned. "Be that as it may, we can't put them in danger."

"So you're saying you don't think the safe house is really safe?"

Her eyes lit with frustration, and she drew her keys from her jacket pocket to wind through her fingers. "Not at all. I'm just saying they'll get in the way." *No offense, Glenna.*

None taken.

Marcus's body language told her he wasn't going to concede this point. He set his jaw, crossed his arms over his chest and leaned back against the sink. She had to block the thought of how gorgeous he was, not wanting to let the dog in on that aspect of her conflict. Surprisingly, his macho posturing actually put her mind to rest, as it told her for certain that he would help her in any way he could. She felt the tension in her shoulders ease a little.

"They both go with me. And Mav won't be in any danger, as magic can't kill him."

Complete shock made her jaw drop, but she gave Marcus credit for not laughing out loud at her. "He can't really be a vampire! There's no way he's old enough to walk around in broad daylight."

Marcus grinned. "He's dyslexic."

"Oh for goddess's sake, Marcus," she hissed, shaking her head. "Your twisted sense of humor is way off base right now."

He held up his hands as if to keep her from attacking him. "I'm serious. He really is dyslexic."

She planted her fists on her hips and squared off in front of him. "I've never heard of such a thing."

"And that means it couldn't happen." Although he looked like he wanted to kiss her, he gave her a pitying stare. "Before he was turned, he was dyslexic. After he was turned, he stayed that way."

She didn't let the burning desire to have Marcus kiss her interfere with her skepticism. Instead, she let the spell take care of her lust. "So he's the opposite of other vampires in that he does everything backwards."

"Exactly." He paused, smiled, then added, "And, he doesn't bite humans. He bites himself."

This time she couldn't hold back. She hauled off and cuffed him on the shoulder.

"Ow!"

"You big baby. I didn't even put any zing behind that." Her reflexive contact with him sent a tingle zipping from her hand all the way up her arm. Startled, she quickly pulled back and scrambled to recover her aloof façade. What in hades had just happened? No time to consider what her reaction meant, but she wasn't going to test her protective magic again any time soon. To cover her confusion, she resorted to sarcasm. "Sure, I buy your 'he bites himself' line. Right."

"Just because you don't believe it doesn't make it a lie." He absently rubbed his shoulder. "I got him a job as a knight at the place I work. That way, he wears chain mail all the time he's on the job, and so he can't hurt himself. His non-work clothes have Kevlar panels sewn into them."

Momentarily, she buried her face in her hands before giving him a dark look. "All right, I'll play along. How does he survive if he's dyslexic and keeps trying to bite himself, but can't because he's wearing chain mail?"

"The Atkins Diet."

Endora knew her jaw literally dropped at that statement because Marcus's eyes lit with amusement.

Expression incredibly smug, he added, "He's got chickens in a pen out back and eats them when I'm not around."

It's not a pretty sight, Glenna grumped from her prone position under the table. *He doesn't cook them, and lots of times he leaves feathers spread all over the place. I'm a carnivore myself, of course, but I rarely hunt and kill anything, and when I do, I don't make a mess while eating it.*

Goddess, that's too much information! Endora returned.

"Mav also eats the occasional coyote or prairie dog if he finds one. And when we first hooked up, I had to convince him that neighborhood pets were off limits."

Endora glanced at the dog. "He ever go after Glenna?"

"No."

He got that bloodlust look in his eye one time when Marcus wasn't around. I just yawned and gave him a good look at my teeth. Canines bigger than his by a long shot, and a jaw that can snap an arm in half. We've never had a problem since.

Smart girl. Endora gave Marcus her most serious look. "All right, gather your troops and let's hit the road. The sooner we get there, the sooner we can take Ashmedai out."

"Why does he get his powers back before we do?"

Endora gave an offhand shrug, but couldn't keep the heat from her voice. "A question I suspect has a very dark answer."

"You're thinking conspiracy?"

His shock was genuine, and Endora had the satisfaction of knowing she'd gotten his full attention. "Apparently, three

Tribunal Magistrates were very supportive of Ashmedai back in the day."

All business himself now, Marcus nodded. "If he gets his full powers in five days, and we don't get him before that, he's going to be very hard to beat."

"A truer understatement was never spoken."

He moved to quickly dry the dishes and put them away. "Actually, counting travel time, we'll have just over four days." He gave her a look over his shoulder. "This sounds more suspicious by the minute."

"Unfortunately, you're right." Endora didn't want to delay, but kept her restlessness out of her voice. "But where Ashmedai's concerned, their not bothering to give us much advance notice is just one in a long list of screw ups. I swear our current Magistrates make the Keystone Cops look like a SWAT team." She stared thoughtfully into space. "I didn't even consider their timing. Maybe we should fly up there."

"With the trouble it would be to get a vampire and a pit bull through airport security, it wouldn't be much faster."

"Point taken. And, regardless of the suspect time frame, we're stuck with it."

"Yeah." He draped the dishcloth over the clean dishes, moved to the back door and shouted for Mav, then started toward the stairs. "I'll get my things. You grab Glenna's food and bowls and throw them in that canvas tote bag. Might as well bring her bed, too."

And don't forget the doggie treats. They're in the pantry. And a couple of chew toys.

Endora smiled down at the dog. "Got it."

I don't really need my leash, but you might want to throw it in. Marcus says it keeps people from being scared of me if they think I'm under control.

Don't take this wrong, but are you sure you're a pit bull? You look more like a chocolate lab-boxer mix to me.

Supposedly, my first master had the papers.

Endora loaded food, treats, bowls and other doggie paraphernalia into the tote, hefted it and the bed over her shoulder then headed for her car, the dog on her heels. *Your first master?*

Some cowboy wannabe from Texarkana. He tried to make me mean.

Doggie gear was quickly stored in the Satellite's trunk, but

Endora kept a couple of treats out, surreptitiously slipping them into her jacket pocket. *Glad he didn't succeed.*

Me too. Glenna gave her an adoring look. *Thanks for agreeing to take me along. I'd go crazy in a kennel.*

I'm with you there. Opening the passenger-side door, Endora pushed the front seat forward and waved the dog in. *And even though Marcus didn't give me a choice, it'll be nice to have another female around. He can be pretty overwhelming when he wants to be.*

He's a great guy, though.

How long have you been with him?

Eighteen months. Too bad he's a man. I could go for him, big time. What a hottie!

Endora blocked her thought of total agreement before Glenna picked up on it. Now she knew maintaining emotional distance was tied up with physical distance. She absolutely could not touch Marcus, since her physical reaction when she had done so earlier proved sexual energy still pulsed between them. Fortunately, the anti-love spell had kept her from jumping him on the spot. He felt it, too, if she'd correctly read his actions since her arrival. Given that she'd been denting the male ego for nearly fifty-five years, she was positive she'd nailed his reaction to her.

I really am very passive for my breed, Glenna continued, a bit apologetically, pulling Endora out of her reflections. *If Marcus, or even Mav, was in danger, I'd fight to the death to protect him. But for the most part I hate conflict.*

Endora reached down and gave Glenna a good rubbing behind the ears. *Sounds to me like you've got your priorities straight, wimpy dog.*

If a dog could grin, Glenna did. *Thanks for saying so, pussycat.*

Endora was still laughing a moment later when Mav came out of his town house carrying a duffel bag and a small crate. Her laughter ended when she saw white feathers sticking out of the crate's slats, and heard a rather alarmed clucking sound.

"Road food," Mav said simply.

"Of course."

Four

Goddess help me, Endora thought five hours into the trip. *I'm going off to fight a depraved, murdering bastard, and my backup is a chicken-plucking dyslexic vampire, a pacifist pit bull, and the only being who totally turns me on, but can't do any magic. I'll be insane before I ever get to Denver.*

Perhaps insanity was a good thing, she reasoned as they rocketed up the highway toward the Mile High City. It would certainly keep her from being frightened to death.

Careful to block her thoughts from the Satellite's other occupants, she tried to concentrate on the task ahead. Doing so proved impossible. Especially with Marcus in the front passenger seat, fewer than fifteen inches from her. She'd infuriated him by saying she had come to Dallas only to ask for his help, and although she felt sorry for that, she still thought it had been the best approach. If they failed to defeat Ashmedai, there'd be no chance of a relationship. If they succeeded, then they could take a look at their future together.

That is, if Marcus was still willing to have one with her. Once on the road, he'd tamped down his anger at her aloofness, but she could still feel emotion radiating from him like steam from a boiler. By keeping their dealings strictly business, had she wounded his feelings? A flash of guilt jabbed her. She hadn't intended to hurt him, but reasoned that her unemotional approach worked best because they could not afford to resume their personal relationship.

Individual wants and needs had to be sacrificed for the greater good. In this case, that was truer than anything. That afternoon when he'd touched her hand, when she'd impulsively cuffed him on the shoulder, she'd almost spontaneously reversed the anti-love spell and leaped on him. His touch had practically ignited her skin. Ditto when she'd touched him. Until that very moment, she hadn't thought she had any acting talent. But she could have given Cate Blanchett a run for her money when she'd maintained a disinterested front. That had been Academy Award worthy. She'd even fooled Marcus into believing she no longer cared for him.

Bitter laughter bubbled up in her throat. Since when in the past forty years had the greater good meant a rat's ass to her?

She'd sworn revenge on Ashmedai, but that was a selfish, strictly personal goal. A payback for Josie's life. But now her motivation covered a far broader base. Why? When had her attitude changed?

A few days ago when I knew I'd see Marcus again.

From the moment the Tribunal's bargain had been made, Endora's life seemed to kick into high gear. Instead of merely seeing each day as exactly like the previous one, she found herself looking forward with all her heart to the future. She allowed a grain of hope to flourish. They were in imminent danger of death, but they had a chance to succeed. Slim, but still a chance. And the thought of absolving herself of past mistakes while saving the universe was a definite plus.

"Let's pull over at the next rest stop," Marcus's deep voice rumbled beside her. "I think we could all use a stretch."

She nearly hissed like a startled cat when he spoke. But feline reflexes saved the day, keeping the car on the road and her emotions in check. She slapped on her protective aloofness and half turned her head to glance, brow cocked, at him.

"It's not smart to just blurt things out when you're in a car going a hundred and twenty miles an hour," she scolded. "The driver could've been startled, lost control and crashed."

Marcus snorted loudly enough to wake Mav and Glenna. "Not likely with you behind the wheel."

Uh-oh, still a bit touchy. "Next time, clear your throat or something," she said in what she hoped was a reasonable tone. Since he merely grunted a reply, it must have been.

"What about it, guys?" Looking in the mirror, she wasn't surprised to see Mav, since he was dyslexic and all, but Glenna was curled up on the seat behind Marcus and out of her view.

"I would like the opportunity to exit this vehicle and walk around," Mav stated. "I need to eat."

And since it's dark, we won't have to watch him do it, Glenna pointed out. *And I could use a shrub break.*

Within five minutes, they were ten miles farther down the road and pulling in to a small truck stop. In front of the shabby-looking café sat a Colorado state police patrol car. Endora pulled in and parked right beside it.

She felt Marcus's stare. "What?"

"Tempting fate?" His question was more approving than disapproving.

"Well, I'm sure the Oklahoma authorities radioed ahead to

their Kansas counterparts about the car they chased for a couple hours. And the Jayhawks most likely have warned the Colorado state police to be on the lookout for a black, '55 Corvette with a blonde female passenger and a Hispanic male driver. So, I doubt they'll give us a second glance."

He gave her the once over. "Oh, they'll give you a second glance all right."

Even though the light inside the car was dim, his stare made her skin sizzle. Had the Colorado air suddenly heated thirty degrees? *Think "greater good,"* she commanded herself. *This isn't about us. It can't be about us.* Mercilessly clamping down on her libido, she sniffed. "Because it's in my nature to do so, I'm taking that remark as a compliment rather than as a suggestion that I look like a criminal." And before Marcus could say anything, she slid out of the car and sauntered into the café.

He got out and stood watching Endora over the Satellite's roof. Just like he'd predicted, he saw every head in the place swivel when she opened the door and moved toward a booth right across from the two troopers.

"She is a striking creature," Mav commented quietly, having also gotten out of the car.

"A man would have to be twenty years dead not to notice her," Marcus agreed. If those two officers noticed her any more intently, they were probably going to burn their retinas out.

"And women automatically consider her a rival."

"What's crazy is, she doesn't even know she's just become the center of attention." Marcus admired her lack of conceit. And her power to ignore the emotions of those around her.

Actually, it was that power to ignore that had him steamed. He'd been half aroused since the moment she'd arrived, yet Endora had acted totally oblivious to him. What in hades was wrong with her?

"You love her."

Marcus knew Mav had no telepathic skills, so he had no trouble lying to his friend. "Until today, I hadn't seen her in forty years. Without encouragement no emotion lasts that long."

Marcus felt his friend's unblinking stare, but didn't turn to look at him.

"Many emotions last an eternity. After forty years, which of yours do you still possess in full?" With that, Mav picked up the chicken crate and moved off into the night.

Starting to feel a headache coming on, Marcus tried to block Endora from his thoughts. Better to concentrate on the near impossible task ahead of them rather than on trying to explore her psyche. He'd go out of his mind in attempting that feat. And if they didn't manage to win out against Ashmedai, chances were good they had no future at all to consider. So, he had to put his needs behind the needs of the entire witch community. Just like Endora had.

Shaking his head at his foolishness, he let Glenna out of the back seat, then accompanied her behind the café in search of a suitable place to take care of her business. Fortunately, the Colorado flatlands stretched out into the darkness with nary a light shining anywhere. Glenna took off like a shot away from the truck stop. Marcus could hear her paws thundering through the grass as if she was a wild mustang. He waited until even with his preternatural hearing the sound was beyond his range, then let out a piercing whistle to signal her back. Within seconds, the footfalls returned, pausing only a short while for what he knew was her rest stop. Then she emerged from the darkness, eyes glowing in the dim light, and followed him back to the car. He tossed her a treat and opened the door. Once she was again tucked away in the back seat, Marcus went into the café.

Endora had struck up a conversation with the two state troopers sitting across the aisle. They were admiring her car. And her legs in the black leather pants she wore. As usual, she paid no mind to that particular type of attention.

You love her.

Mav's words sprang into Marcus's head, and he couldn't deny their truth. Four decades ago, he had loved Endora enough to throw away his career. Now, it seemed, that emotion had grown to the point where he was willing to throw away his life. But either she was doing an amazing job of blocking her emotions from him, or she really didn't care for him at all. He'd gotten no indication that what she'd said that afternoon at his duplex wasn't the complete truth.

Seized by an abrupt need to rattle her like she'd rattled him in Dallas, Marcus slid onto the bench opposite her. Then he gave the troopers a nod.

"Evening, officers."

Although they returned his greeting, he felt their sudden

tension, like wolves sensing the threat of another male's presence. He almost laughed aloud at the subtle posturing they displayed. Being macho types to begin with, they resented his encroachment on the female they'd targeted as theirs, and he could almost smell the testosterone spike in the air around them.

She's out of your league, boys, he thought smugly. *Out of your universe, in fact.*

"Honey, you know I like it when you wear your hair back." Endora couldn't kick him under the table without the action being seen, so he reached across with his right hand and tucked a lock of her black hair behind her left ear. Then he ran his thumb down the side of her throat to her shoulder. The sparks in her eyes promised retribution, but he knew she wouldn't do it right then.

He knew a major payback was in the cards, and he couldn't wait to see what form that retribution would take.

She continued to glare at him. Then her ear suddenly twitched as if she were in cat form and fending off some pesky insect. That startled her as much as his touching her had, if her shocked expression was any indication. She leaned slightly to her right, toward the two state troopers. Although she clearly meant to break contact, Marcus felt a flash of triumph. At his caress, her pulse had leaped beneath his thumb.

Her eyes slitted, but she spoke with saccharine sweetness. "And we know I always do things the way you like them, don't we, sugar cakes?"

He had to back down or get fried by her eyes. But he couldn't resist giving her a smug little grin before momentarily conceding. "You're so good to me, darling." He drew his hand slowly away from her face before turning to give the troopers a rueful smile. "I bought my wife that Satellite out there, but she just doesn't do it justice. If I'd known she'd only drive it sixty, I'd have kept it for myself."

"The speed limit *is* seventy, ma'am," the younger officer said helpfully. "It's a shame not to let that big ol' V-8 do what it was built to do."

Marcus looked back at Endora. "See, honey, that's exactly what I've been telling you."

"But, sweetie-kins, you know how I hate to drive fast." Endora batted her eyelashes like a debutante on speed, then pulled a perfect, spoiled-deb pout. "I could never drive seventy. It just isn't in me to be reckless."

Practically choking on suppressed laughter, Marcus dared again to reach across the table. This time, he patted her hand, noting that her left ear started twitching the moment he made contact. "That's all right, sweetheart, I–"

The crackle of a police walkie-talkie interrupted. "*All units west of Burlington, all units west of Burlington. Move to apprehend a '55 Corvette westbound on interstate seventy. Suspect is fleeing Kansas state police at a high rate of speed.*"

"That's fifteen miles east of here," the older trooper stated. "Let's roll, kid."

Both officers jumped to their feet, the younger throwing bills onto the table as they hurried to their patrol car and sped off into the night.

Marcus shot Endora a look. "Thought that 'Vette would have been long gone past here by now."

"Those troopers looked like they needed something constructive to do." Endora shrugged. "So I messed with their radio."

"They'd have been perfectly content to stay here ogling your legs." Was that jealousy Marcus heard in his own voice? In order to bluff his way past those words, he added, "Maybe the 'Vette had a mechanical problem."

"Mechanical problem? Not a chance. That car's almost as awesome as my Satellite." Endora rummaged through her purse for money, found a twenty. "No, the driver probably detoured up into Nebraska to see Carhenge, or one of the dozen other tourist attractions that particular state has to offer."

"Carhenge?" Marcus asked, quirking his eyebrow to broadcast his skepticism.

"Some guy got a bunch of huge old junker cars and arranged them in the pattern of the Stonehenge monoliths. If I remember correctly, it's somewhere in Nebraska."

Marcus signaled the waitress for their check, then looked back at Endora. "You're kidding, right?"

Expression grave, she pushed the twenty at Marcus. "Would I kid about the most sacred Druidic site in the entire world, reproduced for our born-again pagan friends on this side of the Atlantic?" She shook her head slowly. "Oh ye of little faith."

"Carhenge," Marcus grumbled. "What will they think of next, pet rocks?"

Endora laughed as she rose with lithe grace. "It's a bit late to cash in on that brainstorm. You'll have to stick with divination."

"Sure, like that's been lucrative for me so far." Marcus followed her out into the night.

* * *

It took them slightly over an hour to cover the remaining hundred and fifty miles to Denver, and around ten that night, they were pulling up in front of the safe house on Larimer Street in the Lower Downtown District.

"Welcome to what's known to the locals as LoDo," Endora said as she climbed out of the car and held the seat forward so Mav could exit.

"This looks like a row of warehouses. Or factories." Marcus climbed out his side and let Glenna escape the back seat.

Endora moved to open the trunk, setting their gear on the curb. "Apparently, it used to be a bit of both, way back when. Not too many years ago, this was a very rough part of town. But the city officials thought to play up the historical angle, renovate the buildings, and convert them to shops and loft apartments. This is now the 'in' place to be in the city." She started toward a door that fronted the street. "We've got the loft on the northeast corner of this first building here. Lots of big windows on two sides."

"Did you happen to bring a city map?" Marcus asked, standing with the door open on the curbside.

"There's an atlas in the carrier behind your seat."

Suddenly, Glenna froze, staring straight at the building's front door. Her hackles stood up, and a low growl rumbled in her chest.

Holding the door handle, Marcus turned. "What is it, girl?"

Glenna woofed. *This whole building is humming.*

Endora reached down and scratched the dog behind the ears. "She's picking up on some magic. Some kind of cloaking spell."

"A protection spell, maybe?"

"Could be one or both." *Nothing to worry about, wimpy dog. You'll get used to it.*

If you say so.

If you can't adjust, let me know. I should be able to do something about that.

Thanks.

Absolutely no problem.

Mav turned a complete circle, nostrils flared to better sniff the air. "I must feed."

Both Marcus and Endora noted the chicken pen was empty. They shared a look.

"There are a couple of terrific steakhouses around here," he pointed out. "Could be some good scraps out behind them."

"I'll reconnoiter."

As Mav glided off down the street, Marcus called after him, "Bring back a copy of the Denver *Post*. I want to read the horoscopes."

Endora would have laughed if Marcus hadn't looked so serious. Instead, she hoisted a load of gear and headed for the loft, tossing "Don't forget the atlas" over her shoulder as she went.

* * *

Mav was only gone half an hour, but by the time he returned, Endora and Marcus knew exactly where they were in relation to the city's landmarks. Situated near the corner of 20th Street, their hideout sat a few blocks from Union Station to the northwest and Coors Field, almost due north of them. Traveling southwest a couple blocks would take them to the convention center. At the eastern end of the city park, between 23rd and 17th Avenues, stood the Museum of Nature and Science. Marcus quickly estimated it was close to a mile and a half due east. They'd both quickly memorized the entire map.

"Looks like we're in the middle of the action." He opened a bottle of beer he'd found in the apartment's fully stocked refrigerator. "Theoretically."

She found she couldn't settle down and wandered around the open living area, checking out the titles of the books in their freestanding cases. It interested her to note that all of them had something to do with magic. "Assuming Ashmedai is actually somewhere around here."

"You have doubts of that?" Mav silently entered the kitchen area and placed a newspaper on the cooking island that dominated the center of the space.

"I don't know what to think, Mav." Endora didn't feel the need to lie to Marcus's friend. Besides, there was no point. "I do know I have zero trust in the Tribunal. And, I know we've got just over four days to find our prey and take him out."

Marcus gestured to their living quarters with his beer bottle. "Our fancy digs aside, the Magistrates haven't exactly given us any advantage against a pathologically evil opponent."

"I see." Mav rested his lanky frame on a nearby barstool. "How can I be of help?"

"Dora?"

Marcus deferring to her judgment startled her, but she didn't miss a beat. "I see you as sort of an 'X factor,' Mav." The vampire's expression went blank. "It's like this. Marcus and I are the only ones who know you're here, so that makes you an unknown quantity. An X factor. You can run errands and check out leads without the Tribunal or anyone else connecting you to us."

"And the less our Magistrate colleagues know about our activities," Marcus continued, "the easier it'll be for us to work."

Mav nodded. "Again, the issue of trust."

"You got that right, buddy."

"So, let's get started." Endora picked up the newspaper, handing Mav the front section and Marcus the entertainment section. She took local news and sports for herself. "I know you want the astrology feature, Marcus. Mav, I want you to look for anything that strikes you as odd for a big city paper."

"And what would that be?"

Understanding that Mav took things literally, Endora thought a moment. "News items that just seem wrong." She turned to Marcus. "Help me out here."

Marcus pointed to the front page of the *Post*. "The stories in this section of a paper are of high interest to lots of people. They could be international, like the recent tsunami disaster. Our trade deficit is of national interest. Denver's in Colorado, so anything that's a big story about the state would likely be in the first section."

Endora pointed over Mav's shoulder. "This covers a murder in the city. Sensational local stories like this, or about natural disasters like floods or forest fires, will be here. Go with your instincts." Carrying a bottle of water into the living area, she chose a comfortable-looking recliner, turned on the floor lamp next to it and put her feet up. "I'm checking out sports and the local scene."

"Sports?"

Endora ignored Marcus's sarcastic tone. "Hey, it's football season. Amazingly buff guys in really tight pants. What more could a woman ask for?"

"Some of those offensive linemen haven't seen their feet in years," he grouched.

She almost laughed aloud. Marcus, jealous of a bunch of overdeveloped jocks? That possibility intrigued her. "Sure, but in the case of the skill positions, the term 'tight end' definitely has more than one meaning."

His grunt told of a direct hit scored. She allowed herself a moment to bask in the thought that perhaps he felt more than lust for her after all. If that was true, they had a chance to form something lasting after all this madness was over.

Endora shook her head to clear the fantasies. Unless she concentrate every one of her faculties on said madness, there would be no future—for her, Marcus, or countless others. She quickly turned back to the task at hand. It hadn't been her original intention to look at the sports section. She'd just taken it to see what kind of reaction she could get from her cosmic twin. Now she knew. Setting the sports section aside, she unfolded the local section, intending, as she'd instructed Mav to do, to skim the headlines looking for items that didn't fit.

On the section's front page, above the fold, the headline glared out at her. "Unique New Museum Opens With Mysticism Exhibit." The hair at her nape raised.

"Find anything?" Marcus had sauntered over to lean on the back of the recliner.

Endora nearly leaped straight into the air. Instinctively, she managed to conceal the headline from him by flipping the paper closed as if in reflexive fright. "By the goddess, Marcus! You nearly scared me out of one of my nine lives."

"Sorry." His rakish grin looked anything but apologetic.

"And all I've managed to find out is that the Broncos are out of town for the next two weeks."

"Drat your luck."

She wanted to tell him the only tight end in the world she was interested in belonged to him, but knew she couldn't do that. "True. So, why are you already bugging me? I thought I gave you your assignment."

The look he gave her was pitying. "Please. These are child's play. But, you might want to hear these particular horoscopes."

Clamping down on her curiosity about the museum exhibit, especially when every one of her instincts screamed "legitimate lead," to instead concentrate on what Marcus was saying took effort. But she managed. Every clue, every observation was critical. "Shoot."

He sat down on the sofa arm just to Endora's right as she moved the recliner back to its upright position. At the same time, she hid the local section of the paper in her lap. She didn't want to closely examine her reasons for not wanting to tell Marcus about this lead, but she suspected it was sudden fear that he'd be hurt. *Can't think about that right now*, she reminded herself. *Listen to what Marcus has to say.*

"The *Post* has a pretty decent astrologer," Marcus commented. "This section not only gives the daily horoscopes, but a month-long reading for each sign."

Anticipation had Endora sitting up straight. "What's our friend Ashmedai's?"

"Scorpio," Marcus read. "A wonderful Arabian aphorism describes the four types of men in the world. Perhaps it also describes the four kinds of Scorpios—'He who knows nothing, but knows not that he knows nothing; he who knows nothing and knows he knows nothing; he who knows but knows not that he knows; and he who knows and knows he knows. Your birthday is coming up, why not see which one fits you by trying one, or all, on for size? Keyword is *reasoning*."

"Great." Endora shook her head. "What in hades does it mean?"

"The first man is a fool," Mav stated matter-of-factly as he joined them. "He is ignorant but does not realize it. The second is simple. The third, asleep. The last man is wise."

Stunned beyond words, Endora just barely managed not to gape.

Marcus jerked his thumb in Mav's direction. "He's my friend. That guy right there. *My* friend."

Mav's pale cheeks suddenly had a bit of color. He folded his long legs and sat on the carpet beside the coffee table, facing Marcus and Endora. "There is more."

"No need to wait for an invitation." Endora leaned forward, bracing her forearms on her thighs. "You're the expert here."

"The proverb says to shun the fool, teach the simple man, wake the sleeping man, and follow the wise man." Mav shrugged. "There are slight variations as concerns the second man, depending on which version you read. The proverb has been attributed to Sanskrit, Arabic, Chinese, Persian, and Confucius himself."

Endora had to ask, "And what are the variations?"

"Sanskrit says the second man is a student. The Chinese say he is willing, the Persians a child, and Confucius ignorant. The solution to all is the same. Teach him."

"Buddy, you're amazing." Marcus stretched across the coffee table to slap Mav on the shoulder. "Where did you learn all that?"

"Before I was turned, I was working on a Ph.D. in philosophy at Berkeley."

Marcus whistled. "Impressive!"

Somehow, Mav's revelation hit Endora right in the gut. Even if they defeated Obsidian Ashmedai, they couldn't help Mav return to his former life.

"Thanks for the translation," she said softly.

Marcus looked back at the entertainment section. "And speaking of translations, our October horoscopes are interesting, also."

"Do tell." Endora reclined the chair again.

Marcus cleared his throat then cut a sidelong look at Endora. "Don't get a big head from this one, Bast. Here's Sagittarius. 'This month, female Sagittarians are definitely not the so-called weaker sex. Aim for impossible heights, since in October turning your powers to your advantage comes even more easily than usual. But you must keep the goal in sight. For Sagittarian males, cooperation is the objective, not attainment of your desires. Sagittarius Keywords, *Make an effort.* "

"Co-op-er-a-shun," Endora sang smugly. "And don't you forget it, witch-boy."

Marcus's glare lacked conviction. "I warned you about the big head thing."

"Sure, sure." She gestured to the paper he still held. "Since we're on the cusp, what's the Capricorn report?"

"Thought you'd never ask." He made a production about smoothing out the page, then read in his best college professor voice, "'Remind yourself, high-reaching Goat, not to stumble over the obstacles hindering you, and your path will be more easily negotiated. Since you could be your own worst enemy just now, look to others of your kind to determine how best to take advantage of some family trait to turn things around for you. Capricorn Keyword, *Affinities.*"

"Those seem a tad more clear than the Scorpio one." *Clear as a bell, as far as I'm concerned,* Endora thought a bit grimly. "Anything else?"

Marcus stretched his shoulders by pulling his right elbow across his chest with his left hand then reversing the process. Watching his unconscious grace on display, Endora just about broke into a cold sweat. "Well, I cast a horoscope for both Ashmedai and the two of us. Interestingly enough, most of his came out as aphorisms from famous people." He shrugged. "It happens. Anyway, I'll give you today's and tomorrow's for all of us. October 27th for Ashmedai is a quote from Josephine Baker. 'It is not the same thing to be naked as to have nothing on.' Ours tells us to plunge into something we don't even understand."

"That sounds about right. What about the Capricorn?"

"A quote from Mada Carreno. 'Today's witches are but the fairies of other times who aged badly.'"

"Is she a friend of yours?" Mav asked Endora.

She didn't know whether or not he'd made a joke. "Personally, I've never heard of her."

"Tomorrow's, which actually takes effect in about fifteen minutes, is rather interesting." Marcus put his feet up on the coffee table and closed his eyes, remembering. "At your peril do you ignore opponents who will try to keep you from your goal."

"We are Ashmedai's opponents, are we not?" Mav asked.

Marcus's eyes opened, and his grin was wolfish. "Score one for the dyslexic vampire. Our Sagittarian one is also a quote, 'There can be little liking where there is no likeness.'"

"Aesop." Mav nodded. "I believe that quote refers to the differences between yourselves and Obsidian Ashmedai. You are all witches, yet the two of you are from the light, and he epitomizes darkness. You two and he are not alike, and thus you are mortal enemies."

"Mav you're right on." Shaking his head, Marcus put his feet back on the floor and sat up. "The only thing Ashmedai shares with Endora and me is witch blood. That's where the likeness ends."

"We've covered two of the three horoscopes," Endora pointed out. "What's the third?"

"Capricorn says, 'Use a corner of your eye for watching instead of just seeing.'"

"Words to live by, there." Endora could relate especially to the latter prediction because she readily understood it. She didn't know what to make of the other ones. Interpreting signs was Marcus's specialty. And Mav's, apparently. So she'd pay close attention to what they had to say regarding omens, horoscopes, everything that dealt with predicting the future.

Feeling the pull of the article she'd set aside, she forced nonchalance into her question. "So, what's your next move while I finish this section of the paper?"

"I'm studying the business section and the advertisements," Mav said.

Endora set the front page of the local news section on her lap, headline down. "Before you abandon the front section, read the editorials. If they're on a rant about something totally irrelevant, I think we can count that as a possible clue."

"I'm going to do some divination." Marcus rose gracefully from the sofa, and Endora found her throat going a bit dry as she watched him. "And, if you don't mind, I'm taking the corner bedroom."

"If it is no bother, I would like the third room," Mav stated. "It only has one window."

And that window overlooked the living area. The company who'd converted these buildings from manufacturing to residential had terrific architects, Endora thought. They must have used existing offices or storage areas above as bedrooms, studies or home offices, extra bathrooms, leaving the living and dining areas open to the high ceiling, and the kitchen, laundry room, and downstairs bathroom tucked under the bedrooms. It worked for her.

"Well, guess I get the middle room, then." She glanced at both the men. "A rose between two thorns."

Marcus wagged a finger. "Big head..." He walked away, chuckling, and Mav soon rose to leave as well.

Alone at last. Endora waited until Marcus and Mav left the living area before she reopened the paper.

Five

She was surprised to see her hands shaking as she turned the article and began to read. Just glancing again at the headline had her heart stuttering once more. It began nearly pounding out of her chest as she read down the page.

> DENVER – Denver's newest museum celebrates its grand opening in fine esoteric fashion tonight, as the Museum of Arts and Culture hosts a gala black tie event showcasing an impressive inaugural exhibit.
>
> The show, entitled "Mysticism Across Time and History," features the world's largest collection of artifacts used in the practice of mysticism.
>
> "Simply put, mysticism is the act of seeking union with the godhead," said the new museum's curator, Daemon Azazel. "It is the belief that direct knowledge of the godhead, spiritual truth, or ultimate reality can be attained through subjective experience, such as intuition or insight."

The curator's name raised Endora's hackles, but she tucked that away for later analysis, forcing herself to concentrate on the rest of the article before giving in to the need to think more closely about Daemon Azazel.

> Many of the different mystical disciplines were represented at the exhibit, from Native American practitioners all the way back to the Druids.

Impressive collection, Endora thought.

> "The exhibit features hundreds of artifacts, many of them ancient," Azazel pointed out. "We've culled them from every esoteric discipline throughout history."
>
> He went on to detail several items,

and thanked the various private and institutional donors. None of this information triggered any red flags for Endora, but she kept reading.

"I am proud to say the preeminent piece in the exhibit is a copy of the central text of Kabbalah, the *Zohar.* This particular text dates back to 1300."

Other mystical disciplines represented in the exhibit include the Gnostic branches of Mandaean and Manichaean, Christian snake handlers, shamans from diverse cultures around the world and across time, the occult, and magic.

"And for those who believe in that sort of thing," Azazel commented with a sly wink, "we even have all manner of divination techniques.

Stop by and try out our Ouija board. Totally interactive."

The black tie reception runs from seven until 11:00 this evening.

No tickets will be sold at the door, but donations to the new museum may be made in care of the Membership Office, 555-5500.

The exhibit closes December 21st.

Okay, besides my personal connection to the paranormal, why did this article attract my attention? Daemon Azazel. Endora closed her eyes and concentrated on the curator's unusual name. Daemon was almost too easy. The variant spelling of demon meant evil spirit. But it also, as concerned Western magic, meant an inspiring intelligence or genius. Given the idea that mysticism in part concerned intuition or insight, this second definition was as appropriate as the first one.

She only vaguely recognized Azazel, but knew exactly where to find a reference. *The Demon Watcher's Field Guide* stood on a living room bookshelf. According to the guide, Azazel "was as important in ancient Judaism as Satan came to be later in Christianity."

"Gotcha, Ashmedai," she murmured. "You think you're a very clever boy, don't you?"

True to form, though. Not only did he consider himself a genius, thus the use of Daemon as a first name, but his pedagogical statements showed he considered himself the fourth type of Scorpio—wise. As for his fake last name, the connection to Judaism followed the pattern of his real name's origin.

She wondered briefly if the disparaging remark about divination was directed at Marcus, or the fact that the exhibit closed on their birthday was directly related to them. She truly hoped neither was, but didn't believe in coincidence. Both those elements were in the article, so she had to assume that, at the least, the exhibit was Ashmedai's challenge to Marcus and her. And if he knew they were in Denver at that moment...Well, all hades could break loose.

Having to rely on the loft's protection spell to keep their location a secret scared her, since presumably the Tribunal had cast it. She sighed. Better not to dwell on their total mishandling of this situation so far, however. There was work to do.

The address put the Museum of Arts and Culture in the same park complex as the Museum of Nature and Science, about a mile and a half away. It was straight up midnight and the gala was long over, but what would it hurt to teleport over there and take a look around?

Her feline nature urged her to go solo, but guilt made her feel she owed Marcus an explanation of her plans. *Of course, then I'm going to insist he stay home and wait for me.*

That wouldn't sit well, with him or any male witch she knew. Her insistence on going solo would set off a row of enormous proportions, guaranteed, because no matter what their horoscope said he wouldn't step aside while she followed a lead. Not without some harsh words and, possibly, broken glassware.

And a stark truth strengthened her conviction to go alone. Since she had plunged into something she absolutely did not understand, a part of their horoscope had already come true. By going to the museum without Marcus, she'd keep him from being involved if she got into a scrape. In her heart of hearts, she knew that his lack of magic made him vulnerable to any Ashmedai might still possess. Her own powers were only adequate for self-defense. If Marcus went with her and disaster struck, the game would be over.

"Any leads?"

At the sound of Marcus's voice, Endora's first instinct had been to shove the *Demon Watcher's Guide* between the cushion and chair arm. Her second, powered by a huge dose of guilt for planning to deliberately deceive him, had her snapping, "Stop sneaking up on me."

Both of his eyebrows shot toward his hairline. "Whoa. I just asked a relevant question. No need to have a hissy fit."

"Well, what do you expect? I don't enjoy being surprised."

"Maybe you were surprised because you were so engrossed in the newspaper." He crossed his arms over his chest and raised his brow as if in question.

She didn't take the bait. Instead, she rose from the recliner, managing to tuck the local section under her arm. But not before he noticed.

"What's going on here, Endora?" He eyed her elbow and the section of the *Post* it pinned to her side. "Pardon the cliché, but you're as jumpy as a cat with a singed tail."

"You're making me jumpy because you keep sneaking up on me."

His expression turned dark. "I'm not buying it, Slick. What are you not telling me?"

Bat guano! Now I'm going to have to lie. "Nothing."

"Then show me what's in the paper."

"All right." She flipped the local section over to reveal the article. As he scanned it, she said casually, "I plan to go to the museum tomorrow to see the exhibit."

He looked up, locked his dark gaze on hers. A stubborn line formed between his brows as they drew down over the bridge of his nose. "Not without Mav and me, you're not."

She suddenly realized he hadn't made the connection between the exhibit and Ashmedai. And in case he hadn't memorized any of the article's details, she needed to keep him from looking at it again. So she pulled the paper away from him and said in her most reasonable tone, "By splitting up, we'll investigate more leads faster."

"This lead's the best we've got, and you're not checking on it alone."

Her own temper spiked, but she throttled it back. She couldn't allow Marcus to sense even a hint of her certainty that this was the *only* lead they should check. If he did, he'd never let her go by herself. "Don't get all macho on me, guy. I don't need backup on a museum visit."

"What happened to 'We're in this together?'"

Endora rolled her eyes for effect. "Togetherness isn't necessary on this particular task."

"Then why'd you ask me to come to Denver with you?" His eyes blazed, and he took a step closer to her. "If we're the only two who can take on Ashmedai, why do you suddenly want to do it yourself? You know I won't let you."

Her poker face was nearly as good as his. "I'm planning to gather information," she lied, "so, don't make it out to be some covert operation."

"Everything is covert as far as that slimy vulture Ashmedai's concerned," Marcus insisted. "You're not going alone."

"If you insist, then feel free to come along." Endora tucked the paper under her arm again. "I plan to be at the museum when it opens at nine tomorrow morning. Make sure you're ready to roll by eight-thirty." She smiled sweetly. "Now, if you'll excuse me, I need to use the restroom, and I'm doing it without help."

"Fine," he grumbled.

Brushing past him on her way to the half-bath just off the kitchen, her shoulder bumped his arm. She had to force herself to ignore the instant tingling sensation assaulting her. And her ear twitched once. *I've got to deal with that somehow,* she thought. *But not now.*

While Marcus was insisting on a group assault of the museum, she had plotted a strategy. The age-old woman's prerogative of staying in the bathroom for hours on end should work just fine. They shared a huge bathroom with two sinks, an amazing shower, and a Jacuzzi tub the Broncos' offensive line could probably all sit in at the same time. The bathroom had a skylight, but she had no desire to be anywhere near Marcus when she pulled her disappearing act. Since Mav had a private bath attached to his bedroom, he wouldn't need to use their facilities. Besides, did vampires even have to bathe? She had no recollection of learning that in witches' school.

Fortunately, the half-bath on the main floor had a window big enough for her to get through in feline form. Since she was already wearing mostly black, she would simply zip up her jacket when she shifted back into human form. That would save her a trip upstairs to change, and get her out of the loft even faster.

She strode into the downstairs bathroom, locked the door, and unfolded the local section of the paper. Using a small spell, one of only a few she could perform, she obscured the museum's address and the details of the gala. Guilt stabbed her again, as she knew Marcus couldn't undo it, simple as it was. It somehow felt as though by using magic to hide the clue, she not only deceived him but taunted him for lacking it. And this was a sin of commission, not omission, as she'd done it on purpose.

Without thinking that yet again she was about to plunge ahead without a plan, she opened the window, shape-shifted into cat form, and leaped onto the sill. In a blink, she was gone.

* * *

Although brand new, the Museum of Arts and Culture resembled a classical building, with Doric columns supporting a balcony over the façade-wide steps that led to the entrance. It reminded Endora a bit of the Parthenon, only with a new-car smell. She scampered lightly down the roof and onto the building's fourth-story balcony, then turned back to human form. After adjusting her clothing to assure that nearly all of her skin was covered in black, she used a small blast of mental energy to open the secured balcony door.

Time for extreme caution. Moving silently into the gallery, letting her preternaturally keen senses reach out in the dim lighting for any whisper of danger, she was almost invisible.

What a cliché. Sneaking into a museum during the Witching Hour to check out an exhibition on mysticism. I could have cased this place during the day when other people were around. But noooo. I have to go skulking through a virtually empty building.

Of course, the reception had been over long before she'd read the newspaper article and made the connection. And, regardless of what she'd told Marcus, she'd had no intention of wasting time until regular business hours the next day before checking this lead. *Hopefully, he doesn't think about the time constraints, figure out what I'm doing, and come after me.*

Although she had no idea what to expect at the exhibit, it was the key to locating Ashmedai. She trusted her instincts completely. Their mortal enemy was close by.

But lying to Marcus and then sneaking out on him bothered her more than she'd thought it would. As much as she wanted to pretend she'd left him at the safe house to protect him, that was not completely true. Yes, his lack of magic was a liability she couldn't ignore, but emotionally she feared he wouldn't trust her judgment. Forty years before, back at the circle, he had been the one in control. He'd had orders from the Tribunal and a plan to carry them out. She, on the other hand, had operated on only her driving need to rescue Josie.

As he'd so succinctly reminded her after she'd located him in Dallas.

Again running on a driving need, this time for redemption, Endora realized their personal styles were already conflicting. She trusted her intuition and went after a goal full out. Marcus, although equally relentless in pursuing a goal, was all about structure and pre-planning. And while she feared more criticism from him for her intuitive style, her biggest fear was that he'd ridicule her for it. She wouldn't be able to stand that from him. Which made no logical sense, given her independent feline nature, but there it was.

By the goddess, I knew I wasn't over him, but I thought the love-resistance spell would at least keep me rational. I'm acting like I've got a junior high crush, and if he so much as looks crossly at me, I'm going to dissolve into a puddle. I'm an idiot.

She pushed worries about the love of her life from her mind. Right now, she needed to find clues to Ashmedai's whereabouts. Impossible if she let concern for Marcus's reaction to her deception get inside her head.

The museum was four floors of galleys that ran along all four outer walls and framed the rectangular atrium dominating the center of the building. She had come in on the top floor of the massive building. A quick glance over the balcony revealed about a seventy percent size reproduction of Stonehenge arranged around the central section of the main floor.

And not a '57 Chevy in sight, she thought wryly.

In the exact middle of that ancient Druidic temple was a stand upon which sat a very large book. Her money was on its being the *Zohar*, since that was, according to beloved curator Daemon Azazel, aka Obsidian Ashmedai, the centerpiece of the exhibit. And the fact it was under what looked to be six solid inches of glass also tipped her off. She'd work her way down to the main floor and get a closer look.

Senses on full alert, she navigated the galleries in quick

succession, making her way—to her complete disgust—down to the main floor without so much as sensing a hint of Ashmedai's presence, not even the residual energy he should have left just by being at the reception that night. Discouraged, she decided to take a quick look around the atrium before slinking back to the safe house to admit to her team she'd been following a promising lead that had turned into a wild hare. She walked through the space between the southernmost stones of the Stonehenge exhibit and approached the *Zohar.*

The tome was absolutely stunning, its ornate gold-leaf cover studded with precious stones Endora knew to be hundreds of years old. The main text of Kabbalah radiated a muted power. But that wasn't what made the hair on her nape suddenly rise.

Brimstone and hades! The bastard's here. How did I miss him? Catching movement out of the corner of her eye, she spun toward it.

Obsidian Ashmedai stood thirty feet away at the atrium's northern entrance, menace in every particle of his body. And she had a feeling he was going to try to make her pay for letting curiosity distract her.

He'd been tall and slender forty years before. Now, he was thin to the point of gauntness. She thought grimly that his evil was probably burning away all his extra flesh, from the inside. But even in the dim security lighting, he still looked devastatingly handsome. His white-blond hair and light blue eyes practically glowed. The Devil's own charming archangel, he'd used his good looks to lure his share of love-struck witches to his circle and his bed. She was profoundly thankful she hadn't been one of them, as she suspected he'd be a cruel lover.

"Endora Bast." Ashmedai's voice echoed hollowly in the cavernous exhibition hall. "Hello, my dear. So nice to see you again."

"The feeling's definitely not mutual, Ashmedai." Her feline survival instincts went into high gear, making her sensitive to changes in heat and light, and she picked up on the unusual levels of electricity in the air. *Something stinks like rotten tuna. If I'd been paying attention, I would have felt him coming the minute he entered the building. And he shouldn't have that much magic. He shouldn't have any magic at all.*

The power she sensed radiating from him swept away any doubts that the Tribunal knew nothing of exactly how dangerous this witch still was. Somehow, he'd gotten his considerable power back. If she'd been a betting person, she'd have wagered the ranch that the witch who stood before her had every bit as much magical ability as he'd had in 1965.

That reality terrified her.

Enlightenment followed, hitting like a fist to the gut and almost bringing her to her knees. Medusa had been right. At least one and perhaps more of the Tribunal had aided him. *Were still* aiding him. How else could she possibly explain his having so much magic?

For whatever reason, Marcus had been set up forty years before, primed to take a fall for another's deeds. Someone on the Tribunal had alerted Ashmedai to Marcus's presence, and by becoming involved with Marcus, she had fallen with him. Now, forty years later, the potential consequences of the traitor's betrayal went far beyond two witches being punished for a serious mistake in judgment. This time the outcome was potentially catastrophic for many, many more.

No chance to consider why events had been manipulated this way, but the reality had to be faced. Her survival became even more crucial, since finding the traitor within the witch community was just as imperative as neutralizing Ashmedai.

Knowing he would see eye movement even from that distance and in that light, she reached out with her other senses to assess her situation. Besides the case holding the *Zohar*, there was no cover nearby. And she really didn't think glass, no matter how thick, was going to stop a blast of magic. She was in big trouble.

"So, the Tribunal has sent you after me." Ashmedai's silky voice did nothing but grate on Endora's nerves.

"Somehow, I can't imagine you're surprised." The stand holding the *Zohar* was just feet behind her, so she took a half step back and to her right, opening a possible avenue of escape. It didn't make her feel much safer, but it was something.

She intended to keep Ashmedai talking as long as possible, reasoning that the longer she delayed an attack, the better her chances. Another consideration was information. Any he might divulge could prove valuable. And with an ego like his, he'd never be able to resist some bragging.

"Nice place you've got here, Ash."

He nodded acknowledgment of her statement, but his eyes lit with temper. Score one for the good guys. Ashmedai hated nicknames, so she'd deliberately used the pet name she and

Marcus had given him back in the circle. It hadn't been an endearment. She knew it would irritate him and needed every favorable odd she could get. Jerking him around a bit was just an added bonus she'd appreciate more when she was home safe in bed.

Sadly, it became immediately apparent that her gain was short-lived. He reined in his anger as quickly as he'd loosed it.

"All alone, or is your lover, Marcus Morion, the Tribunal's white knight, with you?"

She truthfully stated, "I haven't been with Marcus in forty years." *In the Biblical sense, that is.*

"Ah, but back then, the two of you certainly were, uhm, how may I put this delicately... *close.*"

His tone was so lascivious Endora had to grind her teeth to keep silent. One of that miscreant's greatest weapons was inducing anger in his opponents. Then he used that distraction to his advantage. Anger clouded reason, and against him that very often proved fatal. Already outgunned, keeping her wits was crucial. He couldn't be allowed to rile her.

"If he was as good as you seem to think he is," she said coolly, "I'd certainly have found a way to be with him."

His smile was more a smirk than anything else. "Back at the circle, I'd planned to bed you myself. To show you what a true witch can do in the practice of the sensual arts. But you always seemed to slip away from me. And also, unfortunately, I often found myself occupied with other, more pressing matters."

Like wallowing in paranoia and planning to kill all your acolytes because you thought someone might have betrayed you? I can believe that. "And I had another witch to occupy me." *And a far better one than you'll ever be.*

"Whatever charms you think Morion has, I could make you completely forget them." He took a slow step toward her, but she held her ground. "Perhaps we could get together now."

His leer turned her stomach from twenty feet away. "When dwarfs sprout wings and fly."

Rage turned his eyes a demonic red, and Endora had a split second to enjoy turning his mind games back on him. Then he said, "I grow weary of discussing sexual matters."

"Me, too." She took a step back, so the *Zohar* display was one step ahead of her position and one step to her left. She could always dive behind it, for what little protection it might offer. "What have you been up to since last we met, Ash?" She gestured around her. "Pull down a couple of degrees in archeology or something?"

"In point of fact, I have spent the better part of the past four decades in Europe, educating the ignorant masses regarding that very subject."

Yup, the 'I'm a wise man, follow me' thing's in play here. Let's see if your ego's as huge as it was forty years ago, you son of a satyr. "And I'm sure your career has been distinguished. You always were an overachiever."

If he was insulted by her innuendo, he didn't show it. "Of course, my career has been stellar, in several of the greatest universities in England and on the Continent. I held the archeology fellowship chair for fifteen years at Cambridge. Taught at the Sorbonne in Paris, and at various universities in Stockholm, Brussels, Prague and Krakow. In each and every one of those venues, I was acknowledged as the most outstanding scholar in my field. I have authored fifteen different books, of course under several different names, all of them regarded as the *vade mecum* of their particular subject."

Vade mecum? If you weren't a pompous windbag, you'd have just said 'handbook.' "And that subject would be mysticism?" He bowed with a flourish Endora ignored. "Now, I can't say as *I'm* surprised. When did you come out West?"

"Three years ago. While waiting for the museum to be completed, I've been teaching classes at the University of Denver. And also organizing societies for the study of the various disciplines of mysticism. I find it completely intriguing how humans are so captivated by the supernatural."

Intriguing, my furry cat tail. You've been scouting for talent. Planning to start another circle after your birthday? Already have a long list of sexual conquests from your adoring students and potential acolytes? That's how you sucked Josie in. Sexual charisma.

"Humans do seem to carry on about the strangest things." She gave an exaggerated look around the atrium and used the gesture to take another subtle step away from Ashmedai. "I'm betting this exhibit is going to prove immensely successful."

"Oh, I know it will be."

His tone indicated he had momentarily tired of bragging, and Endora knew she couldn't keep him talking much longer. Time to turn tail and run. She glanced quickly to the side. The

Stonehenge monoliths were still a bit far off for comfort, but she would do her best to get there.

Her skin prickled at the subtle increase in energy Ashmodai was generating. *Uh oh.*

"All this small talk is getting us nowhere." He stopped moving toward her, crossing his arms over his chest. "It's time for you to either join with me, or die."

As far as ultimatums went, that one was pretty much right to the point.

* * *

"Glenna, go lie down. And get away from the bathroom door. You're probably making Endora crazy."

The dog had been restless since Marcus came downstairs half an hour before and Endora had retreated to the bathroom. How anyone could sit on a toilet stool that long was beyond his comprehension, but he supposed she was still miffed at him and so was stretching out her stay there, hoping he'd go up to his room.

He cocked his head to listen. Pretty quiet in there. "Hey, you doing a year's worth of the New York *Times* crossword puzzle?" he called out teasingly, resisting the temptation to pound on the door to try to get a rise out of her. In part, his consideration wasn't so much because he was a nice guy as it was purely his preservation instinct taking over. Her temperament since she'd reentered his life had pretty much been two degrees shy of freezing. And she hadn't been at all happy with him earlier. He didn't need frostbite.

But despite her treating him like a virtual stranger, he harbored no illusions as to his feelings for her. That had been driven home yesterday afternoon when she'd walked up the driveway to his duplex. She was the only woman he'd ever loved.

Glenna had paced almost nonstop for thirty minutes, while Marcus halfheartedly read tarot cards. He didn't feel like doing more in-depth readings, as he already had highly detailed ones for each of the major players in this little drama. But unfortunately Mav had decided to explore LoDo, so there was no one around to talk to unless he wanted to shout through the bathroom door. Maybe he should take Glenna out for a walk. She seemed completely preoccupied with being a pain in his backside just then and could probably use the exercise.

When Mav got back, Marcus planned to bounce strategies

off him and Endora. They had to devise a plan to take on Ashmedai in as quick and efficient a manner as they could, starting with their trip to the museum. The clock was running.

He knew they could come up with something solid, if only he could get Endora to talk to him with minimal hissing and spitting. He glared at the door currently separating them. That particular female had been twisting him up inside for the better part of four decades. Now that she was back in his life, he felt completely off-balance. Given the task ahead, it was a dangerous place to be.

Shifting in the recliner he'd taken when Endora went into the bathroom, he bumped his hip against something hard. He reached down between the cushion and the chair arm and pulled out the *Demon Watcher's Field Guide*. Instant suspicion hit him. "Endora, what were you looking for in this—"

A cold, wet nose pressed against his thigh, snapping Marcus' attention to Glenna. She barked, wagged her tail, then did the leaping, turning dance that said she had to be let outside immediately or dire consequences would follow.

Sighing, he rose from the recliner. "All right, all right. Keep your fur on. There's a bit of lawn out back for you to use."

The closer he got to the back door, the higher Glenna jumped. She was practically levitating when he turned the knob. The moment the door opened, she shouldered through the opening and bolted into the night.

"Wow. That's some nature's call," Marcus grumbled.

When he finally realized she wasn't stopping to do her business in the back yard, she had already vanished. *What in hades has gotten into her?* He whistled a piercing signal. "Glenna! Get back here!"

Hurrying to the bathroom door, he rapped sharply with his knuckles. "Dora, the dog just took off like a bat out of hell. I'm going after her." No response. Even worse, his hand tingled where it had contacted the wood. *Magic.* He tried the handle. Locked. "Dora?" He rapped again. "Dora, answer me." She'd given in too easily on the museum trip. That's because she hadn't planned to wait. Fear building inside his chest, he raised his foot and kicked the door in. He knew before looking that the bathroom was empty. "Son of a bitch!"

On the sink sat the local section of the *Post*, radiating magic. Fear turned into rage as he contemplated what this meant. She'd not only gone out on her own to investigate the museum, but she'd cast a spell on the article to erase the evidence. What hurt more than anything was the thought that she knew full well he wouldn't be able to counter the spell. Then panic hit when he realized he remembered only that there was a museum exhibit on mysticism.

Why didn't I read the article more closely? he chastised himself. *Because I was too busy bullying her into taking Mav and me with her. Like that worked.*

She had gone after Ashmedai alone, and he had almost no idea of where to find her.

* * *

"Join you?" For every step Ashmedai took forward, Endora retreated one, trying to narrow the gap between herself and the monoliths. "You sucked my best friend into your black magic cult, then killed her and one hundred and one other witches when the Tribunal came after you. You're purely evil, and you're butt-ugly to boot. I'd never join you."

"Come, now, Endora, you can't escape me." His voice was almost hypnotic. He indicated the exhibit with his right hand. "Wouldn't it be nice to be on the winning side for once? We'd make a fine team."

"You can go to the deepest pit of hades."

His chuckle froze her blood. Then he sighed theatrically. "So predictable, my noble Endora. I never thought you'd accept my offer, you know. You were always on a crusade. Thinking you and Marcus were the perfect team to rid the world of my evil. But you failed, didn't you? Failed utterly."

She took another step back. "I'm beginning to think that failure wasn't so much of our own doing as it was the result of help from others."

"You only took forty years to come to that conclusion? I thought you were far more clever than that." He lowered both hands to his sides. "Last chance to take my offer."

"I gave you my answer."

"Ah, yes. The noble response. Pity. I could have used your talents." His laugh was sinister. "Of course, once you're dead, I'll have all your talents for myself, anyway."

"I'm not dead yet."

"Purely a matter of semantics. Good-bye, Endora. As I am an honorable witch, I promise your end will be quick and painless."

"Honorable my a—"

In a move so quick she almost didn't see it coming, Ashmedai raised his hands and sent a bolt of pure energy blasting from his fingers, sizzling like lightning and heading directly at her chest. Only her catlike reflexes kept her from dying right then, but she didn't escape unscathed. As she dove behind the nearest monolith, the blast connected. Its impact spun her half around, sending her sprawling awkwardly to the floor.

"Goddess," she hissed through clenched teeth as waves of agony rolled up her leg.

A smoking hole the size of her fist had been burned into her left thigh, exposing bone. She grabbed her leg with hands that trembled uncontrollably and fought to remain conscious in the face of excruciating pain. It was a near thing. But her motivation was strong. If she passed out, she died.

Suddenly, Ashmedai' silky voice enveloped her. "Still among the living, Endora, my sweet?"

I've got a few lives left, you soulless son of a Hecate.

"Ahhhh," he crooned. "Your telepathy is perilously weak, but very much intact."

She didn't waste energy calling him a pompous, intellectual ass. His voice grew more clear. He was getting closer. She was literally a sitting duck, but his immense ego played to her advantage. By stopping to taunt her before moving in for the kill, he had inadvertently given her a small window of time. Hopefully, enough to make an escape. Gritting her teeth until her jaw hurt, she slid farther behind the stone, bracing her back against it. She had to slow her breathing with a deliberate effort, concentrate her energy and focus. Her life depended on intense, uninterrupted focus.

"Now you die." Ashmedai leaped around the monolith, hands poised, fingertips crackling with energy.

No one was there.

Six

Glenna, I need help.

Endora raced up the four flights of stairs as fast as her three good legs could carry her. Her instincts had been right. A cat with one severely injured leg was far more mobile than a one-legged human. She had escaped from her hiding place seconds before Ashmedai pounced, and since he'd thought to find a badly wounded witch, his shock at finding nothing had bought her more time. For someone who considered himself a genius, his ego had interfered with the age-old adage about warfare: Know thy enemy. Having no clue she was a shape-shifter meant he hadn't anticipated she'd be anywhere but lying behind the monolith, set up for an easy kill. She'd been long gone before he even comprehended the fact she wasn't there.

But blocking the intense pain in her leg required all her energy, making teleportation impossible. She needed help to make a clean escape.

Glenna, I'm at the new museum, over in the park. I'm hurt really badly, and need you to get me back to the safe house.

Thought you'd run into some trouble, so I came to investigate. I'm half a block away, on the entrance side.

A wave of relief broke over Endora as she slowed to check her bearings. *Run right across the front of the building,* she instructed. *I'll be coming off the balcony.*

Be there in ten seconds.

Although she knew Ashmedai would zero in on her telepathic signal and locate her, it couldn't be helped. Glenna was her best chance at getting away relatively in one piece. Endora gathered herself for one last effort. Ignoring the pain in her left foreleg, she pushed on toward the end of the gallery, firing a bolt of mental energy at the balcony doors even as she went. When she heard the lock snap open, she breathed a bit easier.

That same breath caught in her throat when Ashmedai's voice echoed around her.

"You can't escape me, Endora." His statement was all the more menacing for its calm certainty.

Every hair follicle she had stood on end as she sensed a

powerful surge of energy building behind her. Without looking back, she pushed through the door, raced across the balcony and leaped into the night. Behind her, the balcony doors and part of the wall exploded in a shower of brick, glass and shrapnel, just missing her as she sailed out into space.

I'm counting on you, buddy. As she flew through the night, Endora tucked her wounded leg tight against her body and stretched her three good legs out in her best Rocky the Flying Squirrel imitation. Glenna's dark coat camouflaged the dog perfectly, but Endora sensed her moving below. Her senses were confirmed when she heard, *Got ya in my sights, wimpy cat.*

It was the sweetest insult she'd ever heard.

The dog, moving like a Pro-Bowl wide receiver on a post pattern, calculated the arc of Endora's leap and timed her drop perfectly. She was traveling at top speed when Endora made a three-point landing right on her front shoulders. Without breaking stride, Glenna raced off into the night.

Welcome aboard the Pit Bull Express. Estimated time of arrival at our destination is eight minutes, depending on traffic lights.

Funny.

A sound suspiciously like a chuckle rumbled out of the broad chest. *Hang on, pussycat. I don't want to lose you out here in the dark.*

Don't worry, stupid dog. You can't shake me. Wrapping her hind legs around Glenna's sides, Endora slid her uninjured forepaw under the dog's collar and rested her head on the powerful shoulders moving in a steady, ground-eating stride beneath her. *And by the way, nice catch. But we'd better maintain radio silence for the duration of the trip, so our evil buddy up in the museum can't track us.*

Affirmative.

* * *

Endora must have lost consciousness, because the next thing she knew, gentle hands were lifting her from Glenna's back and placing her on her side on the sofa. She had just enough energy to shift back to human form.

"What in hades happened?" Marcus' voice was rough with concern as he carefully rolled her to her back and pushed a pillow under her left knee.

"I ran into our friend Ashmedai at the Museum of Art and

Culture." She bit back a curse when Marcus jarred her slightly, sending bolts of agony along her nervous system. "Ouch! Take it easy."

"Sorry."

He raised concern-filled black eyes to her face, and Endora noticed his hands shaking almost as badly as hers had when Ashmedai first blasted her. Her heart gave an odd little half-beat. If she hadn't been in so much pain, she'd have reached out and stroked his cheek to reassure him she'd be all right. That thought scared her so much that she fell back on irony. Gritting her teeth against a throbbing ache, she said matter-of-factly, "It's just a flesh wound."

He didn't even crack a smile. "You're going to an emergency room."

Endora had to breathe in through her clenched lips to keep from screaming with pain. "No."

Marcus's jaw bulged where he gritted his teeth. "Your leg looks like steak, medium rare. You need help."

She didn't feel up to this fight, but had to do it. "How could I explain this? Used a blow torch to dry off wet leather pants while still wearing them?"

"I'm sure they've heard wilder tales."

"Marcus, please. Magic caused this. No medical doctor can heal it." Unbidden, tears filled her eyes, and she cursed her weakness. "Get hold of Cassie. She'll know what to do."

He stared at her a moment, so much caring in his eyes she thought her heart would break from seeing it. "What's her number?"

Her mind was clouded by pain, or she'd have caught the tension in his voice. "What?"

"What's her phone number?" He stood up abruptly, looming over her. "Because I don't have any magic, Endora, so like any human being, I have to use a damned telephone to call people."

"It is three-thirty on the East Coast," Mav said, gliding in unheard. He was completely unaware of the byplay going on around him. "Won't your friend be sleeping?"

"Most likely." Endora closed her eyes, gathered her scattered thoughts. "But she's not going to be for long." *Cassie? Cassie, it's Endora. Sorry to bother you, but I'm in a really bad way.*

Cassie's reply sounded perfectly lucid. *Dora? Where are*

you?

   Denver. I'm in bad shape.

Within moments, Endora had the phone number of Medusa's friend, Trish, a talented energy healer in New Orleans. Endora passed the number on to Marcus.

Even though it was two-thirty there, the call was answered almost immediately.

"Energy Healing."

The soft voice on the other end was completely alert, and Marcus breathed a silent sigh of relief. "Is this Trish? A former client of yours, Medusa Morlock's daughter Cassandra, gave me your number. Her friend Endora has been badly injured and needs your immediate help."

"I know. Tell me how this happened."

Marcus was a witch. Statements like that didn't surprise him. So, he gave the requested information, then listened intently as instructions poured out of the phone. "Mav, check in the pantry for snakeroot and valerian root." He listened some more. "Make snakeroot tea, and steep the valerian in non-boiling water for twenty minutes. Cover the pan so the oil doesn't evaporate."

As Mav hurried to help out, Marcus held the receiver to his chest and said to Endora, "I've got to get you out of those pants."

"Boy, if I had a dollar for every time I've heard that line."

The crack would have been more humorous if she hadn't been gritting her teeth while she said it, but the fact she could even think clearly enough to come up with it encouraged Marcus, and admiration and love for her nearly overwhelmed him. Her injury had to be excruciating, but she was playing her devil-may-care persona to the hilt. He suspected it was, in part, to keep him from panic. Admittedly, her ploy was working.

Mav brought in the tea, having used the modern wonder of the microwave to quickly brew a large mug full. He handed it to Marcus, who laid the phone on the coffee table then knelt beside Endora. Fighting the urge to kiss her cheek, he held up the mug. "This is a tranquilizer. I'm going to give it a couple minutes to take effect, while I get everything else I need ready. Then, those pants are coming off."

"Sweet talker," Endora rasped, her eyes clouded with pain. "I don't suppose there's any way to save the slacks. I really, really love them."

Sliding his right arm under her shoulders, Marcus slowly

raised her head and brought the cup to her lips. "It's rather shallow to love things, don't you think?"

"So sue me." She drank deeply of the tea, paused for a breath, then finished the mug.

"Good girl." He lowered her back to the pillow and pushed her bangs back off her face. It didn't surprise him to feel a slight fever beneath his fingertips. "Don't go away."

"Strange, but I suddenly have the irresistible urge to square dance." When he raised an eyebrow, she sighed. "All right, party pooper. I'm going to lie right here and dream of converting my slacks into a skirt."

He had to smile. "Based on where the hole is, it'll have to be a miniskirt."

She was already starting to go under as he picked up the receiver again.

"There's a large chrysocolla crystal on the bookshelf," Trish's disembodied voice instructed. "It's turquoise intertwined with a mineral that looks like silver."

"Got it." Marcus brought the palm-size crystal over to the coffee table.

"You'll place this right next to the wound, as it heals the body's cells." There was a slight pause. "It also can be used to bless the past and forgive old hurts, but I believe that use is for another time."

Startled, Marcus held the phone away from his ear and stared at it as if he could see Trish through it. He heard her soft chuckle on the other end of the line. To keep himself from being more embarrassed, he turned to his able assistant. "Is the valerian root turned to oil yet?"

"I will see." Mav glided back into the kitchen. He lifted the lid on the pan and called back to Marcus, "Yes."

"Okay. Turn off the heat and leave the lid on."

Marcus put the phone on speaker to free both hands. Trish's voice immediately filled the room.

"You'll need two more crystals besides the chrysocolla. I sense there's a very large quartz sitting on the window sill behind you. Put it on the coffee table. Last, you need a beryl crystal. The large egg you took to Denver with you to enhance your divination skills will be perfect, Marcus."

That statement did surprise him. "How did you know that?"

He actually heard the gentle humor in her voice when she replied, "I sense great power in and around you."

"I'll be right back."

He raced to his bedroom and grabbed the beryl egg off the window ledge where he'd set it after doing his tarot readings. In under a minute, he was back at Endora's side. Noting that she seemed to be sleeping easily, he tried to feel relieved. But there was still so much to do. Just the sight of the seared, gaping wound in her thigh was reminder enough of that.

"It will be easier to keep her warm if you don't remove her pants completely, so cut off her left pant leg just above the wound."

"You're ruining my fantasy here, lady," he muttered, then gulped when a chuckle came over the speaker. To cover his discomfort at being caught thinking lascivious thoughts at a totally inappropriate time, he quickly cut the supple leather, sliding it off Endora's leg without letting it touch the wound. "Done."

"Now, place the beryl crystal on her stomach. Put the quartz on her right thigh, exactly level with the wound. The chrysocolla must go next to her injury but not on her body. The sofa cushion will do, as close to her skin as you can get it."

"Okay."

"Now, your hands will be mine. Spread your fingers as wide as you comfortably can and hold them just above her leg. Don't touch her. I want you to concentrate on feeling the warmth that will be coming through your hands and out your fingertips then spreading out over the wound. Focus your thoughts on that and nothing else. I'll take care of the rest."

Marcus turned to Mav and said tightly, "You're going to have to be as silent as the dead, buddy. I've just been recruited to do this energy healing thing."

"Have you any skill at energy healing?"

"What do you think?" Marcus snapped.

"I would think the answer is no," Mav replied calmly in the face of Marcus's sudden outburst. "And your fear of failure is making you short-tempered and hostile to your friends."

Marcus could feel his face heat from embarrassment. "Hey, sorry, Mav. You're right. I'm scared to death I won't be able to do this. Shouldn't take it out on you, though."

"I will leave you to your task." He looked down at Glenna, lying by the recliner, tensely alert. "And I will take the pit bull with me for a walk, to protect me from attack."

"Mav, you made a joke."

"I did." He motioned to the dog. "Come, Glenna. Let us prowl what is left of the night."

"Thanks, Mav."

As the vampire left, the dog at his heels, Trish's voice came clearly over the speaker. "There's no need to be afraid, Marcus. I truly sense great power in you. Follow my instructions, and you'll enhance my talents. And Endora will mend that much faster."

Those words were like a balm to Marcus's badly damaged ego. *Unfortunately, Endora doesn't trust me anywhere near as much as you do, Trish.*

"I think you'd be surprised."

He didn't acknowledge the healer's last remark. Instead, he took a deep breath and let it out slowly, cleansing his mind of outside distractions. Then, as instructed, he held his palms flat above Endora's injured thigh, moving them slowly back and forth as he concentrated on evenly distributing the heat pouring from his hands. Before his eyes, the seared flesh began to mend.

Endora moaned softly. "By the goddess, you're good."

He'd thought her completely under from the snakeroot tea, and her comment startled him, breaking his focus. Nonplused, he almost blurted out that he was even better at other things, particularly of the sensual variety. The gentle admonition to concentrate filled his ears and kept him in line. Hades and brimstone! Caught out a second time having naughty thoughts. The energy healer must think him a complete dog.

Trish's chuckle again carried over the speaker.

"I should be charging a sin tax for my fantasies," he murmured, and Trish's chuckle turned to a laugh. "All right. I'm concentrating."

Thirty minutes later when he lowered his badly shaking hands, only a fist-sized patch of pink skin marked Endora's wound.

"That was nicely done," Trish said in her soft voice. "Now you need to get the valerian oil. Massage it down Endora's leg from just above the wound all the way along the bottom of her foot. Work away from her body to drive the pain out and promote cell repair.

"The foot, as you likely know, is a major healing center. Knead the sole with both thumbs, starting from the midline and working to the outside. Cover the entire surface. Use your fingertips to massage the top of her foot while you're massaging the bottom with your thumbs. Ten minutes should be enough. Then hang up the phone and get some sleep."

"I'd kiss you if you were here, lady," Marcus said, his words slowed by exhaustion. "As it is, you'll have to settle for my profound thanks."

"You and Endora must visit me some time soon, and you can deliver on that promise."

Marcus had no way to describe how much hope the energy healer's words gave him. Trish thought he and Endora had a future together. And if they had one, the rest of witchkind had one. He could only pray she was right.

"Rest well," was all he could manage in response to her invitation.

"And you."

Endora was sound asleep, but her left ear twitched several times as he massaged the oil into her skin. Paying close attention to what he was supposed to be accomplishing, he followed Trish's instructions to the letter.

Once done, he wiped his hands on a dish towel and returned the crystals to their respective places in the living area. Slipping the beryl egg into his pocket, he returned to the sofa. And couldn't stop himself from taking a long moment to look down at Endora as she slept. Her wound was nothing more than a pink patch of skin that would likely heal without any trace. She was going to be upset about her favorite leather pants, but there was nothing to be done to salvage them. The size of the hole in the pant leg…In her leg….

Abruptly, Marcus had to fight an overwhelming need to vomit, a tidal wave of nausea he'd managed to ignore during the healing. But now, the remembered horror of Endora's wound, the smell of burned flesh and the sight of exposed bone nearly brought him to his knees. Thinking it best to sit for a moment before he fell headfirst on top of his patient, he plopped down on the coffee table and steadied himself with a bit of yoga breathing. Finally, he knew he wouldn't embarrass himself by losing his supper. But it had been close. Not used to feeling this weak, he decided he disliked the sensation. Very much.

He reached the short distance between him and Endora to grasp her left hand between both of his. Thankfully, his were steady again, instead of shaking as if palsied. A combination of tenderness and hurt radiated from his heart as he studied her.

And relief. Had she not been so resourceful and Trish not so skilled, Endora could very well have died that night. Obsidian Ashmedai would again have taken away something dear to Marcus.

Perhaps that was why he'd been so badly hurt when Endora had lied to him about her plan to go to the museum. Her solitary hunt for Ashmedai violated Marcus's every protective instinct, his every need to safeguard what was his.

He released her hand and sat back. That could be the problem, and he just couldn't admit it. He saw Endora as his, and she didn't. Her feline nature made her stubbornly independent, but he had assumed, perhaps wrongfully, that their being cosmic twins would offset that self-reliant streak. Now, he had no reason to assume anything. The horoscope he'd read earlier had detailed their challenges. He to cooperate, she to excel. And his tarot readings not only reinforced this but added more to the picture. For him, a male witch trained to believe he should control every situation, it was damned hard to sit back and play the passive role.

But it looked like that was exactly what it was going to take.

He gently ran the back of his hand up Endora's cheek, then anchored a loose lock of hair behind her ear. Her left ear twitched once.

"You're so beautiful, Dora," he whispered. "I love you so much I can barely stand it. And I can barely stand that you didn't trust me enough to tell me your plans." Another deep breath. "But I'm trying to deal with that."

Kneeling, he gathered her into his arms and carried her to his bed.

* * *

Endora woke before dawn, disoriented by something intangible. Pain? Remembering how the blast of Ashmedai's energy force had burned like hellfire, she carefully stretched her left leg. Stiff, but not at all sore. The miracle of that reality staggered her. Trish's healing energy, coupled with Marcus's hands, had proven impossibly effective. She ran her fingertips carefully along her thigh. There was no obvious scarring, which defied human logic. But, of course, she was a witch, so human logic held no sway with her. However, she had a healthy respect for power. And even though Endora knew Trish was human, the energy healer had that in spades.

But Endora's acceptance of Trish's talents wasn't what had awakened her. She assessed the situation. Well, her leather pants were gone, and she was in her panties and an oversized tee shirt that wasn't hers. Her nose twitched. Marcus's alluring masculine scent permeated the garment, but it was more than just smell that she sensed. *Heat.* And something else. It only took a moment to realize that for the first time in what seemed eons she felt safe. Ridiculous, given the current circumstances and the fact she'd very nearly been killed earlier that night, but she went with the moment and didn't question her feelings.

She could feel Marcus at her back, sleeping beside her yet not touching her. A twinge of guilt pricked. Likely, he was still angry she'd lied to him about going to the museum. That would have to be dealt with, but right then she had to see to her own needs.

Whether it strained the anti-love spell to the breaking point or not, she had to touch Marcus. Rolling over until she faced him, she laid her hand on his chest and her head on his shoulder, then snuggled up close. Her body tingled everywhere they touched, but she wouldn't back away. His heat and the feel of his skin against hers were things she'd craved for forty years. Although lust threatened to build to real heat, it was banked by her physical condition and the spell. Physically, she was in no shape for intense lovemaking, and knew they couldn't come together any other way. Intellectually, she understood that defeating their enemy had to take priority over their own personal needs.

Still, she could enjoy the feel of Marcus's body. And she did, running her palm over his broad chest. The dark hair sprinkled across it felt like silk. Goddess, he had a terrific physique.

She hugged him. *My hero.* Hours before, he'd put aside his anger at her and helped save her life. The reassurance of his steady heartbeat under her ear abruptly brought her to the verge of tears, which she refused to shed. A cynical, jaded witch such as she did not succumb to emotional displays, even if the reason for that display was unaware of his effect. *We're going to talk about* us, *Marcus,* she silently promised. *Soon.*

When his arms closed around her, her ear twitched once before she drifted back to sleep.

* * *

The next time she woke, it was mid-afternoon and she

found herself alone in Marcus's bed. She stretched cautiously, trying out her injured leg and glad to discover that her lack of pain wasn't just some leftover hallucination from the snakeroot tea.

She lay back down and closed her eyes, concentrating. *Cassie, you there?*

Telepathy over two thousand-plus miles didn't hide the relief in Cassie's reply. *Dora, thank the goddess! I've been worried sick. Are you all right?*

Amazingly, I'm fine. A bit stiff, but nothing major. Trish is incredible. Endora ran her hand down her left thigh, still astonished the flesh was completely healed. *Sorry I woke you up in the middle of the night last night.*

Don't even go there. I'd never have forgiven you if you hadn't contacted me. Besides, Heckle and Jeckle spent the entire evening kicking my kidneys around like soccer balls. I wasn't anywhere near asleep when you connected with me.

Well, I'm grateful.

There was a long pause. *Besides the obvious near-death experience, how are things going out there?*

Not good. But after last night, I've got a definite idea of exactly what we're up against.

We're up against? Speculation was clear in Cassie's thought. *So, Marcus came along?*

He did, actually.

Why do I get the feeling this little excursion last night didn't include him?

Admitting her boss knew her so well was annoying. So Endora chose not to comment on her feelings regarding that fact. *Probably because you would be right.*

Now, exasperation crackled across the telepathic connection. *Endora, why are you putting yourself at unnecessary risk? I thought you needed Marcus's help.*

It's complicated, Cass.

Another long pause. *How's the anti-love spell holding up?*

Thankfully, very well.

My mother knows her magic.

She certainly does. Endora didn't want to think about Medusa's advice after they'd cast the spell, but she had the feeling she wasn't going to get what she wanted in this case.

And it was time to face Marcus.

Cassie, I've gotta go. Thanks again for bailing me out of a tight situation. And tell Medusa her friends are worth their weight in gold.

So are mine.

Endora took a long, hot shower to remove what little muscle stiffness remained. And, she had to admit, to put off for just a bit longer the inevitable confrontation with Marcus. *Scaredy-cat,* she chided herself. *Damn right.*

It was a little after two o'clock when she got to the kitchen. Ravenous, she made a beeline for the fridge. She normally tried to avoid cooking at all costs, but in a pinch she could navigate the realm of food preparation with a modicum of skill.

She poured herself a huge glass of milk and another of orange juice, and was rummaging around for omelet ingredients when Marcus walked in.

Pulling her head out from behind the refrigerator door, she tried to gauge his mood. But he wouldn't meet her eyes. *Evasion tactics, eh? Well, let's see if the way to a man's heart is through his stomach...* "Hungry?"

"No."

Okaaay...Extreme anger, disguised by that male-witch aloofness we females are so not *fond of. Understandable, his acting that way, though.* "Mind if I fix myself breakfast while we talk?" When he didn't answer, she took that as no objection and proceeded to chop up ham and mushrooms, then started sautéing them. While they simmered, she grated cheese.

"When I read the article about the mysticism exhibit at Denver's new Museum of Arts and Culture, the curator's name caught my eye. Daemon Azazel translates into a Hebrew devil which loosely is the equivalent of Obsidian Ashmedai. So I went to investigate. Turns out, the curator is in fact our old friend." Marcus remained silent as she whipped the eggs into a froth then poured them into a second frying pan. "He was there, and I let him get the drop on me. Can't believe how stupid I was not to pay better attention."

"Stupid being the operative word." He sat down at a stool by the breakfast counter, but it was obvious he wanted to pace.

By telling herself she had earned his wrath, she controlled her temper. Whether or not she deserved it was an argument for later, but the fact remained that she'd given him reason to be angry. After removing the omelet from the flame and transferring it to a plate, she looked straight into his furious eyes. "You're spoiling for a fight, so have at it."

He wasted no time taking her up on that invitation. Anyone besides Endora would tremble in the face of the anger radiating off him in waves. She merely braced for it.

"How could you be so careless, Endora?" he asked tightly, emotions barely in check. "You were certain Ashmedai would be there, but kept that to yourself. You lied about when you planned to go to the museum, then put a spell on the article to delay Mav and me if we figured things out. But dumbest move of all, you went in without either of us to back you up."

"What was the point of bothering you over something that might have been a waste of time?" She knew her lame explanation was given all the credence it deserved when his eyes turned to ice.

"Bat shit," he spat. "You said yourself that no clue, no matter how mundane, should be ignored."

"I wasn't ignoring it, I—"

"Having second thoughts about asking for my help? Well, it's too late for that, Slick. We're in this together, whether you want to be or not. So stop the Wonder Woman act."

"I haven't got the boobs to hold up Wonder Woman's costume."

"Don't I know that."

Oh yeah, her deception had definitely hurt his feelings. She forgave his nastiness because she understood its source. If their places had been reversed, she'd have been spitting mad, too, and just as likely to say something spiteful. "I really did just go to check things out. I didn't think I needed help."

"Didn't think you needed help, or didn't believe I could be any?"

She couldn't stop her flinch. *Hit the problem on the first try, Marcus.* Crunch time. Ashmedai was far more powerful than either of them had bargained for. If they had any chance against him, they had to work together. But cooperation was doomed without honesty and trust between them. It suddenly felt like she had a football-sized hairball lodged in her throat.

"All right." She looked straight into his angry eyes and said, "I did think you'd be more of a liability than a help last night. And after running into Ashmedai, I know I was right."

Seven

Marcus's Adam's apple worked furiously a moment, but his voice was even when he stated, "I'd have had your back. By the goddess, Endora, that bastard nearly killed you."

Steeling herself against the pain she saw in his face, she said flatly, "Well, he didn't."

He rose from the stool and started pacing. "If I'd been there, we'd at least have outnumbered him."

"That's where you're wrong." She wanted to shout, but forced her emotions down and kept her tone level. "Put your ego aside and think for a minute. He almost amputated my leg with one energy blast. If I wasn't a shifter, I'd be dead. What would he have done to you?"

That stopped him cold, and she could see him working out the reality in his head.

"Why put a spell on the newspaper?" he asked.

"I explained that."

"So, since I no longer have any magic, I'm not someone you need on your team?"

It was tempting to throw the frying pan at him. Instead, she blew a frustrated breath up into her bangs. "Do *not* put words into my mouth. That's not what I said, and you know it." She focused her most intense feline stare on him. "As it is, my hunch turned up some valuable information. Ashmedai's far more powerful than he should be, considering his birthday's still over three days away."

His jaw set stubbornly "But you didn't know that last night."

"I went on instinct. It's what cats often do."

"Don't get cute with me, Endora."

That did it. She slammed the spatula down on the counter, sending remnants of egg and mushrooms flying in several directions. Then she squared up on him, jabbing her index finger into his chest.

"I'm not getting cute, you lunkhead! I told you the truth. No, I didn't think you could help, and yes it was because you don't have any magic. But that's not the issue. The issue is that Ashmedai has all his powers. We *don't*. We're in bat guano up to our necks right now. So, we can stand here and have a pissing match over whose feelings were hurt and why, or we can sit down like adults and make a plan that might just save our sorry asses and the world as well."

A look that could have been embarrassment crossed his handsome features. He glanced down at her finger, poised an inch from his chest, then looked back into her eyes. "You called me a lunkhead."

"Well, you were acting like one."

"But a *lunkhead*?" He put his hands on his hips, cocked his head to look at her. "Come on, Endora. What kind of insult is that?"

She blinked, then nearly shouted for joy. Ego crisis averted. "Well, I wanted to say self-centered, egotistical, pompous, macho, male chauvinist witch, but I needed a shorter term. For impact, you know."

"Of course." He looked at her plate. Smiled wryly. "You'd better eat that before it gets cold."

Without another word she took her breakfast to the table, returned for the glasses, then sat down to eat. "Is Mav around? We need him to be in on this discussion."

"Up in his room." Marcus moved quickly to the stairs and shouted for his friend.

While she waited for everyone to appear, Endora wolfed down her food. *Hey, stupid dog. You asleep?*

The dead couldn't sleep with all the caterwauling going on between you and Marcus. You two really know how to fight. Glenna rose from her pallet near the bookcase, stretched, then sauntered over. *What's up?*

Marcus returned with Mav right behind him.

Meeting of the minds. I'd like you to sit in.

No problem. Glenna plopped down on the floor near Endora's chair.

"You should give your mutt there a raw egg with her next meal," Endora said to Marcus as he took the chair to her right. Mav sat down opposite her. "She's just a dog, of course, but she earned her keep last night."

"Sure enough, Slick."

When everyone had settled, Endora looked at each of the men, then bent down to pat Glenna's broad head and stroke her ears. "I confess that when we started this, I had very real reservations about bringing Mav and Glenna along." She smiled at Marcus. "But I'm glad you insisted. If you hadn't, I doubt I'd be sitting here right now."

Glenna gave a low woof. *I'm always glad to do my part*

for interspecies understanding and harmony.

And you do it well. Thanks, Wonder Dog. "Based on my encounter with Obsidian Ashmedai last night, I realize we're all going to have to play to our strengths to defeat him."

Marcus rubbed his chin with his hand. "What about the Tribunal's restrictions on who can take Ash on?"

"To hades with them." Just remembering the feel of Ashmedai's power brought equal parts of anger and horror racing back into Endora's mind. "This is nowhere near a level playing field, so I say we cheat to even things up."

"All is fair in love and war?" Mav asked.

"Exactly." She turned from looking at the vampire to focus on Marcus. "Besides, the Tribunal didn't specifically say we couldn't use outside help. The restriction was against augmenting our existing magic. We've already utilized a human, a vampire and a pit bull, so I say let's plan a strategy using the skills of our little Gang of Four here."

Looking suddenly uncomfortable, Mav shifted in his chair. "But what can I contribute?"

Endora smiled at him. "You're the X-factor, remember? No one knows about you, and you can move in complete silence. That will help us the next time we meet the enemy. He'll be able to sense the rest of us, but I think he'll have a very hard time detecting you."

Marcus reached over and slapped Mav on the shoulder. "That's going to be a huge advantage. Individually, we can't outgun him, but we can certainly use our numerical advantage to make him spread his powers thin."

"We need to organize this." Endora left the table just long enough to locate a pad of paper and a pen. Seated again, she put four columns down the page, with each of their names atop one column. She looked at Mav. "Okay, what are your strengths and weaknesses?"

"I keep biting myself."

"Weakness." Endora wrote it down. "But you've got the silence thing on the plus side."

"As well as nearly superhuman strength and the ability to move like the wind," Marcus stated.

With a nod, Endora added those to Mav's positives, continuing to write as they brainstormed the group's virtues and liabilities. Extreme height for Mav, and the power of divination for Marcus. Glenna's large teeth, speed and power, and Endora's shape shifting and ability to teleport in cat form. The fact that she and the dog could communicate telepathically was a positive as well.

Once they'd exhausted their list, she itemized everything she had learned the night before about Ashmedai's current magical abilities. The list was no less intimidating for being short.

Held up against his formidable power, they looked like children playing at war games.

"Understanding Ashmedai's psyche will help us, too," Endora stated.

"That's great, Sigmund," Marcus responded, "tell us what you know."

She lightly slapped his shoulder, this time enjoying the zing of electricity brought on by touching him. "This is all stuff Medusa told me."

"Are you speaking of the original Medusa?" Mav asked, eyes alight. "The goddess with snakes for hair?"

"Sorry, no." Endora shook head, miffed at herself. "I forget sometimes that you don't know my friends. A witch named Medusa Morlock gave me some insight on Ashmedai."

Marcus snapped to attention at the name. "The Medusa Morlock who was a Tribunal Magistrate in the first half of the Twentieth Century?"

"The same."

Respect flared in Marcus's eyes. "Where'd you get such powerful friends, Dora?"

She shrugged. "Fate, maybe. I've been familiar to Cassandra Hathorne-Sandor almost since the Tribunal punished us. Cassie's my best friend, and she happens to be Medusa's daughter." She didn't inform them about the spell to keep her from jumping Marcus. Or the advice Medusa had given her regarding the spell. "Medusa told me that, according to lore, Ashmedai in demon form has three heads, facing different directions. A bull, a ram, and an ogre. He has the legs and feet of a cock and rides a fire-breathing lion."

"All creatures associated with lust," Marcus stated. Endora and Mav gaped at him. "Hey, I went to witch school. Graduated top in my class."

"Impressive," Endora drawled, but she smiled her approval. "Ashmedai's other areas of power are wrath and revenge. His favorite place is the bedroom."

"Not surprising." Marcus turned to Mav. "Since Ashmedai's a Scorpio, the body parts his sun sign rules are the sexual organs."

The vampire nodded. "Added to the creatures of lust his name is associated with, we must assume that he sees sex as power."

"That was certainly his m.o. at the circle." Endora blocked thoughts of Ashmedai's comment about wanting to be her lover. "Medusa also pointed out that his choosing such a repulsive name for himself indicates he thinks of his magic in extremely dark terms."

"So, he wasn't born Obsidian Ashmedai?" Marcus leaned forward on his elbows and studied Endora.

"Apparently, he took that name as soon as he could." Endora thought a moment. "Maybe that's why he hates nicknames. He about blew a fuse last night when I called him Ash."

Marcus raised an eyebrow. "You called him our pet name for him?"

"I sure did."

A smirk spread across his mouth. "Slick, my admiration for you grows and grows."

With difficulty, Endora tried to ignore the warmth his comment and the look in his eyes brought her. "Medusa said she couldn't believe the Tribunal let him take that name, since it has so many fiendish connotations."

"It seems your witches' tribunal has several members who do not have the group's best interests in mind." Mav wrote a short note on the paper front of him.

"You're absolutely right," Endora said

"We are *so* going to kick his ass," Marcus said lightly. "All we have to do is taunt him to death by calling him Ash."

Endora managed a wry smile, then played with the pen a moment, stalling to give herself time to find the words she needed. Suspicion had become certainty in the past twelve hours, and they needed to deal with it. Inwardly, she sighed. No sense beating around the bush.

"There's something else I need to throw out here," she said quietly, "just so everything's on the table, and we can start to form a plan that considers all the facts." Marcus and Mav both looked intently at her. "At least one member of the Tribunal is dirty. Seeing Ashmedai convinced me that he's been supported, even protected, by some Tribunal members since he took his demonic name."

Marcus got up from the table and went to the stove. Fiddling with the teapot, he lit the burner and put on the water. "Impossible."

"Is it?" Gently rubbing her thigh, Endora stared across the room at him. "Think back forty years. To the night you and I spent together. How were we able to slip away undetected from a nightly ritual service? The security at Ashmedai's circle was tighter than Fort Knox."

"All right, I'll give you that." He met Mav's gaze, explained, "I was sent by the Tribunal to work my way into Ashmedai's inner circle. Only three other witches were in that elite group. I was making progress toward that objective when the whole thing went to hades."

Endora continued, "Unless you were one of Ashmedai's elite, you were watched every moment. But the two of us snuck off, found an empty cabin, and had an all-night tryst without anyone interfering." She glanced at Marcus. "That doesn't sound just a bit suspicious to you?"

He shrugged, then rose and went to the stove. "We cast an excellent protection spell."

"Which anyone in that compound would have sensed, and Ashmedai would most certainly have tried to counteract."

Surprised, he looked up from where he was lighting the burner. "You're right. But, to our knowledge, no one knew what we were doing. And there was definitely no attempt to breach the spell. I certainly never thought about that. At all."

Endora found she'd been unconsciously doodling on the note pad. Lines and squiggles that looked suspiciously like bolts of energy radiating from a sphere took up an entire corner of a sheet of paper. She laid the pen down. "And how can Ashmedai have all the powers he had forty years ago, maybe more, given our punishment for not stopping him?"

"He should have permanently lost his magic." Sighing, Marcus leaned back against the counter. "Mav, I failed at my mission, and Endora was deemed an accessory to my failure. For that, I lost all my magic except divination and her magic was reduced to almost nothing."

"Because I'm also a shape-shifter, I can still teleport in cat form, and I've also still got my telepathy," Endora added. "But we were both punished as severely as Ash was."

"As I said, your Tribunal has an agenda that is not for the greater good." Mav stood a moment and stretched his long arms up over his head. Then he sat back down.

"For what that black-hearted bastard did, they should have executed him." The teapot whistled, demanding Marcus's attention. He poured boiling water into three heavy mugs and took them to the table. After setting one in front of Mav, he sat down, then pushed the third mug to Endora. He took a slow sip of his own tea before stating flatly, "Letting him live makes no sense. He's a totally evil, rogue witch."

Mav nodded. "I believe you have just made Endora's argument."

"I guess so, Mav."

Endora cupped the mug to warm her suddenly cold hands. "So, how do we deal with this unforeseen disadvantage?"

"It seems we must anticipate what he will do next, and then lure him into a trap." Mav bit the edge of his mug, as if he was teething. "How accurate are your methods of divination, Marcus?"

"Depends on which one I use, but I can be close to one hundred percent."

She whistled low through her teeth. "That's going to help big time."

"Remember that Horace said, 'To know all things is not permitted.'"

Both Marcus and Endora stared at Mav for a moment before she said, deadpan, "Well, close to one hundred percent fits into that old adage, I guess. So, we're safe."

Marcus rolled his eyes. "What I'll also do is use every method I have available. That way, the predictions that come up in all of them will be the completely accurate ones. Any deviations across any of the methods can be put into categories. The more times each of the deviations shows up, the more concerned we should be about that particular factor." He emptied his mug in one long swallow. "I've already got tarot readings for you, me and Ashmedai. It won't take me long to do ones for Mav and Glenna." He closed his eyes a moment. Calculating. "I can have all the other divinations done by seven o'clock tonight."

Mav put down his own mug and looked at Endora. "What should we do in the meantime?"

"We're going shopping." When both men gaped at her,

Endora stated blithely, "I want to get my hands on some fireworks."

"Fireworks?"

She ignored Marcus's skeptical expression. "Something to cause a distraction. I'm not above using any cheap, underhanded trick we can think of."

"Fort Carson is over in Colorado Springs," Marcus said half-seriously. "Bet you they have lots of things that blow up."

Endora shook her head. "I'm not interested in military weapons, although an Apache helicopter strike against Ash has tremendous personal appeal. All I want is lots of small stuff that will go boom and create billowing clouds of smoke."

"Perhaps there is an amusement park nearby," Mav suggested. "Or, an establishment like Medieval Festivals. We use pyrotechnics in each show."

"That's brilliant!" Marcus jumped up. At the bookshelf he pulled down a Denver phone book, leafing through it as he brought it back to the table. "If there's a place around here like Festivals, we're in luck."

Endora took the book from his hands. "Mav and I will check this out. You need to get started on your predictions."

"Sounds like a plan."

* * *

Four hours later, Mav and Endora were unloading boxes of bottle rockets, flash pots, Roman candles and pinwheels from the Satellite's trunk and bickering back and forth over who had found the coolest stuff. As they hauled the stash into the condo, Marcus came to investigate the commotion.

He surveyed the boxes and crates. "Looks like you did go to Fort Carson. Think the government will miss this stuff?"

"We purchased much of this from a legitimate dealer," Mav stated gravely.

"The rest we got from a less than legitimate roadside shop out south of here on Eighty-five," Endora added with a sly grin. "We drove almost to Sedalia."

"I'd say it was worth the trip." Marcus hefted a box and moved it to the side to clear a space for walking. "We could do the Fourth of July justice with this stuff."

She sensed a reticence in Marcus that hadn't been there following their shouting match earlier that afternoon. Wondering what was going on but hoping he'd be forthright about it and not leave her guessing, she said smoothly, "Let's hope it serves to distract a certain evil witch we know."

"We also bought igniters." Mav showed Marcus the three butane lighters they'd found in a discount store in Littleton. "We did not purchase one for Glenna, as she lacks opposable thumbs."

Marcus glanced over at his pet, decadently sprawled across her bed beneath a front window. "And here I always thought she was just clumsy."

Sure, go ahead. Make fun of the dog.

Endora laughed. "They're just teasing, Wonder Dog. Boys do that because they care."

"Either we tease you, or we slap you on the butt," Marcus agreed, but to Endora his wit seemed a bit forced. "If it's all the same to you guys, I'll bring kitchen matches as a backup. I don't have much luck with the fancy lighters."

Endora went to pour herself a glass of milk. "Suit yourself." She paused a minute and looked Marcus straight in the eye. "We've got to attack him tonight, you know. I stopped and got a bunch of willow branches. I'm going to make a witch's ladder out of them."

"What good will that do?" Mav asked.

"Knots can bind energy," Endora explained. "And willow has very powerful magic. So, I'm going to take the thinnest branches and make a net using nine knots. Theoretically, we can rob Ash of his power by throwing it over him."

"Theoretically?" Mav cocked an eyebrow.

Endora sighed. "I'm not sure I've got enough magic to cast the spell effectively. That's why we have to get him to expend as much energy as possible before I drop the net on him."

"He can't be completely recovered from last night," Marcus pointed out. "The five o'clock news carried reports of a huge explosion near the new museum. Over a hundred people phoned the police and fire departments, many reporting a fireball. Funny thing, though. When authorities checked out the place, there was no damage to any building in the area."

"Ash blew the balcony door and the top quarter of the building right out into the street." Endora's eyes lit up with the call to battle. "To repair that much damage, he would have had to expend an incredible amount of magical energy. He can't be at full power right now. This is our best chance to nail him."

"Let's get to work, then. I've got all the divinations finished.

Be right back." Marcus quickly returned from his bedroom, a hefty stack of papers and charts in his hands.

"That's a lot of information." Endora's observation was genuinely admiring, but she noted he didn't seem to give it much credence. Knowing he doubted her sincerity saddened her. She had lots of bridge-building to do, and it rankled that she'd have to put it off. That wouldn't stop her from being honest, though. "You work fast."

"Indeed, I do. Let's go over these."

It had been worth a try, she thought.

Endora and Mav took seats at the table while Marcus spread out the papers between them.

"Remember, Scorpio's key word for October is reasoning," Mav pointed out.

"And Sagittarius is 'make an effort,' and 'affinities' is for Capricorn." Endora winked at him. "You're not the only one with a good memory."

"I am impressed, Miss Endora." Mav gave her a half-bow as a show of respect.

She also remembered that her October Capricorn horoscope warned against stumbling over obstacles and being her own worst enemy. And the words *look to others of your kind to take advantage of some family trait to turn things around for you.* Those told her she'd be relying heavily on Marcus, magic or not. That particular thought stayed private.

"Okay, now that we've got the mutual love-fest thing out of the way," Marcus said mildly, "let's push on with the nitty-gritty."

"Yes, oh slave driver." Endora smiled sweetly at him.

"There are general statements for each of the days. October Twenty-ninth is 'time is the most personal possession.' 'Find an oracle you can believe in' covers the Thirtieth, and 'nothing spent can be completely restored' covers the Thirty-first."

Mav pressed his fingertips together in a posture of contemplation. "Time is critical for all of us right now. This could merely be a reminder of what is at stake."

"And we can't deny this is personal for us, too." Endora was once again doodling. It helped her concentrate. "Tomorrow's aphorism seems a bit obscure. Unless the oracle is someone real and not a metaphorical omen that could have numerous interpretations."

Mav looked at Marcus and Endora in turn. "Marcus is our

oracle, is he not?"

"Yes." Marcus's expression told Endora he was desperate to ask if she believed in him. She just as desperately wanted to be able to answer yes. Right then, however, she couldn't say for certain. And she'd sworn to be honest with him. "But since we know that, isn't the more important question who is Ashmedai's oracle?"

If he was disappointed in her answer, Marcus didn't show it. "Knowing his ego, he probably thinks he's his own."

"Of course!" Mav actually smiled. "The Scorpio must find out what type of man he is. Obsidian Ashmedai considers himself wise. A leader all others should follow."

"Makes sense," Marcus said. "He's already proven that with his circle."

Endora nodded as she drummed both index fingers on the table. "And now with the museum exhibit. I got the feeling from the newspaper article, and then from things he said last night, that he's canvassing for those with supernatural ability."

"Why would he do that?" Mav pushed the mug back and forth across the tabletop from hand to hand.

Endora shrugged. "A talent search for acolytes, maybe? He could be planning to start another circle."

"Brimstone and hades," Marcus swore. He started to crumple the paper in his hands, then placed it deliberately onto the table and smoothed it out before plunging his fists into his pockets. "That makes more sense than I care to admit. And, by the goddess, that possibility terrifies me."

"Agreed. But we knew when we started he was shooting for uber-witch status."

"I guess I just never wanted to seriously think about the ramifications of his meeting that goal." Marcus gripped the table with both hands, squeezed until the knuckles went white, then relaxed. "I'll give him one thing, he's convinced he's smarter than any of us."

"And he not only thinks he's omniscient, but omnipotent as well. The only witch intellectually as well as physically equipped to lead a circle of ultra-powerful witches. He wouldn't believe in anyone but himself." Endora again drummed the table. "So, his ego could very well be his biggest weakness."

"Make sure you add that to your assets and liabilities sheet," Marcus said.

She did. "All right, if we can't nail him tonight or tomorrow, for D-Day, we've got 'nothing spent can be completely restored.'" Seeing Mav's puzzled look, she explained, "Ashmedai's birthday is the Thirty-first. He regains all of his powers and can steal the ones we possessed before our punishment. So, that's our personal Normandy Invasion day."

Marcus got up to stretch. "Expending energy, in this case through magic, would apply here."

"If we force him to use huge amounts of magic tonight, maybe he won't be able to get it back at all." Endora underlined her sketch of the lightning bolts. "That's where all of our pyrotechnics come in. Drain his magic, trap him in the witch's ladder, take him down."

Marcus started to say something, then hesitated and shrugged. "Possibly. And we're certainly going to expend lots of energy by the time November first rolls in."

He wasn't sharing something, but Endora truly felt if it would endanger the mission, he would. So she didn't push him. Instead, she again studied the chart. "Energy expenditure's a given. As for today's horoscopes, Ashmedai's is 'attack is the reaction.'"

"That gave me chills when I first read it." Marcus paced a few steps then turned back to the table. "I'm not any warmer now."

"But you know what ours are, also."

He gave Endora an ironic smile. "Sagittarius says 'he who limps is still walking.'"

"Damn right I am."

Endora studied the horoscopes again. "I see a theme here with our buddy Ash. October thirtieth and thirty-first deal with death and the afterlife."

"And when you combine our horoscopes with Ash's, that theme's just reinforced," Marcus pointed out.

"Not very cheerful," Endora cracked, "but very, very true. But how can we use our foreknowledge to our advantage?"

"Consider the power of All Hallow's Eve." Mav sipped his tea before continuing. "The veil between this world and the next is very thin, thus it is the traditional night to celebrate an ancient pagan ritual."

"Followed by All Saint's Day on November first," Endora pointed out with a bit of a grin. "So the Christian saints can purge from the world all the evil spirits that got in the night before."

"You are being facetious," Mav stated.

Endora winked back at him.

"Ahem." Marcus cleared his throat, placed the horoscopes on the far side of the table, and picked up another sheet. "Another factor to consider. Not only is Halloween Ashmedai's birthday, making it a particularly powerful time for him, but there's a full moon that night as well."

"Oh bat shit! We're thinking ahead, but not thinking about right now. Given that today's Scorpio reading says attack, should we assume Ashmedai is going to come after us here? Soon?" Endora mentally checked the protection spell, found it was solid all around.

"I found no indicators in any of my divinations that he would. He's furious, and he'd like to fight back, but he doesn't know where we are."

"Do we know where he is?"

Eight

Marcus shrugged. "I can only pin him to is the museum. Even when I'm scrying, he only shows up there."

"At museum," Endora mumbled, writing the words down. "Makes sense, as it's likely his center of power. The place is a virtual lodestone for paranormal energy. He's got a model of Stonehenge in there, not to mention an ancient copy of the *Zohar*."

"The book of Kabbalah."

"Give the vampire a cookie." Endora got up, gathered everyone's empty mugs, and took them to the kitchen. "Refills, anyone?" Both Mav and Marcus indicated yes, so she poured them a round. "The exhibit has literally hundreds of artifacts, representing every type of mysticism throughout history. He'd be a fool not to use it as his base."

"And as we know," Mav said as he accepted more tea from Endora, "Obsidian Ashmedai is not a fool."

"At least not in his own mind." Endora set Marcus's mug in front of him, then resumed her seat. "If he thinks we're trying to destroy the exhibit, thus weakening his power base, he'll pull out all the stops against us. And since the success of tonight's campaign relies on his wasting and depleting his magic, that works in our favor."

"We need the museum's floor plan so I can determine where he keeps himself when he's not doing his curator thing. And to chart where the nexuses of power are. If there are more than one, we could use them against him." Marcus looked at Mav.

"The building's open until nine," Endora stated. "And the docents at the information desk will be more than happy to provide you with a map."

"I'll be gone no more than fifteen minutes." And Mav was out the door.

"Who says you can't get good help anymore?" Endora cracked.

* * *

It was nearing eleven-thirty that night when Marcus and Mav parked the Satellite at the corner of Twenty-sixth and Clayton, beside the municipal golf course. The roof of the Museum of Nature and Science could be seen across the fairways and to the east. The Museum of Arts and Culture sat directly across the course from them, lurking in all its Grecian glory like a temple to the ancient gods.

Glenna climbed onto Marcus's lap, a tight fit behind the wheel and, leaning her chest against his, put her head on his shoulder. He gave her an idle pat on the back, his mind on Endora.

"She should have given the signal fifteen minutes ago." His hands were shaking, so he gripped the steering wheel and squeezed. "We should go in."

"She will signal us when all things are ready."

"But maybe she needs—" A rumbling growl from Glenna brought him up short. "What in hades has gotten into you, Mutt?"

Mav looked at the dog, then at Marcus. "If Endora had encountered trouble, she would have signaled Glenna, and Glenna would have in turn alerted us."

"But what if she can't signal? What if Ashmedai's got her?"

"As her cosmic twin, could you not sense if she was in danger?"

"I didn't sense it last night," Marcus snorted.

"Of course you did. It was just obscured by the anger you felt at being excluded from her plan."

Biting back an oath, he released the steering wheel. "All right. You've got a point."

"Yes, I do." Mav took a long pull from a straw in a covered cup that Marcus thought smelled suspiciously like blood. "We will await Endora's signal, as we were instructed."

"It's her show," he agreed testily. That reality frightened and angered him, for reasons he didn't care to examine. And, perhaps, because he knew how things were going to turn out that night. He'd seen it in his divination.

"I followed both Endora's and your instructions to the letter." Mav opened the glove compartment door and set his drink in the shallow depression that had passed for a cup holder in the mid-1960s. "The fireworks are set up at the corners of the top floor, centers of the middle two floors, and behind each Stonehenge monolith on the main floor. If nothing else, they will make tremendous noise and choke the area with smoke."

Marcus set aside his misgivings. "How about the storage area?"

"Firecrackers which I believe are called M-80s and cherry bombs are set to be ignited via a long fuse." Mav looked over toward the museum. "If, in fact, Obsidian Ashmedai resides in that area, he will receive a sensory shock of impressive proportions."

For some reason Mav couldn't explain, he could be seen in mirrors but not on camera. Endora had hit on the idea that, since he wouldn't trigger any museum security cameras, he would play the role of saboteur and plant the explosive devices. Brilliant plan, actually, and Marcus had to admit he was a tad jealous he hadn't thought of it himself. But he knew his part in this drama, although it didn't sit well with him. Cooperation. Endora led, he followed and helped out.

I'm a former agent for the Tribunal! Why do I have to take a back seat to an amateur? Before his resentment took the bit in its teeth and ran off with him, he mentally shook himself out of his pity party. *Bat shit! My ego's getting as big as Ash's. Not good. Not good at all. I've completely lost my focus on the big picture*

Right then, Glenna's head came up off Marcus's shoulder and her tail began to wag. She gave a low whine, looking him directly in the eye as if to say, "What are you waiting for?"

"She got Endora's signal," he said, opening his door. "It's show time."

*   *   *

Endora was hanging on to her nerve by her fingernails. To check Mav's preparations and make sure the trap for Ash was set, she'd entered the museum alone through a back upper-floor window. Good thing. Both Marcus and she had forgotten the vampire's dyslexia. While Mav's instructions were to screw all the fuses in counterclockwise, he'd in fact done just the opposite. None of them were operational.

She'd had to shape-shift to human form to fix the problem, thus giving up the cover provided by her small feline stature. And the amazing night vision that went with it. Her human eyes functioned well in the dark, but you just couldn't beat cat-ray vision.

She knew Marcus was ready to fly apart at the seams because she'd been receiving regular updates from Glenna on the situation in the Satellite. But unless they all wanted to die within a few minutes of starting their raid, she had to delay the operation to correct the munitions problem. She had reported the same to Glenna, who in turn replied that Mav and she were doing their best to keep Marcus from jumping in to play hero. She even said she was prepared to use her teeth if necessary to restrain him. Fortunately, it hadn't come to that.

Finally! Got the last charge primed right. Glenna, the front door's open, so bring 'em in. Don't forget the net. I'll meet you by the monolith nearest the door.

Unlike last night, she could sense Ashmedai's presence in the building. It had been especially strong near the southernmost storage room. Marcus had been right. The storage area was Ashmedai's sanctuary. Well, they were just about to rock that foundation of safety right out from under him.

"Mav, take the right side of the fourth floor," Endora instructed as Marcus, Mav and Glenna came quietly but quickly into the museum. She caught Marcus's questioning look when he handed her the willow net. The look died when Mav sprinted silently up the staircase to the left. "I'll explain our delay later. Take the right side, third floor." When he moved off, she looked down at Glenna. "All right, girl, over to the *Zohar*. Get your forepaws right up on the case. I'll light the fuse for the storage room firecrackers. When you get my signal start barking your throat out."

Got it.

Endora stashed the net out of sight behind a support pillar by the entrance, shape-shifted, then teleported to the fourth floor. Storage was near the back of the museum, the end of her fuse line halfway back along the upper gallery. She had to shift back to human form to ignite the fuse, but as soon as the flame had burned a few feet toward its target, she shifted back to feline and melted into the shadows. *Now, Wonder Dog.*

Glenna set up a racket fit to wake the dead. And when the pressure of her large paws on the protective glass case set off the museum's alarm system, the din increased seemingly by another decibel. Sadly, the door to the security office had somehow been jammed tight, trapping the guards inside and leaving only the museum's curator free to investigate the problem.

Which he wasted no time in doing. Ashmedai came racing out of the storage room, roaring. "Security! You incompetent dullards. What has happened to the *Zohar*?"

"They're indisposed, Ash." Endora relied on the gallery's

acoustics to distort the direction her voice came from. "They won't be rushing to check out the alarm for you."

"Endora!" Hands raised and ready, he turned a complete circle, looking for her. "I thought you would have died from our encounter last night. That blast you absorbed should have killed you."

"Fortunately for me, *should have* isn't the same as *did*. Besides, I couldn't die before we finished the business between us."

"Ah yes, still angry about that incident forty years ago." His laugh was cruel. "You can't bring back the dead, Endora. Even I can't do that. Yet."

"You're not going to get the chance to gain that much power, you twisted bastard." She caught the anger in her voice, throttled it. Refused to let him get inside her head. "It's just you and me, Ash. For Round Two."

At that moment, the M-Eighties and cherry bombs Mav had set around the storage rooms started popping like the opening salvo of Armageddon.

Ashmedai whirled back toward the storage rooms, blasting away with a burst of power that opened gaping holes in a section of the wall between the two doors.

"Naughty, naughty, Ash," Endora taunted from a safe distance away. "What will your museum patrons think of their curator when they see this? I doubt they'll appreciate you redecorating so soon after the grand opening."

He whirled toward the sound of her voice, and obliterated a support column in the opposite direction of where she hid.

The smoke had barely cleared when Mav lit the fireworks on the other side of the top floor.

Multiple bolts from each of Ash's hands scorched the walls behind where the charges had ignited. But by the time the echoes from one hundred firecracker blasts had died, he had gathered himself.

"Very clever, Endora. But your plan to drain my magic is doomed, of course."

She saw him subtly moving toward where he thought she was hidden. It gave her great pleasure to see his eyes light up with anticipation when she said, "You can't blame a girl for trying, now, can you, Ash."

He lunged toward the seared column he'd torched, firing energy at the area in back of it.

Behind him, a feline Endora leapt from the balcony, aiming for the gallery the next level down. Her loud laugh was another taunt. "Missed me!"

"Bitch!"

By the time he turned toward the sound of her voice, Endora was safe behind another column. But that didn't stop Ashmedai from letting loose a blast which missed her by a good fifteen feet. However, it hit the glass display case containing several of the Gnostic artifacts. The case exploded, scattering glass shards and exhibition pieces over a ten-foot wide blast footprint.

"Down here, witch-boy." Again, the acoustics carried her voice from a seemingly different location on the third floor. "I'm going to wreck your entire exhibit and cut off your power source."

"Impossible!" He sent an energy bolt hurtling downward. It took out a ten-foot section of the third floor banister opposite where Endora hid.

Just as the bolt left Ashmedai's hand, Marcus set off the charges in the corner of the third floor directly under Ash. From her position across the atrium, Endora watched the smoke roil up, its sulphurous smell permeating the air.

A cry of rage burst from Ashmedai's throat as he sprinted to the closest staircase. In less than two heartbeats, he was on the third level, hands glowing with unleashed power.

Endora kept to the shadows as she slunk down the stairs at the opposite end and moved to the second level, reached the landing and changed back to human form. With impeccable timing, she was just at the rail when Marcus set off the charges across from where Ashmedai moved along the third-level balcony. Retaliation was swift and vicious. She could hear the energy hissing through the air as Ashmedai's magic blasted across the open space and slammed into the wall on the floor above her.

"Not even close," she called from the level-two railing. Then she deliberately laughed. "You can't hit what you can't see, I guess."

"Then come out into the open."

"Now, now, Ash," Endora said reasonably. She moved behind the nearest column, peeking around its base to locate him. "What fun would that be? I really don't want to die right now, especially since I'm having such a great time destroying your plans once again. So, I think I'll make you chase me some more."

With that, she lit the fuses to the second-floor charges and raced down the stairs to the main level, firecrackers and cherry bombs going off behind her. She knew her plan to rattle Ashmedai was working, as evidenced by the fact that he hammered the second-floor balconies with blast after blast of energy.

Got under your skin, didn't we, Ash, old buddy?

He was definitely taking out some frustrations on the architecture. Without her preternatural hearing, though, she wouldn't have detected a most welcome sound. The blasts were no longer as loud as before. His magic was weakening.

Realizing he still had plenty of firepower, she refrained from a celebratory dance.

Glenna, bring the net.

The dog rose from where she'd been lying by the museum entrance guarding the willow contraption Endora had fashioned. Grabbing several branches in her mouth, she quickly dragged it to the Stonehenge monolith nearest the *Zohar*. Endora moved behind it.

Drop it right here. Good girl. Now go find something sturdy to hide behind. The fireworks are nowhere near over.

I'll just go right over there, behind that other big stone.

Good idea. Stay out of sight, though. Don't want Ash blowing holes in my favorite mangy dog.

Har, har.

As Glenna trotted off, Endora sensed Marcus and Mav positioning themselves at opposite corners of the main floor.

"Where are you, Endora?" Ashmedai roared from the second floor.

"You're about to find out, scumbag," she whispered. Firing up her butane lighter, she ignited yet another fuse. "Now!"

The flame crept toward the base of the stand holding the *Zohar* as clusters of bottle rockets were launched from opposite corners of the atrium. Shrieking like banshees, they rose to the third balcony level and exploded with loud cracks, adding more smoke, sound and confusion to a scene that had begun to resemble a Civil War artillery duel.

A blast of magic from the second level obliterated the Stonehenge monolith directly in front of Mav's position. Endora hoped he had stayed true to form and moved to his left when she'd told him to go to his right. Otherwise, he was going to be moving into Marcus's next position, leaving the bottle rockets in the far corner of the museum unlit.

The next attack was directed at Marcus's former position, but to Endora's relief, another round of bottle rockets launched from the other two corners of the museum. Ash's retaliation was swift, but his blasts were noticeably shorter and with less punch.

"Let's see what happens now," Endora said quietly, watching the fuse she'd lit approach its target.

This explosion was muffled. The reaction it drew from Ashmedai was anything but. As thick black smoke engulfed the *Zohar*, he screamed as if tortured by Satan himself.

Endora stepped back behind the monolith when he leaped from the second-level gallery, landing beside the display. His magic quickly cleared the thick cloud of smoke, revealing the stand and the sacred book of Kabbalah completely intact.

"Endora!" He roared, eyes pure red with rage.

Shifting to cat form, she leaped atop the monolith she'd hidden behind. "Up here, Ash."

The blast of his magic tore the top of the stone away, but she'd already leapt clear.

Marcus stepped from hiding directly across the atrium. "She's pretty hard to hit, isn't she, Ash?" As soon as he spoke, he rolled to his right, behind a five-foot wide display case. He kept rolling while plaster on the wall behind where he'd been standing shattered to dust.

"Marcus Morion." His name on Ashmedai's lips was a vile curse. "I should have known Endora would lie. She's so embarrassingly in love with you."

"Actually, I didn't lie," she said from her new position several stones clockwise from where she'd started. "I told you I hadn't been with Marcus in forty years. That's the goddess's honest truth."

Ashmedai didn't even look at her, just pointed his fingers back over his shoulder and fired a bolt of magic in the direction of her voice. It missed with room to spare, but she had to give him credit for almost catching her flat-footed. She'd expected him to look toward her when he loosed the energy. That would have given Marcus a chance to move again. He'd moved some, but he wasn't as well-protected as she'd hoped he'd be at that stage of their operation.

His lack of good cover didn't seem to bother him. Instead

of staying hidden, he stepped boldly from behind a display case. "I've recently learned that you plan to become the most powerful witch on Earth, Ash," he said calmly. "I can't let you do that."

"When I take away your former powers, and the powers of your whore, no one will stop me." Ashmedai sneered as he added, "Although right now your magic is laughable."

He showed his contempt by blasting the display case Marcus stood beside.

Foreknowledge saved Marcus from death. His divinations had revealed that Ashmedai would use all the cunning he possessed to win this fight, so instead of going with instinct and diving back behind the display, Marcus dove in the opposite direction. But he no longer had the speed and strength of a witch. He wasn't completely clear of danger when the blast destroyed the case, and everything in it became deadly shrapnel. A ceremonial pipe struck the back of his head, and he was barely conscious as he hit the floor. Adding to his pain, the concussion from the explosion propelled him across the polished floor at a rate of speed he couldn't achieve by himself. He slammed up against a support column, which knocked the wind from his lungs.

"Marcus!" Endora couldn't stop her cry of horror as she saw him lying motionless, pieces of glass and metal embedded in his back and arms.

Immediately back in human form, she signaled Mav, who was off to her left about ten o'clock. Then, she was in a dead sprint to grab the willow net. Mav, silent as always, leapt on Ashmedai's back, clamping inhumanly strong arms around the witch's neck.

"Beelzebub!" Ash cried, twisting and writhing in an attempt to break free of his attacker.

But Mav proved every bit as physically strong as his asset column said. Locked together, they struggled to gain an advantage, to land a crippling blow. They swore and grunted, staggering across the open space of the main floor, neither able to overbalance the other and take him down.

Although terrified that Marcus was mortally injured, Endora couldn't leave Mav and chance his getting into trouble as she went to help her incapacitated hero. Deciding not to abandon Mav for Marcus tore at her heart, but it was the right decision.

She stayed out of the way of the fight, looking for an

opening so she could make her move. But they gave her no opportunity. Forced patience was not one of her strong suits, yet Endora had no choice. So she waited.

Equally matched, Mav and Ashmedai continued the fight. The air resounded with the sound of striking blows, of fierce effort. Fangs bared, Mav was going for a neck bite when Ashmedai gathered himself and, with an extraordinary burst of power, threw the vampire across the atrium. Mav landed on his back, skidded a yard, then regained his feet and charged again.

Ashmedai stopped him with a blast of magic. But Mav maintained his feet and, pushing with all his strength against the energy field, forced the witch to use extreme magical power to keep him at bay. As Mav made hard-fought progress toward Ashmedai, the witch struggled to maintain peak output.

Sensing Ash's struggle, Endora saw her chance and raced forward, tossing her net over his head in one fluid motion. Immediately, his force field died. Mav, now without resistance to push against, nearly fell face down at Ashmedai's feet. He caught himself before that happened and stood panting, fangs bared, two paces from his enemy.

Ashmedai whirled in fury on Endora. "I'll kill you, you traitorous hag."

"Obsidian Ashmedai," she said as calmly as her fear for Marcus would allow, "on the authority granted me by the Witches Tribunal, I'm arresting you for high crimes against the witch community."

"Do you actually think your pathetic spell can hold me?" Ashmedai taunted. Raising his arms, he began to chant.

The hair on Endora's nape rose a split-second before Ash's entire body started glowing. "Bat shit!"

She had no time to get to cover before the blast of magic tore her willow net into a thousand pieces and launched her into the air. The force blew her through an existing break in the second-level railing. Just before she landed, she saw Mav flying through the air in much the same manner she had. He was headed backwards in the direction of the museum's entrance.

Marcus, I'm sorry, was her last thought before she blacked out. *I wasn't supposed to get you killed.*

* * *

The sound of inhuman howling, curses and growls snapped Marcus from his stupor.

What in hades is happening?

His head pounded, his entire back felt aflame. But he ignored the pain and pushed himself up onto his hands and knees. When he turned his head toward the melee he saw Ashmedai and Glenna locked in a death struggle two yards away. They rolled on the floor, Ash beating the dog's head and back with his fists, howling and cursing as they fought. Glenna had sunk her teeth into the sorcerer's thigh and, despite being soundly pummeled, was hanging on as tenaciously as any of her breed. Growls of pure malice rumbled from her throat, adding to the cacophony of Ash's cries.

From the amount of blood spraying across both combatants, Marcus guessed she'd punctured a femoral artery. He also guessed, based on the increase in the electrical charge surrounding the pair, that Ash was readying a magical blast to kill Glenna. Knowing he'd be nearly worthless to protect the dog, he nonetheless rose shakily to his feet. His vision blurred, and he cursed his weakness, sagging heavily back against the column he'd slid headfirst into. That only drove shrapnel deeper into his back, increasing his suffering. He struggled to stay upright and conscious.

Gotta get into the fight, he thought, nearly mad with worry, trying to clear his blurry vision and steady himself. *If I don't, Glenna's dead.*

Pushing himself away from the column he leaned against, he took a step toward the two combatants. Fell to hands and knees. Curses he'd never even heard before spewed from his mouth as he began to crawl.

But he hadn't gotten very far before the sound of shattering glass pulled his attention to the center of the atrium. He saw Mav, a fire axe in his bony hands, smash the cover protecting the *Zohar*. Endora snatched it from the pedestal and dashed toward Ashmedai and Glenna, Mav in her wake.

"That's enough!" Cradling the sacred text in her left arm, she raised her butane lighter with her right hand. "Kill that dog, Ash, and I destroy your exhibit centerpiece." To drive home her point, she clicked the lighter's trigger.

It failed to ignite.

For one breathless moment, all five combatants froze. Endora's gaze briefly locked on Marcus's before she looked back toward Ash and screamed, "Glenna, move. Now!" As the dog released her hold on her foe's leg and retreated, Endora tossed the *Zohar* high into the air in his direction. "Catch, Ash." He lunged for the book. She shape-shifted in an instant, leapt onto Glenna's back, and shouted to Mav, "Get Marcus. We are leaving!"

Moving with incredible speed, Mav covered the fifteen feet between himself and Marcus, hefted his injured friend in a fireman's carry and was to the exit, right on Glenna's heels, when Ashmedai caught the book.

* * *

"Don't say it."

Marcus's voice was muffled as he lay facedown on the sofa while Endora carefully removed various types of shrapnel from his shoulders, back and arms. She'd put an ice pack on the large bump on the back of his head, warning him to stay as still as possible.

"Say what?"

A chunk of glass clinked as she dropped it into the cake pan she was using for a surgical basin.

"I told you so."

There was a pause. Then she sighed quietly. "I have no intention of doing that."

You'd certainly be justified. I was almost no help tonight. Worse yet, he'd known the outcome before he went into the museum, yet hadn't told Endora or even Mav. He wanted to think that, if his liability would have meant serious injury for any of the others, he'd have said something. Scratched himself from the mission. But he couldn't be completely sure of that.

Pride was sometimes a terrible thing.

He stifled a groan as yet another foreign object was pulled from his flesh and tossed into the cake pan. "I guess you're getting enough of a payback by torturing me this way."

"I'm really sorry to have to do this, Marcus." Her voice held only sincerity. "You heard Trish say you'd heal faster if all the debris is gone before she does her thing."

Mav had brewed snakeroot tea as soon as they got back to the condo, but fearing Marcus had a concussion, Endora watered it down to prevent his going totally under. As a result of the weaker dosage, he was quite uncomfortable. But realizing he probably felt about a tenth of the pain Endora had endured less than twenty-four hours before, he resolved to suck it up and take it.

"It's nearly two in the morning," he ground out between her pulling loose what felt like a baseball embedded in his left triceps muscle and removing a pencil-sized splinter from his left shoulder. "Which means three in New Orleans. Doesn't the woman need sleep?"

"Of course she does. But she's like all those old-time doctors who made house calls years ago. When their patients need them, they get out of bed to help."

He felt another twinge of pain in his shoulder and heard what sounded like iron drop into the pan. "By the goddess, Dora, how big is the stuff you're getting out of me?"

She was silent a moment, and he could hear scraping sounds, as if she was sorting through something in a metal pan. Which, he admitted, she was.

"Sizes vary. The one from your triceps is a short piece of tubular metal. I had to pull hard because only the very end was still exposed. It must have penetrated over an inch into the muscle. That's why that one probably hurt so much coming out."

"Thanks for the graphic description. And you're right, it hurt like unholy hades."

"Hey, you asked. If it's any consolation, I think that's the worst one of all. The one from your shoulder blade looks like a human head. About the size of a big marble. Went in close to half an inch."

"Great. It's probably some type of voodoo artifact, and now I'm cursed."

She chuckled. "Voodoo dolls are cloth. You know that. And, since I don't see any pins sticking in you, you're reasonably safe. On the other hand, it might be an effigy..."

"That's it. I *am* cursed."

At that dry comment, she laughed out loud. "Don't worry, we won't light any fires around you, so you won't have to worry about doing a Guy Fawkes impersonation."

"You're all heart," he groused. Secretly, he wanted to kiss Endora until she couldn't breathe. Guilt for making her worry about his injuries had been riding him hard, and hearing her easy laugh brought immeasurable relief.

"Sure, yuk it up," he grumped, capitalizing on her improved mood. "You're not the one who's going to have your manhood fall off any time soon."

She snorted. "Or any time at all, for that matter."

Her hands again took up her task. He could feel twinges and pulls here and there, but the overall climate in the room had eased. And so had his pain.

"Where're Mav and Glenna?"

"Off doing some vampire-pit bull bonding. The sight of all the blood at the museum got Mav pretty revved up. So, he's out working it off."

"Why'd he take Glenna with him?"

"Being an expert on fangs, he cleaned up her teeth, checked them over for chips and cracks. No damage from her encounter with Ash's thigh. Now, she and Mav are buddies."

"Ash didn't hurt her?"

"With her skull? She's like a fur-bearing battering ram." She must have sensed that he was still concerned, because she added, "Nothing more than bruises. She's fine." Another piece of metal hit the basin. "He went to retrieve the car, after they checked the museum to see if the authorities found anything."

"Like Ashmedai's dead body?"

Nine

"We should be so lucky." Lifting the ice pack from his head, she went to the kitchen to replace the melted cubes, then was quickly back. She gently probed the area before reapplying the ice. "This lump back here's getting smaller."

"Guess it goes to show you can't dent rock." He took a deep breath before saying, "Thanks for getting me out of there tonight."

"Thank Glenna and Mav." Her breath caught when she sensed him getting ready to apologize for almost ruining their plan, but she spoke before he could. "I don't think you saw this, but Mav jumped Ash and nearly managed to bite him in the jugular."

Marcus tried to turn his head to look at her, but pain stopped him. "He actually went for someone else's veins?"

"Yeah. It must have been an adrenaline rush of such massive proportions that it short-circuited his dyslexia."

"So, he went for Ash."

"I was so proud of him!"

"But he didn't connect."

Endora actually sighed. "No, but not from lack of effort. As strong as Mav is, Ash kept him from sinking his fangs in." She described the struggle and how her net had temporarily robbed Ashmedai of his magic. Then her tone went grim. "But what I was afraid might happen did. My magic couldn't hold him. He blew the net to atoms, threw Mav and me off like we were weightless. I blacked out when I landed on the second-floor balcony."

"Goddess, Endora, are you hurt?" Pain be damned, this time he did turn to look at her.

She gently pressed his head back down onto the sofa cushion and readjusted the ice pack, which had slid off. "I'm fine. Minor bruises and nothing permanent."

"But you said you blacked out."

"I couldn't have been unconscious for more than a few seconds, because when I got to the railing, Ash was standing over you, ready to deliver the *coup de grâce*. If I'd been out much longer than a minute, he'd have already killed you and moved on to Mav."

"So, that's where Glenna comes in."

"You should have seen her, Marcus." He wasn't sure if Endora could hear the pride in her own voice, but it came through to him loud and clear. "She flew across the atrium so fast it looked like her feet weren't touching the floor. Ash was just raising his hands to zap you, and she hit him like a freight train. Completely unbalanced him. His blast took down one of those thirty-foot-long pennants hanging from the ceiling. She spun him away from you, knocked him down, then went for his throat. I think he was a bit winded after prematurely shooting his magic, but he kept her away from his neck, just like he had Mav."

"So she got his leg instead."

"Pit bulls are apparently less discriminating than vampires as to what body part they'll bite."

He would have nodded if he thought he could move his head without dislodging that damned ice pack. "She must have bitten all the way to the bone. There was so much blood flying."

"Almost all of it his."

Endora pulled his right arm away from his body and ran her hand gently down his ribs. Abruptly, pain started to move toward his lower abdomen and transfer to heat. He had to concentrate hard to hear what she was saying over the sudden rush of blood in his ears, not to mention another place.

"I'll tell you one thing. I'm never going to get her mad at me. She was like sixty-five pounds of Satan's wrath."

Marcus forced himself to chuckle. "Wish I could have heard Ash scream when she nailed him."

"Horror-movie victims don't reach those decibel levels."

He carefully lifted his head to look at her. That sudden twinge of pain yanked him back from sensual fantasies. A relief right then as it got him refocused on their discussion. "Who thought to grab the *Zohar*?"

"I did. But without Mav, I'd never have been able to break the glass. For a scrawny dude, he's amazingly strong."

"It's that undead thing he's got going for him."

She snorted out a laugh. Then he heard water dripping into a basin. A wet washcloth brushed his neck, and Endora started carefully working it downward.

"I'm washing the blood off so I can see your wounds better. I think I got every piece of shrapnel that hit you, but if I missed something, you're going to feel a poke."

"Thanks for the warning."

"Don't tough it out if you do feel it. I've got to get everything out of your skin before I call the expert healer back."

He relaxed his muscles, waited for a pain that would indicate she hadn't seen all the damage. "Quick thinking after the lighter wouldn't ignite. Ash's expression when you tossed the book in the air was a Pulitzer Prize-winning photo op."

"We had to get out of there. The only way I could think of to buy time was to threaten Ash's baby. Since we'd tricked him into pretty much blasting everything else in the museum, the *Zohar* was our best bet."

"Well, it worked."

She had finished, plunked the washcloth into the basin. "That's it. Time to up your dose of snakeroot."

He heard her walk away, run the water, and key the microwave. "Now that my suffering's pretty much over."

"Couldn't risk your falling asleep." She returned with a steaming mug and helped him sit up to drink it. "Your real treatment's about to begin, so we can dope you up." She looked straight into his eyes. "But before that tea takes effect, we've got to talk."

He knew what was coming. "We threw everything we could at Ashmedai and still couldn't beat him."

"Even after we'd drained his magic in every possible way we could think of."

"Glenna hurt him badly."

Endora nodded. "An added bonus for us. The energy he's going to have to expend just to repair his leg will be substantial."

"Think that was Glenna's payback for you?"

"Not at all." Endora smile slightly. "She told me the day I met her that she'd fight to the death to protect you."

That thought cheered him. "Really?"

"Straight from the dog's mouth."

"That's pretty amazing." And warmed his heart, even though he was too macho to admit that. He returned to the topic at hand. "If Ash is true to form, the museum will be completely restored before anyone sees it today. Mav will tell us if the mess got cleaned up when he and Glenna get back."

She nodded. "Ashmedai's going to have to ensorcell the guards who were on duty, so they don't question what happened. That will also burn some energy."

"True. And he'll have to deal with the security tapes." He

caught her grave look. "You're thinking that, even if he expends the magic it will take to put everything to rights, we still can't take him."

"I don't see how." She caught the mug from his hand before it hit the floor, then carefully guided him back onto his stomach on the sofa. "But you're not in any shape to discuss this any more tonight. When you wake up in a few hours will be soon enough."

"Okay."

Endora was rubbing valerian oil into Marcus's right palm when Mav and Glenna returned half an hour later. His wounds hadn't been nearly as severe as hers, so the healing had taken half the time. The crystals again sat on their respective shelves, and all that remained was for her to massage Marcus with the oil, then get him to bed. Since the shrapnel had hit his upper body, Trish instructed her to apply it to his arms and hands exactly the same way he'd applied it to her leg and foot.

"How is he?" Mav asked.

Endora smiled up at the vampire. "He'll be fine. But if it hadn't been for you and Glenna, he'd be dead. Most likely, I'd be, too. So, thank you. For both of us."

"It was a, what's the sporting term? A total team effort." Mav sat down in the recliner.

"Well, you and Wonder Dog were the heroes of the team." *Thanks again, Glenna. That's two I owe you.*

I'm keeping tabs.

Of course. How do you like your steak?

Raw.

How'd Ash's leg taste?

The dog actually bared her fangs. *Like rancid meat. He's pure evil, and that kind of stain goes through an entire body.*

Although that's a horrifying thought, it makes sense. How'd you get so smart for a dog?

I read the Wall Street Journal *every day.*

Good one. I took you more for the gossip magazine type. When the dog just gave her a baleful look, Endora chuckled. Then she reached over and patted Glenna's broad head. *Well, pal, guess I won't be serving you spare ribs Ashmedai any time soon.*

Angus flank steak, raw, will do.

You got it. She looked over at Mav. "I'm almost finished

here. Would you carry him up to his room when I'm done?"

"Of course." Mav tipped his head back and stared at the condo's high ceiling. "Ashmedai has already completely restored the museum."

That wasn't surprising, but it disheartened her completely. "I figured he would. But, hellfire, I was hoping he wouldn't have enough magic left in him." She finished her massage of Marcus's hand and wiped the oil from her own. "At least not this soon after the fireworks display he put on earlier tonight."

"He is terrifyingly powerful." Mav sat up, then rose to hoist Marcus into a fireman's carry.

"You've got that right." Endora preceded them up the stairs, turned down Marcus's bed, removed his jeans, then saw that he was comfortably settled. "You're no slacker yourself, Mav."

The vampire looked down at Marcus then moved to the bedroom door. "You have no explanation for why Ashmedai's magic is so potent?"

"Just what I've already told you. Suspicions only. Nothing I can prove." Endora ran both hands through her hair and stood looking grimly down at Marcus. "Forty years ago, someone sold Marcus out. Ash told me as much last night."

Mav's black eyes gleamed with an unholy light. "He admitted someone on the Tribunal is helping him?"

"Hinted at it, then asked me why it took me forty years to figure out that we didn't fail on our own." She turned out the bedside lamp and moved toward the door and Mav. "Someone wants Ashmedai to become the most powerful witch on the planet. And that witch or witches think they can control him."

"But you have your doubts of that possibility."

"Think what happened in the museum tonight." She couldn't stop a shudder. "Given what he can do right now, if he gains the magic Marcus and I had, no one on Earth, in heaven or in hell will exert any control whatsoever over him." Endora grimaced at the image.

"There would certainly be no single witch capable of it. Not even a cadre of two or three."

"Not even the entire Tribunal," Endora stated. She rubbed a hand across her face. "And with our powers limited and his greater than ever, I have no idea how to stop him."

Mav looked over her shoulder at Marcus, and then back at her. "I think you have a very good idea of what needs to be done in order for you to defeat Obsidian Ashmedai. You just have not yet decided how to go about implementing it." He nodded respectfully. "Sleep well."

* * *

A short time later, Endora slid into bed next to Marcus. In case he needed something in the night, it seemed natural to lie beside him as he had done her the night before. He lay on his stomach, head turned toward the wall. She moved close enough for their shoulders to touch, ignoring the twitch in her left ear, enjoying the warmth of his skin against hers. As it had the night before, a feeling of security crept over her. Ridiculous, really, considering their circumstances.

The full dose of snakeroot tea had knocked Marcus out, but lacking its sedative benefit, Endora couldn't sleep. Right then, she doubted if a double dose could have completely sedated her. Too many thoughts rushed at warp-speed through her head, and she couldn't power them down. Sleep would have to wait.

Plenty of time to sleep when I'm dead, she thought bitterly. *Which may be a lot sooner than I'd planned.*

It was now October thirtieth, which meant they had fewer than forty hours to devise and carry out another plan. If they didn't kill Ashmedai—and it was now apparent they would have to destroy him to stop him—then all would be lost at exactly midnight on November first. Ash's birthday would have run its course. He would have full powers. Terrifying to think he could be even more powerful than he was at present. Then there was the even grimmer reality of his taking Marcus's and her magic.

And what options did they have? Well, running away and trying to hide had a certain amount of appeal. Of course, they'd still die when the Solstice came and he stole their magic. And if she and Marcus couldn't stop him now, before his birthday ended, how in hades did anyone stand a chance against him afterward?

Mav's words flashed into her head. *You have a very good idea of what needs to be done....*

As usual, the vampire had been completely right. She knew a path to follow. Medusa's advice, and the incantation to reverse the anti-love spell, were fresh in Endora's mind. Now, it was just a matter of gaining the cooperation of her cosmic twin. The love of her life. The witch she wasn't certain still completely trusted or loved her.

Too restless to stay still any longer, Endora rose to go and plan another campaign. This one against Marcus.

✤ ✤ ✤

It hadn't worked.

Marcus had slept five more hours after Endora left him. She'd spent that whole time trying to marshal all her reasoning, logic and rationale to approach him about what she saw now as their only chance to triumph over Ashmedai. The facts were in her head, nothing else. No glib phrase or seductive come-on to induce him to go along with her idea. Nothing original came to mind.

Perhaps stark reasoning would work. Marcus knew Ashmedai was too strong for them to destroy, even if they enlisted Glenna and Mav again. No, they had to increase their own magic. She could think of only one possible way to do that.

Her conversation with Cassie yesterday had put an idea into her head she couldn't shake, no matter how hard she tried to argue against her own reasoning. But both Cassie and Medusa had warned her repeatedly not to discount the power of love. And she felt Marcus's sensual pull so strongly, she'd had to use an anti-love spell to counteract the magnetism they shared.

What if they stopped fighting the attraction? Gave in to their mutual need for intimacy? And she knew it was mutual. Marcus had been radiating pheromones since she'd shown up on his doorstep in Dallas, and Medusa's spell was all that was keeping Endora out of his arms. If love truly was the most powerful force in the universe, then why not use it to their advantage?

But she had to ask herself if it was really love she was talking about, here, and not just lust. They definitely felt lust for each other...but what about deeper emotions? Because if all they had was lust between them then her idea was dead from the start.

She closed her eyes and recalled their one night together, the memory as fresh as if it had happened that morning rather than forty years before. Of course there had been overwhelming attraction, basic lust, amazing passion. But they hadn't just had sex. She and Marcus had made love in the most profound way. So profound, the experience seemed nearly sacred.

And although their relationship had been extremely short, had never been tested by the challenges of the long haul, she didn't doubt now that it would have withstood anything thrown against it. She loved him with her entire soul. Even if he didn't return the depth of her love, hers would be enough for them both.

It's like we're acting in a terrible parody of Romeo and Juliet, Endora thought wryly. *But, hopefully, we'll still be alive at the end.*

On the other hand, if lovemaking didn't augment their magic, then they'd at least die happy when Ashmedai caught up with them.

Endora's breath clogged in her lungs the moment she heard the door to Marcus's room open, the pad of his feet on the hardwood floor. Clicking sounds on the boards indicated Glenna was right behind him. The dog had climbed into bed beside Marcus after Endora left early that morning, taking over Endora's protection and comforting duties.

Marcus wore only the briefs they'd put him to bed in, and as he ran his hand through his thick, black-brown hair, his black eyes locked on hers and lit up. "Good morning." He flashed her the grin she'd seen in her fantasies for forty years. "It is still morning, isn't it?"

Unable to speak coherently, she nodded. The sight of his broad chest with its dark hair dusting lean, powerful muscles dried up all the saliva in her mouth. As she watched him move toward her, seemingly with no leftover pain from his injuries, she had to clear her throat in order to manage a simple, "How are you feeling?"

He flexed his shoulders, and her salivary glands kicked back in with a vengeance. "Fine. No pain or stiffness anywhere."

Well, she was sort of hoping there was stiffness in a certain place, at least in the very near future, but she could wait. "Hungry?" *Goddess, can I come up with a more clichéd line?*

"I could eat a horse."

Apparently, she didn't have the market on clichés. She started to move toward the kitchen.

"No offense, Endora, but I'd rather cook my own breakfast."

He flashed her that grin again, and she'd have forgiven

him any insult. So she went to sit on a bar stool and watch him cook, determined to bring up what was on her mind while she had a somewhat captive audience. And Mav nowhere in sight.

But if her suggestion was going to make Marcus angry, she preferred he didn't have extremely sharp weapons readily available. With that in mind, she held off broaching the subject until he'd scrambled eggs, made toast, fried up a panful of hash browns and taken his heaping plate to the table to eat. Pouring herself a glass of milk, she joined him.

Once he was busy tucking into his meal, she took a deep breath and prepared to tell him the truth about the anti-love spell, and her idea of how to defeat Ashmedai. Her mouth opened. Not a sound rolled off her vocal cords.

Panic stabbed her. *What in hades is wrong with me? I'm never speechless. Ever.* She tried again. Nothing. Her mind raced frantically, commanding her vocal cords to cooperate, trying to force words over her tongue and past her teeth. She thought of faking a seizure to get his attention, but discarded that as far more melodramatic than she was willing to get.

While contemplating sign language, she must have made some sound or other because Marcus suddenly looked up at her. "You all right?"

"Uh, yeah. Fine." *Come on, brain, engage!* She took a quick drink of milk, then tried again. And prayed to the goddess her face wasn't flaming with embarrassment, or that the six feet separating them would prevent his noticing if it was. "Uhm, Marcus, after you're done eating, we have to finish the conversation we started before you conked out last night."

He took a healthy bite of food, savored it with a connoisseur's appreciation. Swallowed. Took a long drink of orange juice. "I think I know where you're going with this conversation."

Oh, I doubt that. I very much doubt that.

But she couldn't force herself to speak. This desperate situation was a golden chance to lay out her reasoning for taking what she knew to be their only course of action. Yet she remained silent. Why? It flashed into her consciousness in a burst of painful realization. Her true fear, what had figuratively welded her mouth shut, came from the thought that Marcus had never really loved her and now, because she'd done so many outrageous things normal witches didn't do, he didn't even lust for her anymore, either. The thought that he might not care for her or want her in any way terrified Endora almost to the point of paralysis. If that was true, she'd be devastated beyond recovery. And her plan to save them and all of witchkind from Ashmedai would fail utterly.

She forced herself to think objectively. Realistically, what if her love was truly unrequited? What would she do if he didn't agree that this was their best chance to beat Ashmedai? Wouldn't agree to intimacy with her?

"Well?" Marcus prompted, interrupting her gloom-and-doom scenario. "I see a plot in those green eyes. What is it?"

Reflexively, she pushed back from the table and rose to move closer to him. This was something that shouldn't be shouted across a table. Sitting down in the chair to his left, she swallowed hard. Then again. "Well..."

When her voice trailed off, he shook his head. "Come on, Dora. Cat got your tongue?"

Bad jokes always yanked her chain. She fisted her hands in her lap. "Not funny. Juvenile and clichéd, but not funny."

"I'll admit it wasn't my best material," he readily stated. He leaned his elbows casually on the table, a smile playing about his firm lips. "But it did seem to shake you out of your catatonia."

She'd have laughed at his corny puns if she wasn't so nervous. *Keep the goal of the greater good in mind. Deep breath. Concentrate. Speak slowly.*

"All right, here's what I'm thinking. Separately, we know we can't beat Ashmedai. And even when we combined our skills with Mav and Glenna's talents, Ash kicked our butts."

He rolled his eyes, crossed arms over chest. "That's not exactly a news bulletin. So, what's really on your mind? It's not like you to equivocate, Endora."

Her mouth went dry again. "I, um, don't want you to take this wrong."

"Take what wrong?" Impatience filled his voice. "I have to have information before I can misinterpret it."

Impulsively, she reached out and covered his hand with hers. When his eyes met hers, she said, "Our only chance is to cooperate fully. I mean, I think we'll increase our powers if we, uhm, if you and I..., well...What I'm trying to say is the two of us need to—"

He stared at her like she'd grown a second head. "Can you put this in a language I can understand on some level?

Because I haven't got a clue and, as you keep reminding everyone, we've got very tight time restrictions here."

Goddess, why can't I just say this? She knew the answer, but given the dire nature of their circumstances, she should be able to ignore her fear and be more plainspoken. "Marcus, I think that, to maximize our powers, you and I need to...We should just..."

She realized he understood her exact meaning when his face went pale and rage flashed in his eyes. In a nanosecond, he went from smiling and casually joking to shaking with fury. The contempt in his eyes almost cut her heart out.

He leaped from his chair as if he'd been propelled by booster rockets.

Bat shit. This is not going to go well.

Ten

"I can't believe you, Endora." Marcus fisted his hands on his hips, as if to prevent himself from hitting something. "You do your Lone Ranger routine, and when you find out you can't handle Ashmedai yourself, you enlist our help. But that plan fails, too. So you're on to Plan C. Which is propositioning me."

She remained seated and perfectly still, trying to wait out his fury so she could reason with him. Although it hadn't surprised her, his reaction inexplicably hurt. And his mockery sparked her own temper. "This isn't what I'd call a proposition."

"How about business arrangement?" He squared his stance to face her. "Does that term work to explain why you suddenly want to get in bed with me?"

"There's nothing sudden about this," she countered, voice heating. "If you'd set aside your ego for a minute and just listen, I—"

"Listen to you justify your lack of common decency? Not a chance," he sneered. "You've stayed at arm's length since you showed up in Dallas. The only exception being if one of us was out cold. Now you want to jump me to increase your powers?" He turned away, yanked his hands through his hair, then spun back to face her. "I won't be your stud, Dora. Go downtown and buy some pretty-boy gigolo for the night if you want some jollies. Maybe that will get your magic back for you."

"I'm not talking about sex." Anger had her on her feet, but she didn't approach him. "This is about increasing our *combined* powers. Not just mine."

"Not about sex?" His laugh held no humor. "Are you suggesting we'll get our magic back if we sit around a campfire, roast marshmallows, and sing 'Kumbaya'?"

For a moment, Endora truly thought he was going to throw something. Likely at her. But he clenched his jaw until the muscles beneath his ear bunched. She knew he was using all of his self-control to fight the urge to lash out physically. She had to try to break through his rage.

She stepped toward him. Reached out her hand. "Marcus, I—"

"Don't touch me!" He pushed her hand away, spun on his heel, and headed for the door. "Glenna, we're outta here. The air in this place stinks." He shot Endora a venomous look. "Don't even think of following us. I won't be responsible for anything that happens if you do."

In a blink they were gone.

Endora stood frozen by the staircase, unable to get her limbs to move or her mind to function. She wasn't even sure if her heart was beating. In fact, it felt crushed. Could that scene have gone any more wrong?

What in Hades have I done? Her legs turned to jelly and she just managed to flop down onto the bottom step in lieu of crashing to the floor. Head in hands, she fought the urge to sob.

"I have never seen Marcus so angry."

She sensed Mav standing behind her at the top of the stairway but didn't raise her head to acknowledge him. "How much of that little imbroglio did you hear?"

"I arrived just as he accused you of propositioning him."

That did it. Endora burst into tears. Instantly, a gold-embroidered silk handkerchief that must have cost as much as an all-day spa session was pushed into her hand. She cried for a good five minutes before, sacrificing whatever dignity she might have had left, she blew her nose, loud and long, into the exquisite cloth.

"Oh, Mav. He totally misunderstood what I was saying."

"In point of fact, I believe he understood perfectly."

Sniffling, she raised her head to look at him. "What do you mean?"

"Marcus loves you deeply, but you claimed upon your arrival in Dallas that nothing but the business of defeating Ashmedai lay between you. This not only angered him, it hurt him." Mav looked down at his hands, and Endora could see a hint of color on his pale cheeks. "Now, you wish to use sex with him to boost your powers. How would you react if he had asked the same thing of you?"

He had a point, but she wasn't about to concede it. "I didn't ask him for sex. He jumped to that conclusion."

Mav shook his head. "Then, you really have no wish for him to bed you?"

Mav's old-fashioned terminology might have amused her if she hadn't been ready to hit her head repeatedly against something hard. As it was, she ignored his quaintness. "There's a universe of difference between lovemaking and sex."

"But Marcus doesn't think you know that difference."

Endora's heart lurched in her chest. *If he truly feels that way, can I convince him otherwise?*

Abruptly, she found herself fighting down sudden panic. If she folded without a fight now, the price paid would be even more than losing her only love. She had to get on top of her game immediately. She closed her eyes and, taking a deep breath, settled herself. Concentrated on her goal. Then, drawing on all the swagger and independent-mindedness of her feline self, she put a glint in her eye and confidence in her voice. "Then I guess I've got to change his mind about that."

"I wish you the best of luck."

"Oh, I won't need luck." She smiled her most seductive smile. "But if it makes you feel better, send it my way all the same."

* * *

Endora found Marcus six blocks away in a park, throwing a stick for Glenna to fetch. His lack of enthusiasm for the game produced an equal lack of enthusiasm from the dog, which took her time retrieving the stick. Then she ambled as though severely arthritic back to where he sat to drop it at his feet. Sensing the anger still radiating from him, Endora almost lost her nerve before she remembered exactly what was at stake and knew that only death could stop her from trying her hardest to reach him.

"Dog obesity's a growing problem in America," she said with all the lightness she could inject into her tone. "Glenna isn't getting much exercise from the pace of that game."

Marcus raised his head, and even at a distance of twenty-five feet, Endora could see the angry light in his eyes. Undaunted, she moved slowly toward them.

He nearly snarled when he said, "I told you not to follow us."

"You can't be surprised I did." Never taking her gaze off his, she steadily closed the gap between her and the bench where he sat.

"Just can't leave well enough alone, can you?"

Now just a couple steps from the bench, she stopped. "There's no well enough to leave alone right now, Marcus. We both know it."

"Go away." He turned his head, looking out across the park as the shadows started to lengthen with the sun's setting.

"We've got nothing to say to each other."

Endora's heart clenched once, hard enough to simulate severe angina, but she ignored it. "Then do you mind if I just deliver a monologue? Because I've got some very important things I need to air out. Don't listen if you don't want to."

Marcus shrugged but didn't turn to look at her. "Free country, and all that. I couldn't stop you if I wanted to, anyway."

A less than gracious invitation, yet Endora didn't have the luxury to be offended by his bitter sarcasm. She sat down beside him, careful to leave a good foot of space between them. "Here's a story you need to hear."

Still not looking at her, he grunted. Then he crossed his arms over his chest and leaned against the back of the bench, staring into space. His studied indifference didn't phase her. She made herself as comfortable as one can on a wooden park bench while sitting next to a hostile party.

"Forty years ago, a young witch's best friend fell in with an evil sorcerer. So, she did what anyone who loved a best friend would do. She tried to help." Marcus kept looking straight ahead, but his hands had tightened on his biceps. He was listening. "Inexperience was her major problem, and she had no idea how to rescue her friend. But she jumped right in anyway." Endora figured her need to touch him was suicidal, so she kept her hands resting in her lap. "By entering the evil sorcerer's circle, she found her friend. And discovered just how powerful the circle master was. She had no hope of a successful rescue all by herself.

"Fortunately, another young witch—her exact age to the minute–had come to bring down the circle. He had skills she only dreamed of. They fell instantly in love and, acting on an attraction more powerful than either had ever known, they made love for an entire night." She caught the bob of Marcus's Adam's apple, and hope started to grow. "He was her first. She his. And their night together was so amazing, so incredible, she knew she'd never have that deep a connection with anyone else. He was her lifemate. The witch she'd spend the rest of her days beside.

"But fate took a cruel hand in their story. The sorcerer killed everyone in the circle and cast suspicions on the pair. Although not blamed for the murders, they were punished by losing most of their magic. Ordered not to see each other for forty years. Grief for her lost love nearly drove her to suicide, but becoming a familiar changed her mind. That, and her need for revenge against the witch who had destroyed her life and slaughtered her best friend.

"Early on, she looked for love with others but quickly realized that only her lifemate could fill the void in her heart. She gave up looking for a substitute. Over nearly forty years in servitude as a familiar, her mistress became her best friend. For the most part she was happy."

Before continuing, Endora paused and swallowed hard to steady her voice. She didn't want to break down and sob through the most important part of her narrative. "When the time came for her punishment to end, fate threw another obstacle at her. The very Tribunal that had taken her powers now needed her help. The evil witch would regain his magic before she and her lover regained theirs. And they were the only two who could prevent his becoming all-powerful—"

"You didn't ask me to stop you if I'd heard this one before."

Marcus's sudden interruption nearly made her jump, and it unnerved her so much she didn't hear his exact words. "What?"

"You were supposed to say, 'Stop me if you've heard this one before' before you told the story. You didn't. Since I've lived it, almost exactly, that counts, too." At last he looked at her. His brown eyes were somber but free of anger, and the spark of hope grew stronger in her heart.

"You haven't heard this part." When he merely raised his brow in question, she said, "Before going to her lifemate and enlisting his help, the witch asked her employer for a favor. She wanted an anti-love spell cast on her, to help her concentrate only on the daunting task ahead." At those words, Marcus became very tense. "Without the spell, she knew she'd think of little else but making love with her mate. And that their irresistible attraction might prove fatal for both. Her friend's mother, a very powerful witch, helped cast the spell. The elder warned her not to ignore the power of love and gave her the spell to reverse the anti-love charm.

"As usual, our heroine thought she knew best and didn't take her friends' words to heart. Until she encountered firsthand their enemy's formidable magic. He shouldn't have had such power, but he did. And she found herself wondering if, by sharing the magic they'd experienced together before, she and her lifemate could become strong enough to defeat him." She couldn't stop herself. She reached over and put her hand on

Marcus's knee. Then she cleared her throat. "When she tried to explain her idea to her mate, fear that he no longer loved her made her fumble her explanation. She—"

Words and breath left her body simultaneously as Marcus hauled her against his chest and kissed her until her breath backed up in her lungs. When he finally let her go, both of them panted from lack of air. His Adam's apple was bobbing, and her ears twitched uncontrollably.

"If we're not careful," she gasped, her throat closing from emotion, "we'll be arrested for lewd acts in a public park." Forcing aloofness into her tone, she nevertheless felt her eyes fill with tears.

His dark eyes were intense with passion and more than a little pain. "How could you think I'd stopped loving you, Endora?"

"Forty years is a long time, even for beings that live to be over one hundred and fifty." She smiled wryly, caressed his cheek. "Out of sight, out of mind, or some such rot. And although my saying this will likely stoke your huge ego, you're incredibly handsome. I'm sure you've had your share of women since we were together."

He shook his head. "You said it yourself. We're lifemates. That part of your story is exactly mine. I tried my damndest to forget you. Forget what we'd had. Couldn't. So I gave up."

Resting her forehead against his, she murmured, "I thought Medusa's spell would protect me from my feelings. Keep me from ignoring these dire circumstances and just jumping you. And it worked almost perfectly."

He whistled through his teeth. "Medusa Morlock's one of the most respected Tribunal members in over two hundred years. Amazing magical skill, and integrity to burn. That must have been a powerful spell."

"Until very recently, I didn't know just how powerful," she said on a shrug. "Marcus, Cassie helped Medusa and me cast the anti-love spell. Since she's pregnant with twins, there was a circle within a circle, and the spell is pretty much impenetrable."

"What did you mean when you said it worked almost perfectly."

Embarrassment heated her cheeks, as she scratched at her left ear. "Well, have you noticed that when you touch me my ear twitches?"

He reached out and stroked her cheek with the back of his hand. Her left ear immediately quivered and he roared with laughter. "Amazing."

"I think it's my body trying to throw off the spell," she admitted sheepishly. "Since it only happens when you touch me."

He shook his head and smiled crookedly. "And here I thought you didn't love me."

"I'm so sorry." She bussed his lips with a quick kiss. "The only thing I could think of to stay on task was ignoring my need for you."

Suddenly on his feet, he looked down at her, eyes burning intensely. Then he pulled her to her feet. "Let's go back to the condo. We have some magic to work."

Her knees suddenly threatened to collapse, forcing her to lock them to remain upright. "If you insist."

* * *

As they walked down Lawrence toward Sixteenth Street, it was like being twenty years old again. Endora wasn't exactly sure how they managed to walk, since they were very actively engaged in lots of hugging, hand-holding and nuzzling. She hoped that, since it was almost dark, the good citizens of LoDo were too busy eating dinner to notice a couple practically mauling each other in public. And if they were noticing, she hoped the shenanigans didn't upset anyone. Of course, if they did, she figured it was the observer's problem, not hers.

* * *

"I have to tell you something before we end up where we're headed," Marcus said quietly into Endora's ear, right after he licked it and saw it twitch. He felt her tense, but squeezed his arm tighter around her shoulders to anchor her. "It's important that you know, so hear me out, all right? Don't speak until I'm done saying what needs to be said."

"Okay." She relaxed marginally against him.

He had to breathe deeply before continuing. "I knew we'd fail last night." Although he sensed she wanted to ask how, she kept her word and stayed quiet. "I didn't give you and Mav all the information I'd gotten from the horoscopes I cast. Mars is in retrograde from October second to December tenth."

Endora whistled softly through her teeth. "Mars retrograde influences conflict." She looked up at him with a wry grin. "Sorry. Couldn't help interjecting some of my own knowledge into the conversation."

"You're incorrigible." He kissed her on the forehead. "But you've got your Mars facts right, witch-woman. I saw it influencing our particular conflict in a surprising way. Victory would not come from aggression. The horoscope recommended using subtlety and strategy to cope with adversaries, that military situations would take unexpected turns and that competitions were prone to upsets." He paused a moment. "This is where you say that, although we took the fight to Ashmedai, we used strategy against him, and even as underdogs, almost upset him."

"Consider it said."

Marcus waited until they had crossed the intersection of Lawrence and Twentieth before he continued. "There's more, and this is the part where I get disgusted with myself."

"I know Cassie believes confession is good for the soul, but you don't have to go there if you don't want to."

He stopped in the middle of the sidewalk and turned to face her. "If we ever hope to trust each other fully, you have to hear this directly from me."

Tears formed in her eyes, and he saw her swallow hard before she said, "You're right. We need complete honesty. There's been too much deception between us as it is."

When she raised her hand to cup his cheek, the emotion her simplest touch evoked in him closed his throat. He put his arm around her shoulders again and started walking. "What I didn't tell you about the horoscopes is this—October Twenty-eighth said, 'Trust your instincts.' October Twenty-ninth is 'protect your soul.' And October Thirtieth is 'work a candle spell.'"

"So, I was right about going to the museum by myself."

They turned up Sixteenth Street, heading toward Larimer.

"Yes." He sighed and slowed their pace. "Lying to me about when you planned to go to the museum sent the message that you didn't believe in me."

"It wasn't so much not believing in you as fearing you'd get hurt."

"I think subconsciously I knew that. But we're talking about male witch pride here. My ego got in the way. That's why I blasted you about that stunt. And the thought of you taking on Ashmedai alone froze my blood." He leaned down and kissed her fiercely. "Don't ever do that again."

"No, sir." She kissed him back, necessitating their stopping

on the sidewalk midway down the avenue called the Sixteenth
Street Mall to reacquaint themselves with each other's tonsils.

When they finally broke apart, his serious look was back.
"One of the reasons I didn't tell you about the horoscope for
the Twenty-ninth was because I knew you'd try to shield me
from danger."

She shook her head. "You didn't have to go, but you went
right along even though you knew you'd be injured."

"I had to help in any way I could," he said on a shrug.
"Lighting fuses wasn't too demanding."

"But what if Ashmedai had killed you?" She could hear
the pain in her voice when she asked that question.

He kissed the end of her nose, then brushed it with his
fingertip. "Not a single one of the divinations I made showed
my death. Or the deaths of you, Mav, Glenna, or Ashmedai for
that matter. I knew I wouldn't leave the museum in the best of
shape, but I'd still be alive when the dust cleared."

"Thank the goddess for that favor." She started to pick up
their pace. "And, since you *are* my soul, the result for the
twenty-ninth is pretty obvious."

"I love you," he said simply. "Have I told you that
recently?"

"Not in the past ten minutes or so."

"I'll do better." He smiled. "I have a feeling 'work a candle
spell' is on the agenda for tonight."

"You'd be absolutely correct."

"And here's something else." He kissed the side of her
head, chuckling when her ear started in again. "Tonight's a full
moon."

"I thought it wasn't full until tomorrow night."

"Just another of my sins of omission. But more important
even than that is the fact there's going to be a total lunar eclipse
at eleven-thirty."

That news momentarily stunned her. She butted his shoulder
with the side of her head. "Thanks for coming clean on that
one."

"We've got about two and a half hours before the eclipse."

"A full lunar eclipse," Endora marveled. "An extremely
powerful circumstance. A night filled with magic."

"Think Ash will try to capitalize on the situation?"

"He might." She smiled with satisfaction. "But lunar events
are goddess-centered events. Female oriented. He can perform

whatever rituals he wants, but he'll never gain as much from them as I will. And, as my cosmic twin, what I gain, you'll gain."

"Works for me."

They turned on Larimer and headed to the condo.

* * *

One look at Marcus and Endora as they entered the kitchen, and Mav signaled to Glenna. "Come with me, my canine friend. We are not needed here tonight."

"Thanks, Mav." Marcus had Endora neatly tucked against his right side, so he slapped the vampire on the shoulder with his left hand.

The vampire looked first at Marcus, then at Endora. "We would only be in the way, so we will seek alternate lodging."

"Steer clear of the museum." Endora smiled.

He nodded gravely. "We will return in the morning."

You're one lucky cat, Glenna told Endora. *Getting Marcus all to yourself for the whole night. Whoooeee. I want details when I get back.*

Endora laughed and lightly thumped Glenna on the back. "See you tomorrow, Wonder Dog."

As soon as Mav and Glenna left, Marcus dropped his jacket on the recliner. Then he turned to Endora, slid her leather jacket off her shoulders and disposed of it the same way.

"Finally alone." His kiss was slow and lingering as he ran his fingers through her hair then down her back to her hips and back up.

"I'm going to enjoy your attention a lot more as soon as I reverse this anti-love spell," she said wryly, tugging on her ear to stop its twitching.

Immediately, he let her go. "How can I help?"

"Well, you can keep your hands to yourself for a little while." She laughed at the pained expression that suggestion brought to his face. "Be brave, lover boy. It's not going to take long to cast the reversal spell."

In order to make good on that promise, she sent him to the pantry to find ritual candles in specific colors. While he was off on that errand, she was quickly scanning the wood box beside the fireplace. She selected a foot-long piece of willow kindling about an inch in diameter. In the kitchen, she lit a burner and charred the first four inches of one end of the stick. It was ready when Marcus got back with the candles.

"Is your beryl egg in your bedroom?" she asked

"On the window sill."

"Good. We can use it in the spell."

He remembered what Trish had told him the night before last, when he'd helped her with Endora's healing. "We might want to bring the chrysocolla crystal, as well." He explained that it could be used to bless the past and forgive old hurts.

Endora thought for a moment before nodding. "Definitely couldn't hurt. And I'm certainly going to need as much of a power burst as we can generate. If we add agate, then we've got three powerful crystals in the room with us."

"Okay, let me think about why we need that one." Marcus grabbed the chrysocolla from the bookshelf and started up the stairs. "Got it. Persuasion and harmony."

Endora followed. "It also gives courage and guards against danger. So, it covers a lot of bases."

"I'll say."

The desk in the corner was covered with charts and horoscopes. The rest of the room comfortably strewn with clothing, shirts, jeans, a pair of shoes, Marcus's running shorts.

"I didn't think we'd be using this room for much of anything, um, romantic." He picked clothes up off the chair and shoved them in a dresser drawer.

Touched by his sudden nervousness, Endora watched him tidying up. "We can use my room if you want."

He knelt down, reached halfway under the bed, and grabbed a shirt. He'd worn it last night during their encounter with Ashmedai. Torn and covered with blood, it was a complete loss. With a grimace, he wadded it up and threw it into the wastebasket. "My bed's a king size."

"Well, that's always a plus."

He stood and, hands on hips, studied the room. Then he turned serious eyes on her.

Wow, something's really bothering him. And it isn't just an untidy bedroom or the thought of finally getting into bed with me again. She waited, giving him the chance to unburden himself.

"I know our main purpose for making love is to find a means to defeat Ashmedai," he stated.

She had to bite her tongue to stifle an emphatic denial. He obviously had to get this out in the open. And she had to let him.

"But, I want you to know that, for me, the main purpose is to show just how much I love you." He gathered her close in his arms, rested his forehead against hers for a moment. "And I do love you, Endora. Only you."

Because they'd been parted so early in their relationship, she'd never had the chance to learn just how romantic he was. That knowledge humbled her. Raising her head, she lightly nipped his chin with her teeth. "Right back at you, babe. In spades." She cocked her head and studied his face. *Something else there.*

He had to clear his throat. "And, I know the greater good is the most important thing...the most important reason for us doing this and all. But I don't want you thinking you, ah, well, I mean...Bat shit, this is hard to say."

"Just speak your mind. You won't scare me away."

Frustration brought his eyebrows together in a slight scowl. He took in a quick breath, then let it out in one long sentence. "The thing is, I don't want you thinking this is some sort of bothersome duty you've got to endure, just so you can get the power to go out and rid the world of Obsidian Ashmedai.

Eleven

Endora wanted to laugh right out loud at his unfounded fears, but she managed to transform the laugh to a sly grin. *Still worried I'm only making love with you as a duty to all of witchkind? Think again, buddy. I'm having my way with you because I've got a forty-year itch that needs a major scratching.*

She mastered her smile and managed to say, in a tone of complete sincerity, "What you're saying is you don't want me having that 'lie back and think of England' mentality when we come together, right?"

He looked miserably embarrassed, yet determined to assure himself she didn't see going to bed with him as a chore. His nod was curt. "Yeah. That's it."

"You're forgetting that I'm an American witch, not a Brit."

For a moment, his expression went completely blank. Then enlightenment hit, and he smiled widely before laughing. Catching her in his arms, he spun her around three times before setting her on her feet in the middle of the floor. "Goddess, I've missed your horrible sense of humor. You're really something, Endora."

"Hey, I'm not doing this wholly for the greater good, lover boy," she said tartly. "Oh no, I'm far more selfish than that. This is for me. And for you. And for the forty years we've lost." She gave him a quick kiss on the cheek before stepping back just as quickly. "If we're lucky, we'll generate enough love magic to defeat Ash. If not, we'll have this between us, no matter what happens tomorrow night."

"Then let's get started." He set the candles and the crystals on the desk.

Her heart gave a painful thump, but it came from the love threatening to leap out of it due to sheer frustration if she didn't get this anti-love spell reversed very soon. "Roll up the rug and shove it under the bed."

Because her magic wasn't strong enough to cast a circle of light, she had to improvise. So while Marcus took care of moving the rug, she drew a pentagram on the oak floor with the charred piece of willow kindling.

Then she set about placing the five candles at the points of the pentagram. The pink one, symbolic of love and friendship, morality, and overcoming evil, went at the topmost point. The most powerful position. Moving clockwise, she placed the green candle on the upper right point. A Sagittarian color, it symbolized healing, luck, and fertility. Orange went on the lower right point, for courage and concentration. The red candle, representing strength, passion, sexuality, and protection went on the lower left point. Finally, she set the purple candle in the upper left position. It was the candle that provided extra power.

Marcus stood watching her, a look of intense concentration, and not a little concern, on his face. "It's been forty years since I've cast a spell of any kind."

She looked up at him, saw his expression, and gave him her most reassuring smile. "And I've only attempted a spell this complex once in all that time. Less than a week ago, with help from two witches who are completely in command of their magic."

"We can only do our best." He looked a bit embarrassed as he said, "I realize that's about as clichéd as it gets. But clichés only get that way because they're true, so people wear them out with overuse."

"Thanks for saying it. Even if it is corny and way outdated." Her smile belied the insult, as she finished placing the candles and rose. "I'll take the lead here, so just relax. Clear your mind and concentrate on hearing my voice inside your head."

"I've lost my clairvoyance." His aggrieved tone pulled at her heartstrings.

"Inside the magic circle, that shouldn't be a problem." She touched his hand. Brought his gaze to hers. "Like you said, we can only do our best."

"Of course, that's an overworked phrase."

"Because it's true." Taking a step toward him, she reached out and brushed his cheek lightly with her fingertips. "Trust me, Marcus. Believe in us. In what we're capable of doing together. Trust *us*."

His smile was brief. "I do."

Mentally, she sighed in relief. He was one of the most inherently honest mortals she knew. If he said he believed in them, he wasn't just saying that to make her feel good.

"We should be skyclad for this ritual," she said quietly.

With a silent nod, he removed his clothes and placed them on the chair beside the desk. Without daring to glance at his body, she removed her own clothes and laid them over his.

They entered the pentagram from opposite sides, facing each other, gazes locked. In his eyes she saw a wealth of love and faith.

His undisguised confidence in her nearly melted her heart. She wouldn't fail him. Them. *Marcus, can you hear me?*

Yes. His inner voice sounded both surprised and intensely relieved. *Coming in loud and clear.*

Endora's delight equaled Marcus's surprise. Telepathy would allow him to "hear" the chants before she actually spoke them. The casting would go more smoothly and be exponentially more powerful if they recited the chants in unison. *All right. First thing on the agenda is to call upon the elements.*

I remember how to do this. His smile was slightly cocky.

She grinned right back. *Then what are we waiting for, witch-boy?*

Just following orders and letting you lead.

Shaking her shoulders to loosen them, she gave him a wicked leer. *And since I'm leading this dance, just make sure you don't step on my feet.*

He smiled again, but this time it was not a playful expression. He was down to business. *You want me to hold the three nexus stones?*

That would be best. Your hands are bigger than mine, so the crystals won't be piled on top of each other. That way, their resonances won't overlap and possibly cancel them out. If we intertwine our fingers, I'll have contact with them, too, adding to their effectiveness.

Sounds right to me.

Placing the agate, the beryl egg and the chrysocolla crystal into his cupped palms, she pushed the stones as far apart as she could. Then she reached up under his hands and inserted her fingers between his. She could feel the pulse of each individual stone, and that steadied her nerves.

Marcus and Endora turned until they touched from shoulder to hip, extending their cupped hands, and thus the stones, toward the pentacle point where the pink candle sat.

"We call upon the elements of Spirit, Earth, Air, Fire and Water," they said together. "Hallow this rite."

They turned counterclockwise and repeated the chant to the purple candle. After completing the chant a total of five times, once to each pentacle point, they knelt and placed the agate, egg, and crystal in the very center of the magic circle.

Rising, they stood facing each other, the crystals between their spread feet, and grasped hands. Again, they twined their fingers together.

"Love is the strongest of affinities for another," Endora intoned. "A bond that can endure time and distance."

The chrysocolla began to vibrate, glowing from within with a turquoise light that enhanced the soft candlelight.

"A spiritual interconnection beyond any other," Marcus continued. "Capable of transcending even death."

As had the crystal, the agate began to glow, projecting a lacy pattern of light in various shades of yellow, orange, red and brown against their legs. The light in both stones gained in intensity as the rite continued.

Endora lifted her hands level with her shoulders, bringing Marcus's up as well. She pressed her palms flat against his, still keeping their fingers interlocked. Gave his hands a brief squeeze. "The affinity I have for you has been suppressed. Powerful magic has stifled the most potent of emotions."

The beryl egg lit up as if a light had turned on inside it. Shafts of green light shot in all directions, illuminating their bodies, and the walls, ceiling and floor with dots of intense emerald. As had the light of the crystal and the agate, the egg's light gradually built in intensity as the spell progressed.

"The time has come to reverse this spell, for the ultimate power of love to be released from its constraints." Marcus smiled down at Endora.

Looking deeply into his eyes, she said, "Lift the spell and let love free."

"With this ultimate power of love, of light, we seek to drive out the darkness."

"Loose the only omnipotent emotion known to mortals." Endora straightened her arms over her head, bringing their bodies together from shoulder to thigh. She could feel Marcus's heart beating just above hers, his crisp chest hair against her sensitive breasts. His erection pressed hot and full against her belly. Heat shot all the way to the tips of her fingers and toes, and for a moment she could think only of how much she had missed such incredible intimacy. The feel of a loved one's body, skin against skin. But renewal of their intimacy had to wait. The spell was not yet completed.

As they stood with hands extended and bodies just touching, a white-blue pulsing light started at the tips of their fingers and began to spread downward. Soon, their hands and arms looked as if they were swathed in electricity. She turned her thoughts from her lover and concentrated on the cocoon of energy that had now moved below their hips.

When their bodies were completely surrounded by this skin of electricity, they chanted together, "Reverse this spell cast three by three. So as we say, thus it must be."

As they lowered their still-locked hands to their sides, Marcus closed his mouth over Endora's. When their lips touched, the room slowly filled with swirling light of every hue and intensity. It danced around them, seeming to draw them even closer together, until they were a single being.

Endora wrapped her arms around Marcus's back, leaned into the kiss as his tongue delved the heat of her mouth. Then her tongue joined the duel.

As the intensity of their caresses increased, so did the strength of the light surrounding them. The stones at their feet fairly radiated as the room became more and more brightly lit. Soon, not a single shadow remained. The two lovers were encircled by blinding, pure white light that made the electricity pulsing from their bodies nearly invisible.

Then the light snapped out as if a giant switch had been thrown, leaving them standing in the middle of the pentagram with only the five candles to provide illumination.

"King-size bed," Endora murmured against Marcus's lips as they broke the kiss long enough to catch a breath. "Right now."

"Umm, hmm." He caught her lower lip between his teeth and gently bit down.

On a throaty chuckle, she stepped into him, overbalancing them both and propelling them toward the bed. He fell on his back on the mattress, Endora sprawled on top of him. She had the presence of mind to close the magic circle before capitalizing on her commanding position by quickly covering his face, neck and chest with kisses and love nips. Working her way down across his pecs, up and across his shoulders, and back to his face, she fanned a flame that had been banked inside him for far too long.

It took only moments for her frantically determined attention to make him break into a sweat. With a quick flip, he reversed their positions, linking her fingers through his and pinning her hands on either side of her head. Then he kissed her fiercely, with all the pent-up longing that had built steadily over the last four decades. Wedging his knees between hers, he rubbed his body against her, pelvis to shoulders, watched her eyes go dark with passion. Felt the crackle of energy along his skin wherever it made contact with hers. His physical response to her first touch was rampant; this full-frontal caress only served to make him more ready. It had been forty years since he'd had a similar response to a female. And it had only been to this particular female. The amazing sensation was like coming home.

"I can't hold back, Endora," he said, trying to control his breathing and return some aspect of sanity to their mating. "I'm way beyond finesse of any kind."

Her smile was purely feline. "We'll go for finesse the next time."

"This could get rough," he felt it necessary to warn her.

When she pulled her hand from his grasp to gently run her fingers through his hair, he almost came undone. "You won't hurt me, Marcus. It's not possible."

On a choking groan, he spread her thighs and entered her, immediately beginning a steady rhythm of deep, strong thrusts. He was helpless to slow down, to gentle his actions, to do anything but touch her in the most elementally intimate of ways. He had needed this, needed her, for too many years to restrain himself. Not knowing just how long he'd be able to last, he put all of his efforts into making every stroke count.

She climaxed within seconds, her long, keening moan breaking the relative quiet of the room. "Goddess!"

As she came apart beneath him, her inner muscles tightening around him, his rhythm broke and his senses scrambled. The feel of her pleasure momentarily seared his nerve endings, rendering him completely incapable of movement for a long moment. As her contractions began to subside, he turned his head to kiss her neck, then raised up long enough to gasp, "Been a long time for you, too, right?"

"Too long."

He had little time to reflect that she'd said exactly what he was thinking, as she had wrapped her legs around his waist and was kneading and stroking his back with both of her hands. He felt like his skin was on fire everywhere they touched, knew that far more than their bodies came together when they made love. That their souls were melded together as well. As he reestablished his cadence once more, she surged under him in response. He found his pace and drove her steadily toward another crest. She reached that summit, knowing it wouldn't be the last one she'd climb that night.

* * *

"I'm sorry, Dora." Marcus lay back on the pillow, with Endora's head cradled against his shoulder.

Without looking up from watching his small, flat nipples tighten as she lightly ran her fingernails over them, she said, "You didn't hurt me, if that's what you're apologizing for."

"That's not it. I'm apologizing for not lasting longer."

At that confession, she stopped caressing his chest and levered herself up on her other elbow. She aimed her best feline stare directly into his somber black eyes. "You're kidding, right?"

"No."

"Well, you should be."

"How can you say that?" He cocked his head and stared intently up at her. "I was done in under twenty minutes."

He looked so cute, lying there all concerned and sexy, that she couldn't bring herself to brain him with the nearest crystal. Instead, she kissed his chin. "Marcus, I had three orgasms. Three. From where I'm sitting, that ranks as an excellent score. Up in the 'master' category, in fact. And twenty minutes isn't exactly a slam-bam-thank-you-ma'am type of conjugal encounter." With her fingertips, she smoothed away the crease between his eyebrows and ran a finger across his lips. "Given the fact it's been forty years since we last did this together, I think things went just fine. More than fine, actually. Fantastic. But just because you satisfied me so thoroughly, don't think I'm letting you off the hook."

His eyebrow rose even as he caressed her hip with one hand. "What do you mean?"

"I distinctly remember, before completely losing my mind three times and being reduced to a moaning, whimpering matrix of spent neurons, that I told you we'd take our time during the second round."

He closed his eyes for a moment. Concentrated, then sighed. "Round two is going to have to wait. It's eleven-fifteen. We have fifteen minutes to prepare to draw down the moon."

Endora leaped out of bed as if she'd been flung from a catapult. "Bat shit! I completely forgot." She ran her hands through her hair, smiling wryly at him. "Your lovemaking really did scramble my circuits."

This time, his smile was closer to a cocky smirk. "Guess I did, didn't I?"

She snorted, then bent down to rearrange the crystals in the pentagram. "So much for an ego crisis."

"I'll go get white candles." Gloriously nude, he left the bedroom, headed for the pantry.

As she watched him go, she realized that the old Marcus would never have doubted his ability to pleasure her. They had both matured in the past forty years. She liked the grown-up couple they'd become far better than the impetuous youths they'd been. Too bad they'd gained their maturity in separate parts of the world, far away from the comfort of each other's presence.

Feline practicality told her it did no good to look back with regret. So she'd look to the future, no matter how brief that time might be, with hope.

She removed the used candles before setting her lodestones—the crystal, the agate and the egg—in a triangular formation outside the pentagram. The crystal went at the apex, the agate on the left and the beryl egg on the right. A circle within a circle.

This time, Marcus placed the candles on the pentagram. Then, with a snap of his fingers, he lit them all at once.

Knowing the sex magic they'd shared had restored Marcus's abilities made Endora want to shout her happiness. But she didn't want to feed his ego. "Show off."

"I haven't been able to do any kind of spell for forty years." His grin nearly went from ear to ear. "I never knew exactly how much I missed that ability until just now when I got it back. I'm sure you understand exactly how good it feels to be able to do magic again."

"Actually, yes."

Bodies glowing from their recent lovemaking, they stepped into the pentagram and stood facing each other, again interlocking hands and pressing palm to palm.

Endora spoke first. "If I command the moon, it will come down. If I wish to withhold the day, night will linger. If I wish to embark upon the sea, I need no ship, and if I wish to fly through the air, I am free from my weight."

Marcus took the role of the high priest. "We call upon the

goddess who goes by many names. Come down and enter the body of our high priestess. Through her, speak. Lend your wise guidance. Enlighten us to the true way."

When Endora began to sway, he tightened his grip on her hands. Only a moment passed before a shaft of muted light penetrated the ceiling of the bedroom and entered her body through her mouth. When she opened her eyes, their emerald green had been replaced by pure white light.

The goddess had come.

"Listen to the words of the Great Mother," Marcus intoned, although his responsibility was to listen, as they had no coven to be the recipients of the goddess's wisdom.

Endora's mouth opened, but her lips didn't move. Still, Marcus had no trouble hearing the words she spoke in another's voice. He concentrated on remembering every small detail of what was happening. The success of their venture depended on his attention to what the goddess told them.

"If ye have need of any thing, when the moon is full, then shall ye assemble in some secret place and ask what ye will of me, who is the Queen of all Witches." Endora swayed more widely, but Marcus wasn't worried for her safety. Her physical self was merely channeling the goddess's spirit.

"I am the Mother of all living things," she continued. "My love is poured out upon the earth. Celebrate, feast, make music and love, all in my praise. Give love unto all beings. Keep pure your highest ideal; strive ever towards it; let naught stop you or turn you aside.

"I, the benevolent goddess, give happiness. I give knowledge of the spirit eternal. I give peace and freedom and reunion with those who have gone before unto death."

Marcus knew his part. "Hear the word of the Star Goddess."

"I call unto thy soul. Let thy divine self be open to the wonder of the infinite. Worship me with a heart that rejoices. Let there be beauty and strength, power and compassion, honor and humility, mirth and reverence within all of you."

Endora's swaying slowed, became more subtle. "Thou who seek me, know thy seeking shall avail thee not unless thou knowest this mystery. If what thou seekest thou findest not within thyself, thou wilt never find it outside thyself. For I have been with thee from the beginning. I am that which is attained at the end of desire."

The moment the last word left her mouth the light left as well, curling to smoke above their heads, and Endora's knees buckled. Still holding her hands, Marcus eased her to the floor. Then he extinguished the candles and closed the circle. Lifting her limp body, he placed it gently on the bed. Her magnificence brought tears to his eyes, and he felt his Adam's apple working rapidly up and down. He stroked her hair back from her face and kissed her cheek. It was encouraging to note that her ear didn't spasm. In fact, neither of her ears had moved from the moment they first entered the magic circle.

Endora was right about her body fighting the anti-love spell. He smiled slowly. *Our lovemaking certainly cured her of her twitch.* And cured him of an itch he suspected she shared with him.

"Hey, Sleeping Beauty," he whispered in her ear. "Time to wake up."

Her lips curled upward. "When I open my eyes, am I going to see a handsome prince, or some ugly dragon?"

He kissed the corner of her mouth, and was rewarded with a languid smile. "See for yourself."

"Eeeeeew! Ugly dragon."

All Marcus could do was roll his eyes and laugh helplessly at her antics. "Goddess, I love you, even if your sense of humor needs a good makeover."

"That goes both ways." She sat up, turned and scooted to the edge of the bed.

When she stretched in a very feline manner, Marcus swallowed hard. They were both still naked, and her actions did very interesting things to her breasts. "You're killing me, here, Endora."

She shot him a startled look which quickly turned seductive. "Deal with it, lover boy. You promised me slow this time, remember?"

"How could I ever forget a promise like that?" He extended his hand, then pulled her to her feet when she grasped it. "Let's see how much magic we got back, okay?" He snapped his fingers, and they were both fully clothed.

"Isn't this a bit counterproductive?"

"Shhh." He reached for her, cupped her face in her hands, and kissed her for a long, slow time. His lips were nearly touching hers when he pulled back, murmuring, "I've undressed you in my mind every night for the past forty years. Now, I want to do it for real again." When he saw tears gather in her eyes, he kissed her tenderly.

They undressed each other with a slow deliberateness that belied their pounding hearts. Then he lowered her to the bed, where they explored each other's bodies with languorous hands and questing mouths. Both discovered four decades of life. Of wear and tear, of experience neither had garnered when they'd last come together. Like connoisseurs, they savored. Relished. Repeatedly came back for more.

Endora slowly licked a path along the crescent-shaped scar on the inside of Marcus's left knee. "Where'd you get this?"

"Old athletic injury." When her look demanded more information, he grinned. "Nosey."

"Curiosity and the cat. That sort of thing."

A sigh that proclaimed him to be much put upon by his lover rumbled from his broad chest. "I lived in Europe in the Seventies. Being the wannabe jock I am, I needed something for amusement that was more physically challenging than cricket or lawn bowling."

"Water polo's a rough sport." With her fingertip, she again traced the path of the scar.

"I was afraid the horses would drown."

She swatted him on the arm. "And you say my sense of humor is terrible. Come on, out with the dirty facts. I'm going to bite you if you don't tell all the details."

"And how, exactly, would doing that make me talk?" When her eyes narrowed in annoyance, he relented. "I played soccer, all right? Mid-fielder on a pretty good team, until I got creamed in the league's championship match by a defenseman from our biggest rival. I don't think he necessarily took a cheap shot, but my teammates definitely took umbrage with his actions."

She propped herself up on her elbow to look down on him. "What happened?"

"Well, mind you, I was laid out on the grass, clutching my knee to my chest and trying not to scream like a four-year-old. So I wasn't in any position to see much of the stadium-clearing brawl that took place."

Endora stared. "Don't you mean bench clearing?"

"Nope. Both teams started mixing it up right on the field, and it wasn't long before over half the fans in the stadium joined in. The people who didn't want to get hurt in the mêlée headed for the exits, but that still left about ten thousand people fighting. It took fifty mounted Bobbies to restore some semblance of order."

"What happened to you?"

"By the time the authorities cleared the combatants, they'd pretty much forgotten all about me. Even through all the pain, I realized I had to get out of there or risk being trampled by a bunch of crazed soccer fanatics. So, while the fight escalated, I managed to crawl to the dressing room and scrounge around for a crutch. I found one, snuck out the back entrance where only players were allowed access, and headed off to the hospital to have it looked at. I'd torn the medial collateral ligament, and my competitive soccer playing days were over."

She stared at him a moment. "You made that story up."

"Goddess's truth. They take their *football* seriously over there." Smiling, he ran a fingertip along her right collarbone. "Okay, your turn. Where'd this bump come from?"

"Nothing so dramatic as a brawl." She abruptly looked sheepish. "I was in cat form and had decided to sneak into a friend's house to surprise him. Thought I was leaping through an open window. Actually, whoever cleaned said window had used a really excellent glass cleaner." When he started to chuckle, she added, "That was one rare time when a cat didn't land on her feet."

He laughed outright at that and kissed the place where the bone had broken. He ran his tongue the length of her collarbone before moving to her breasts, where he laved each in much the same way.

He was rewarded by a hitch in her breath that indicated she was certainly not indifferent to his actions. Then he used his mouth, kissing and slowly suckling each breast in turn, rapidly accelerating the tension in her body. Until she grew restless beneath his mouth. Until her fingers clutched at his hair and drew his head tighter to her.

Taking her restiveness and low moans of pleasure as signals, he moved down to pleasure even more sensitive areas.

Although it wasn't possible, he thought he could spend the rest of his life in bed with her like this. Since that time frame might only be a few hours, though, he decided he'd do his best to live what remained of his life to the fullest.

Twelve

It was midmorning, and they were in the kitchen cleaning up from breakfast, when there was a knock on the back door.

"It's Mav and Glenna," Endora said without looking up from the pan she had scrubbing in the sink.

"Why'd they knock?" Marcus unlocked the deadbolt by pointing at it and making a twisting motion with his finger. "Mav's got a key."

She shot him a smug look, purring, "Maybe they were afraid they'd catch us in a compromising position." Leaning into him where he stood beside her at the sink, she kissed him slowly.

"Of all the positions we tried last night," Marcus replied when the kiss ended, "I didn't think a single one was compromising."

She laughed before calling out, "Come on in, you two. We're in the kitchen, and you have my word that we're decent."

"We didn't do anything indecent in my book, either," Marcus whispered. Then he turned toward their roommates with a genuine smile. "Hey, guys. How's the Denver night life?" *How'd you sleep, Glenna?*

Just inside the doorway, the dog stopped dead in her tracks and cocked her head at Marcus. Then she barked twice, did her happy dance across the kitchen floor, and leaped at his chest. *You can talk to me!*

He caught her in his arms, cradled her bulk against him, then kissed her soundly on the nose. *You bet your canines, Killer.*

How?

It took a little magic and a lot of faith, Endora interjected.

Glenna enthusiastically licked Marcus's face, sparing not a single inch of his skin from ear to ear and chin to hairline. *Outstanding! Of course, Endora and I won't be able to talk about you telepathically anymore. But that's all right, I guess.*

That's fine with me, too, Marcus stated wryly as he set Glenna back on the floor.

We've both been checking out your butt.

Too much information, Wonder Dog, Endora interjected, shaking her head. *Don't bolster his self-esteem any more.*

It's already off the charts as it is.

Checking out my butt, eh?

Ignoring the smug look on Marcus's face, Endora looked down at the dog. "See what I mean?" Then she turned to Mav. "Have you eaten?"

The lanky vampire took a seat on one of the bar stools near the butcher block. "Both Glenna and I are satiated."

Not wanting to know exactly what that meant, Endora gestured to the dirty dishes. "This won't take us long to finish, then we need to convene a war council. So, stick close."

"It is October Thirty-first," Mav said on a nod. "Obsidian Ashmedai will gain full power at midnight tonight."

"Believe me, Mav, we're going to have a big say in the matter." Marcus hung his dishcloth on the oven's door handle and went to the dining table. He stood, hands on hips, looking down at the charts and papers he'd set out just after they'd finished eating. With a glance at Mav, he gestured at the accumulated stacks. "We've got another surprise planned for our buddy Ash."

Mav moved to look over the pages Marcus had indicated. Then he looked at his friend. "From all appearances, your spell casting was successful."

"Beyond my most outrageous hopes," Marcus confirmed with a slight smile. "But we still don't know exactly how much magic we regained. Or if it's going to give us enough power to bring Ash down."

"Will you test the extent of your powers before you engage Ashmedai once again?"

Marcus shook his head. "Doing that is problematic, for a couple reasons. First, we'll have to go somewhere remote to see just how much we've got. There's always a chance some hiker or rock climber will happen on the scene, forcing us to wipe out his memory."

"That takes time," Endora commented from the kitchen. "Up to a half hour if you want to make sure you're not hurting the person whose memory you're altering."

"The other problem with testing our powers is that we run the risk of depleting them before we really need them."

Mav took his favorite chair at the table and sat down. He steepled his fingers, pressing them to his mouth in a posture of contemplation. "Yes, I see how those factors could present problems. But, how will you know what powers you have available?"

Wiping her hands on a dishtowel, Endora joined the males. "We're trying little things right now. Ironically, if we can do the simple stuff, we can likely do the more complex. Especially if we concentrate and don't have to maintain any one spell for long." When her hands were dry, she wadded the towel up and tossed it toward the refrigerator. Halfway there, it shook itself out of its spherical shape and floated quietly toward the handle, where it threaded itself through and settled. "Want another crack at Ashmedai, Mav?"

"Yes," he answered succinctly.

"Glenna?"

The dog's enthusiastic bark confirmed her eagerness to take another chunk out of the witch who'd nearly killed her master.

Endora smiled. "Are we all gluttons for punishment, or what?"

"What we need to do first," Marcus said as Endora joined him at the dining table, "is go over what the goddess told us when we drew down the moon." He quickly caught Mav up on what exactly that particular rite entailed and why it was important to their cause.

"Since the goddess used me as her mouthpiece," Endora said, "I heard nothing. So, Marcus will clue us in. Then we'll use her advice to eliminate Ash's threat for good. How about it, lover boy?" She gave Marcus a quick hug before stepping back a pace. "What did we learn in school last night?"

"That we've got all the power we need," he stated firmly, looking from his lover to his friend and back. When Endora and Mav just gaped at him, he continued. "The goddess said what we don't have already inside us we'll never find outside ourselves."

Endora frowned. "Was she talking about magic?"

"Not exactly, although magic is definitely part of the equation. My interpretation is that she was talking about the spiritual. The command she gave was to keep our highest ideal pure, to strive toward it always, and to let nothing stop us or turn us away from that path."

"Well, wanting to see Obsidian Ashmedai writhing in Hades has certainly been my ideal for a very long time," came Endora's wry comment. "Somehow, though, I doubt that's a noble path the goddess would endorse."

"Yet the two of you have an ultimate goal which is, in fact, noble."

Marcus turned to Mav. "What's your theory?"

"The goal you ultimately seek, even at the risk of losing your own lives, is the elimination of a threat to your world and all those who dwell in it. Many religions speak of the honor of self-sacrifice so that others may live and prosper. In Christianity, it is considered the ultimate of great deeds to lay down one's life for a friend. Thus, your goal is a very noble one in any philosophy."

"It all gets back to the greater good." Endora startled the vampire by going over to his chair, bending down, and kissing him on the cheek. "That's first-class insight. I'm calling you Socrates from now on, buddy."

"I think you're demonstrating another of the attributes of power, Endora." Marcus pointed to a legal pad containing notes from the drawing the moon ceremony. "Look at this comment here. We're commanded to give love to all beings. You do."

Endora felt her cheeks heat. "Because I kissed Mav, that gives me a power attribute?"

"No, it is because you accept me, even though I am what I am." Mav looked earnestly up at Marcus and Endora. "Since I met you, Endora, you have not once looked at me with mistrust or repulsion. You have included me in every step of this venture. And you have no idea what that has meant to me."

"Oh." Endora shuffled her feet. "Well, you're Marcus's friend, after all. And I've always said anyone who's a friend of his is a friend of mine."

Marcus gathered her into his arms for a quick kiss. "Don't sell yourself short, Endora. You've got the biggest heart of anyone I know. You also have beauty, strength, compassion, honor and reverence. Those are the other attributes the goddess told us we needed." Then he shot her a sly grin. "And even though your sense of humor is completely warped, that counts as mirth."

"You're damning me with faint praise here." She gently nipped his chin.

"I said it counted." Marcus's eyes lit with mischief. "You do have to work on the humility, though. That's gonna be tough for you, I'm afraid. But it is an attribute of power according to the goddess."

With a laugh, Endora pushed out of his embrace. "And

156 Laurie C. Kuna

becoming humble won't be at all tough for you, ego-boy." She left Marcus's side to sit at the end of the table opposite Mav. Then she reached for the sheet of paper closest to her.

"Actually, as your cosmic twin, what you've got, I've got." Marcus's tone didn't indicate he was aggrieved in any way by this situation.

Mav started shuffling papers, piling similar ones neatly together. "His ego is legend, as you already know."

"Thanks for the support, pal."

"Maybe we can find an ego farm, sort of like a fat farm, where we can send you to get help." Endora smiled as she scanned a page, then looked up at Marcus. "I'm sure the Internet has information on programs like that."

"Remember, where I go, you go." Instead of sitting down, Marcus put both hands on the table and leaned forward to study the information. "Here's another tidbit that may or may not relate to us. The goddess controls the door to the Land of Youth, the cup of life, and the Cauldron of Cerridwen, the Holy Grail of Immortality."

"She mentioned that during the rite?" At Marcus's nod, Endora's eyes hardened, posture abruptly straightening to military deportment. "What if we were wrong to assume the *Zohar* is the central piece of Ashmedai's mysticism exhibit?"

"I'm not following you," Marcus stated, looking down at her from where he stood, hands still on the table, stiff arms supporting his upper body.

"He's assembled the greatest collection of mystic artifacts ever seen," she answered tightly. "Why not assume he got the Cauldron of Cerridwen as well? If it truly grants immortality, wouldn't Ashmedai want it?"

Mav rubbed his chin with his hand, then began straightening and re-bending a large paper clip he'd taken from a stack of papers. "Yes. In fact, I believe he conceived of the exhibit for the express purpose of acquiring the cauldron."

"How'd you come to that conclusion?" Endora asked.

"As you know, in witchcraft, cauldrons are emblems of the womb, from which all life flows," Mav stated. "Also, the Cauldron of Cerridwen is known to the Celts as the Cauldron of Regeneration. Since Ashmedai's mysticism exhibit has artifacts from the Druids, the Hebrews, witchcraft and every other culture of mysticism, isn't it odd there are no cauldrons?"

Endora felt her eyes go wide. "You're absolutely right.

He's likely got a cauldron, maybe even the Cauldron of Cerridwen, but he didn't acquire it for the exhibit."

Marcus started to pace slowly across the living area and back, speculating aloud. "Makes sense. Get hired to run a museum, then pick an occult theme for your opening exhibit. Once the artifacts start to come in, you pull the best stuff for your personal use."

Endora nodded. "And even though the *Zohar* is Kabbalah's most sacred book, it's just window dressing to Ashmedai. He has no use for any artifact from that particular branch of mysticism, no matter how powerful. There is no way to gain personally from it."

"Although it gives legitimacy to the exhibit, it's nothing to him beyond that." Marcus turned the chair back-to-table and straddled it, leaning his crossed arms on the top of the back.

"Then why did he panic when Endora threw the sacred book into the air?" Mav asked.

"I think I know why." Endora covered Marcus's hand, squeezed once, then released him. "And the other night in the museum, I certainly counted on my hunch that, although he's a complete monster, Ash respects the sacred."

"Indeed," Mav noted, "there are many examples of that duality. Adolph Hitler was a great lover of art."

"Agreed," Marcus said. "While Ash practices black magic to become powerful, he doesn't destroy anything that is at all sacred. And that includes artifacts from such belief systems as Christianity, which has had little nice to say about practitioners of the magickal arts." He indicated a layout of the museum exhibits. "So, he uses the *Zohar* as his centerpiece, and he hides the cauldron. As the museum's curator, he had knowledge of every piece they were getting for the exhibit. It would take very little effort to falsify receipts and tuck a particular artifact in his storage room home. Only he would know it was even on the premises."

"And with the Cauldron of Cerridwen, the Holy Grail of immortality, in his possession," Endora stated gravely, "he wouldn't just be the most powerful witch on Earth; he'd be a god."

"I'll do a scrying and find out if he's got it." Marcus got up from the table and started up the stairs. "Then, I think we need to send Mav in to steal it."

The vampire's smile was as broad as Endora had ever

seen it. So broad, it showed his gleaming fangs. If he hadn't been a friend, that sight would have disconcerted her. Royally.

"I would be more than pleased to take that particular object from Obsidian Ashmedai," Mav said, obviously relishing the opportunity. "He has caused too much pain and suffering to my friends for me to let him go unpunished. And he is a threat to all creatures on Earth, as well."

Endora leaned back in her chair and crossed her arms loosely over her chest. "Wouldn't it be best if we send Mav for the cauldron while we're distracting Ash? If he goes in there alone, against a pissed off witch who's just about to become omnipotent, really bad things could happen." She looked at both males alternately.

"A very good idea," Marcus agreed. "Mav? Want to coordinate with us one more time?"

"Of course." Mav looked at Endora. "And I have an idea for using the teachings of Kabbalah against Ashmedai."

"I'm all ears," she said immediately.

"According to the *Zohar*, red string wards off evil spirits." Mav's eyes lit with mischief. "I propose that we each wear strands of red string around our necks, where Ashmedai can see them."

Marcus laughed. "I love the irony there, Mav." He left to find red string among the supplies in the pantry.

By noon, they had included Mav and Glenna in their revised plans. Deciding to wait until the museum closed at nine, they had the entire afternoon and early evening to prepare.

Endora and Marcus chose his bedroom for their preparations.

As they undressed quickly and moved into each other's embrace, Endora sighed. "I could get used to this kind of activity with you." She kissed him lightly on the mouth. Ran her hands slowly down his chest.

He pulled her closer, suckled then licked the juncture of her shoulder and neck. "You'd better get used to it, since I'm not going anywhere."

A moment's doubt seized her. In a few hours, they both could be dead. Was this the last chance they would ever have to make love together? She knew he felt her anxiety just as if it was his own because his eyes instantly locked on hers, their black depths intense.

He ran his hands up and down her back in a reassuring

caress. Kissed her cheek softly. "We have to do our best, love."

His words touched her heart, the warmth of his caress soothed her agitation. "Pray to the goddess it's enough."

"I have a feeling it will be."

Surprise had her eyebrow shooting up. "Did you divine the outcome of tonight's big showdown?"

"No." He pulled her head onto his shoulder and hugged her so close she could feel his heartbeat inside her own chest. "No desire to know the outcome. I'll trust the goddess and have faith in us, the Gang of Four. And, of course, we'll be wearing red strings."

She laughed. "How could I have forgotten that important element of our arsenal?"

His expression turned serious, and he kissed the top of her head before saying, "I especially have faith in you, Endora."

"I love you." Her throat tightened with emotion as she reached up to pull his mouth down for a long, maddening kiss. "No matter what happens tonight, I'll love you."

"Beyond death."

"Beyond even that."

He sank to the floor, pulling her onto his lap as he went. She wrapped her legs around his waist and pressed her body to his, feeling the electric current that hummed between them when their skin touched. They kissed and caressed with slowly building intensity, until finally he lifted her, positioned himself, and lowered her carefully onto his erection.

Her moan was more a purr. "You feel so good inside me." She knew he'd understand she didn't just mean in this physical way. That she meant his spirit being inside her as well.

"We make our best magic together," he said as he skimmed his hands up her sides and down her back from shoulders to buttocks, alternating a slow stroke with a quick one.

Busy combing quick fingers through his hair, she paused to smile. "That's because of our affinity. We're two sides to the same coin." She gasped when he rolled her nipples between his fingers, managed to hiss out, "Like produces like."

He surged up, and neither of them spoke any coherent words for a long time after that.

* * *

They were dozing from their fourth and most intense bout of lovemaking, when Glenna scratched at the bedroom door.

Guys, get up! Something's very wrong.

"It's just seven o'clock," Endora said, her inner clock providing the time in lieu of any mechanical device.

But they both leaped from the bed without question or hesitation, thick red string wrapping itself around their necks and clothes flying onto their bodies as they rushed to let the dog in.

Marcus was first to the door. He opened it to find Glenna and Mav in the hallway. "What's going on?"

The protection spell is gone.

They had no time to debate the significance of that, as the windows of the living area exploded in a hail of flying glass.

And Obsidian Ashmedai materialized in the middle of the room.

"Spread out," Marcus ordered. "Glenna, with me. Mav, stay with Endora."

"Follow me." Endora leaped over the balcony, landed between the dining table and the bar separating dining from kitchen, and then vaulted over the bar. Mav was practically on top of her when the blast of Ashmedai's magic hit the heavy oak woodwork, rattling the pots and pans hanging above the butcher block and stove.

She had seen Marcus and Glenna heading toward Mav's bedroom, so knew they wouldn't be in the direct line of fire, as that room was to the right of the staircase.

"Surprised to see me?" Ash taunted. He sent a bolt up the stairs, but only Endora's bedroom door took any damage.

"Nothing you do surprises me, Ash."

The rattling cookware gave Endora an idea. With the flick of her finger, she sent pot after pot after frypan hurtling at Ash. But she didn't have to see that none of them hit their mark. Not a single one gave off that satisfying thump of metal against flesh. Lots of pinging sounds from disintegrating metal, nothing else. She sent the cutlery next. Same result, but it was gratifying to realize she could teleport things other than herself. And it was keeping Ash off balance. He most likely hadn't expected resistance like this.

"A parlor trick," Ash roared. "You have no real magic." He sent another blast at the bar they crouched behind, but the solid oak withstood it.

"He is a pompous ass," Mav said simply, fingering the red string around his throat.

Endora started to chuckle, noticed his fangs elongating,

and stifled her mirth. "Uh, Mav." With her finger she gestured at his mouth. "Do you know your teeth are—"

"Yes."

"You're not going to start biting yourself, are you?"

"No."

We need to get over to the museum, Marcus said in Endora's mind. *Give Mav some cover. I'll do the same for Glenna.*

Are we playing into his hands by going there? It's his power source.

Not if we steal the cauldron. Tell Mav it's in the farthest storage room, behind a three-panel decorative screen. But before he grabs it he needs to take all the white candles in the storage room and set them up on top of the Stonehenge monoliths and on the second floor balcony railing. Seven per monolith, but don't worry about numbers for the rest of them, as long as they form a circle all around the main floor. Then he has to grab the cauldron, take it to the lion's den at the zoo and throw it over the fence.

That's going to piss off several of my distant relations.

We can't worry about a bunch of angry cats right now.

I know that. I was just trying to lighten the moment. Endora...

She relayed Marcus's message. "All right, Mav, ready? When Marcus signals, I'm blasting Ashmedai with my own force field. That should distract him enough to get you and Wonder Dog out of here and on your way to grab the cauldron. Glenna will let us know when the candles are in place."

"I will be very swift."

"I'm counting on it, buddy."

"Now!" Marcus shouted.

Immediately, beams of power flew from the stairs. Endora stood up so her hands would clear the top of the bar. She sent two quick blasts at Ash, then ducked back down as his retaliation strike was almost instantaneous.

"Think that got his attention?" She looked at Mav. "All right. I'll give a count of three, then I'm gunning for him again. Stay down so the bar will shield you from his sight, and get the hades out of here." She winked at him. "Good luck." Her fingers began to glow, and she flexed them several times to loosen them up. "One, two, three!"

With the scream of a jungle cat on the hunt, she popped

back to her feet and sent three quick strikes right at Ash. He parried them, but nearly was scorched by Marcus's simultaneous volley. In the fury of their magic battle, Mav and Glenna slipped undetected from the condo.

Let's give them as much time as we can, Marcus thought. "So, how'd you manage to find us, Ash?" Marcus called from above.

"I had dearly hoped you had been mortally wounded during our last encounter, Morion," Ashmedai said coldly. "And that hope grew when neither of you came to the museum last night to harass me with your pathetic diversions. Imagine my surprise when I learned you were both still alive, and in a safe house here in Denver."

"So, which Tribunal member tipped you off?" Endora asked, hidden once again behind the bar. "Was it your old champion, Arthur Morass?"

A slight pause preceded Ash's laugh. "There's no need to conceal such information from the likes of you. You both will be dead, and my secret will die with your last breaths."

We're not dead yet, Marcus and Endora thought at the same time. She laughed silently. It was good to have a partner.

But Ash was at his pretentious best right then, using a tone and cadence that would have made many an evangelical preacher take notes. "That unctuous toady, Morass, has indeed championed me for many years," Ashmedai stated. "But he and his three cohorts supported me merely because they thought to control me. They delayed returning my powers, the fools."

I've got a feeling I know what's coming, Endora told Marcus.

"So, I killed two of them as a warning to the remaining pair."

Bingo. "So, Morass masterminded the entire operation."

Ashmedai's unpleasant laugh filled the condo. "Morass has delusions of his own importance. No, he is neither the mastermind of my rise to power, nor is he the most powerful member of the Tribunal aiding me. Not in the least. That would be Mordecai Montrose, the Head Magistrate."

Goddess, are we in trouble.

Think about your powerful friends. Marcus's thought was the epitome of calm. *Unless I'm a complete moron at reading character, if we survive tonight, I'm betting Medusa will have a hand in bringing down our two rogue magistrates.*

Just then, another voice filled their minds. *Hey, guys, all the candles are set up. Mav's on his way to the zoo with the cauldron.*

Glenna, find a safe place to hide, then sit tight, Marcus told her. *We'll be there in just a few minutes.*

Endora didn't like to admit it, but the realization that they really were going there gave her a jolt of momentary panic.

Endora, I need cover so I can get down to you.

Marcus's request snapped her out of her momentary lapse. *You've got it.* She jumped up and fired off three quick blasts of energy. Paused a heartbeat and repeated the sequence two more times.

He was crouched by her side before the second trio of blasts were finished.

Nice to see you. She gave him a quick kiss on the cheek.

Thanks. His look was smug. *I'm thinking we should let good ole Ash know just what we've done with his precious Cauldron of Cerridwen.*

He'll be a very unhappy camper.

And, hopefully, a careless one.

I like your criminal mind. Endora leaned over and kissed him again.

Since you're the one who dragged me into this mess, you should have the honors.

She chuckled. *My pleasure.*

Goddess, you're so sexy when you have that "I'm going to kick somebody's ass" look in your eyes. His wide grin showed perfect white teeth and made Endora's heart thump extra hard.

Remember that thought for later because I'll be cashing in on your observation. "Hey Ash," she called, quirking an eyebrow at Marcus as she did. "Thought you might like to know that, since it's your birthday and all, Marcus and I got you a present."

A bolt of power destroyed the refrigerator across the kitchen from them.

"Aw, now that reaction would hurt my feelings if I really cared whether you liked your gift or not." Endora gave a theatrical sigh. "But the truth is, I think I'm going to enjoy it more than you are."

"Don't be obtuse , Endora," Ashmedai said.

"Obtuse?" she asked in her best Valley Girl intonation. "Does that, like, mean, like, hebetudinous, or are you, like, saying I'm slow-witted?"

Hebetudinous?

Endora smiled. *Hey, my best friend's a writer. She's got a great synonym dictionary, so I've picked up a few things.*

Like hebetudes? Sounds like a disease I wouldn't want to get.

Ha, ha.

"Your ridiculous attempts to be erudite are not amusing, Endora."

"All right, now you are hurting my feelings. But, since you just don't think I'm scholarly, I'll cut to the chase. We replaced your old cauldron."

"You did *what?*

Neither Marcus nor Endora had ever heard such a note of panic in Ashmedai's tone. When she turned her surprised gaze to him, he was grinning like the Wolf with Red Riding Hood in his sights.

We got to the black-hearted bastard! "Hey, that moldy pot is two thousand years old if it's a day," she stated matter-of-factly. "Lots of wear and tear, exposure to all those fires, moisture from the rain spells. Dings and dents from being hauled to every Black Mass. So, we decided to replace it with a shiny new one."

"You couldn't be so foolish."

"Well, according to you I could," Endora retorted. "Obtuse, remember? Marcus and I wanted to make your birthday extra-memorable, so we went down to Cauldron's 'R Us and picked you up a brand new, shiny pot to cook your potions in. The old one's probably being melted down right now."

"NOOOOOOOOOOOOOO!"

Endora and Marcus teleported out of the condo a split-second before Ash's blast leveled the entire kitchen.

Thirteen

Marcus and Endora positioned themselves on either side of the *Zohar*. Glenna sat behind the monolith directly to their left, and Mav stood behind the monolith directly to their right. They didn't have long to wait until Ashmedai joined them.

The front doors blew nearly off their hinges, and a whirlwind hurling black bolts of lightning swept into the exhibition hall.

"Rather over the top for an entrance, don't you think," Marcus observed wryly.

Endora shrugged. "That's Ash for you. Never do something simple when a grandiose gesture will garner more attention."

"Guess he didn't think he should conserve his magic."

"And that kind of attitude so appeals to my inner bitch." Endora's expression was feral. "I very much enjoy rubbing someone's nose in their own arrogance."

The whirlwind died, and Ashmedai stood where the vortex had been.

"Showtime, Endora." Marcus quickly glanced her way. "I love you."

"I know."

"What have you done with the Cauldron of Cerwidden?" Ashmedai bellowed the moment his whirlwind dissipated.

"I told you, we got you a new one." Endora's force field deflected the witch's furious blast. "Temper, temper."

"You'll give it back to me immediately, or I'll—"

"You'll what, Ash? Kill us? Steal our magic?" Marcus's tone was pure ice. "Not without a fight, you won't."

"And the fight will be fair," Endora added, "since the Holy Grail of Immortality isn't here to boost your powers."

Ash's roar of fury shook the monoliths, but both Marcus and Endora repelled his magic when he sent it blasting toward where they hid.. She wondered if either of them could withstand a direct, full-powered attack, but their plan was meant to assure that wouldn't happen. Guerilla warfare was the only way they stood a chance against superior firepower. So, they would alternate their attacks, keep all magic spells short and briefly intense, and only combine their powers when absolutely necessary. And it was imperative they keep him fighting on more than one front. To that end, they both took several sideways steps, opening a larger gap between them, broadening the field of fire.

"Obsidian Ashmedai," Endora said calmly, "I arrest you in the name of the Tribunal for crimes against witchkind. Those crimes being murder, conspiracy, bribery, and the illegal practice of black magic."

He laughed and raised his hands.

Her agility carried her to safety, and Marcus's counterattack prevented Ash from immediately blasting at her again. But the sight of the spot where she'd stood—now a blackened hole three feet across and three feet deep—sobered her.

Of course, Ash didn't need to know that.

"Be advised," she stated as if nothing unusual had just happened, "if you do not surrender yourself willingly, I am authorized to use deadly force."

Ash answered that declaration with a shot that brought one of the huge banners suspended from the ceiling crashing down on her.

Or at least on where she'd been.

"Missed, Ash. Losing your touch? It happens as the birthdays start to pile up. They say the eyesight is the second thing to go. Right after your sex drive."

He fired at her again, but the bolt seared only the Stonehenge exhibit. "You can't kill me." His shout echoed around the cavernous space.

"Come on, Ash, let's be reasonable here," Marcus taunted. "You're outnumbered, and it's four hours until midnight. A pretty long time to fight us off while you wait for a power boost."

Marcus tucked, rolling toward the north side of the gallery as a wall disintegrated far behind where he'd just been.

"You forgot to add that we're way better looking than he is, too."

"Bitch!" Fury increased the potency of the energy Ashmedai sent this time. A support post and part of the second-floor balcony crumbled beside Endora. She stepped safely away.

Who are you calling a bitch? Glenna raced from cover and leaped at Ashmedai's back. But before she could lock her jaws on the back of his neck, his magic had hurled her head over tail toward a huge support column on the hall's west side. Suddenly, Mav leaped from cover and caught the dog around the chest just before she crashed headlong into the support. He continued to run, Glenna in his arms, to the shelter of the alcoves behind the monoliths.

To distract Ash from noticing Mav's presence, Marcus opened up with a barrage of fireballs that occupied all of his target's attention. As he tired, he moved steadily to his left, getting himself into a flanking position.

"Why doesn't he ever call you names?" Endora complained to him. "This is definitely not gender equity here."

She deflected a white-hot ball of flame then sent a trio of blasts back at Ashmedai.

"At least he didn't call you a lunkhead." Marcus, now directly opposite Endora, forced Ash to turn his back on one to attack the other.

The moment he did so, going after Marcus using a two-handed cast, Endora toasted the sorcerer's backside with a well-placed fireball of her own.

Ashmedai roared, spun, and sent a wild bolt in her general direction. It hit somewhere on the third floor.

"I have to admit, Ash, you didn't lie and call me a stupid bitch." Endora sent a shot that ricocheted off the floor at his feet, and she could barely stifle a huge grin when he had to dance fast or lose an appendage. "Because I'm not stupid."

"You are a buffoon!"

Endora laughed aloud, even as she dove away from flying plaster and wood chips. She knew her quirky sense of humor annoyed some people, but no one had ever called her names over it before. Ash was really losing control if he was letting her get to him in that way.

But to her mind, that was all to the good.

Keenly aware that the clock was moving relentlessly, Endora and the gang stalked and attacked, counterattacked and dodged, keeping Ash constantly off-balance, scoring minor hits at an ever-increasing rate. Glenna, although more cautious following her close call, still roamed the perimeter of the fight, her barks and growls drawing immediate fire from Ashmedai. By using his superhuman strength to lift display cases and hurl them at Ash, Mav presented another front to defend. The witch deflected each one of these projectiles without appearing to be struck by any of the artifacts, but this rigorous defense contributed to the dissipation of his magic. More and more frequently, his blasts were not carefully aimed, which sapped his strength and led to slower reflexes. But he was still frighteningly powerful.

And it was approaching midnight.

Goddess, I can't believe this guy, Endora said a bit

breathlessly. *We've been hammering him for over three hours, but he's still on his feet. He must be on supplements or something.*

Witches take supplements? Glenna's eyes glowed in the dark where she crouched beside a shattered display case.

Some witches do. It was too easy, but she had to take the opportunity or lose it forever. *They believe in the saying, "A steroid a day keeps the witch doctor away."*

If dogs could groan telepathically, Glenna did it. *You're twisted, you know that?*

Thank you.

Marcus effectively ended the banter. *All right, children, let's focus here. Time to use the candles and the willow net.* From his position diagonally across from Endora, he fired two quick power blasts at Ash, then ducked back behind cover as the counterattack came. *At this rate, we won't wear him down until after the Witching Hour. And then it'll be far too late.*

Endora popped up, sent a ball of magic rolling at their enemy, who was crouched by the stand holding the *Zohar.* The ball rolled quickly toward Ash, struck him from behind and engulfed him in a puff of choking purple smoke. As he coughed and sputtered out the counter-spell, Endora told Marcus, *I'll draw him into the center of the floor to increase the candles' effectiveness.*

All right. Glenna, give Mav the signal to get the willow net.

Endora saw where Ashmedai leaned heavily against the holy book's pedestal, and even from thirty feet away could detect his labored breathing. "Ready to surrender?"

The magic he sent against her had nowhere near the kick his previous efforts had achieved, but it still made her arms tremble as she held her protection spell against him. When the duel ended, she was numb from shoulders to fingertips from the effort. Yet she stood straight and still. "Can't beat a girl, Ash? That's pretty pitiful."

The insult was too much to bear. With a growl of rage, he charged her.

Only to be stopped in the middle of the exhibition area by the containment spell she cast. He spun away, found himself completely engulfed. And Marcus directly behind him, supporting Endora's casting.

"You can't have this much magic," he screamed. "It's impossible!"

Marcus shook his head sadly. "Ash, Ash, Ash...Tsk, tsk. I thought you of all witches would know enough about magic to realize nothing's impossible."

"This can't be happening!"

Ashmedai spun frantically in a circle, testing the boundaries of the spell with his hands. All three witches knew that attempting to blow a hole through it was far too dangerous to even consider. And his insanity didn't extend to foolishness of that magnitude.

Endora prayed hard to the goddess that Ash was too enraged to think clearly about his predicament. If he did, he'd realize that neither she nor Marcus had much experience with casting spells of such intensity. Having lost their magic so young, they'd never even practiced something requiring the amount of concentration it took to hold the containment. And even with Marcus's help, she could feel the spell starting to waver. *The net had better work this time.*

It will. We cast the spell together.

Bolstered by Marcus's confidence, she calmly said, "Now, Mav."

Just as the vampire reached Ashmedai, Endora and Marcus cut the containment spell. Mav threw the willow net over their captive's head, then stepped away from the instantly thrashing, writhing figure Ash became as the fully-charged willow strips settled over him.

"Happy Birthday, Ash," Endora crooned.

"Here's a light for your candles." Marcus snapped his fingers, and five hundred white candles lit in sequence, illuminating the tops of the monoliths and the entire balcony above them.

Endora extended her arms out shoulder high, palms facing toward Ash. Then she raised her hands above her shoulders, and the candles flared high, brightening the darkened museum with the most ancient form of illumination. "Let light drive out darkness."

Marcus stepped forward, stopping the exact same distance from Ashmedai as Endora was opposite him. He raised his hands as well, and the candles became torches. "Let love drive out hate."

Both Marcus and Endora took a step toward each other, tightening the cage they'd trapped their enemy in. After each had spoken a line of the chant, they stepped forward again.

"Let warmth drive out cold," Endora continued.

"Let courage drive out fear."

"Let knowledge drive out ignorance."

"Let kindness drive out cruelty."

They were now three steps away from Ashmedai as he cowered beneath the willow net, struggling against his constraints. His body trembled as if palsied, and his face was twisted in agony.

The candle flames burned three feet high, lighting the entire museum in an ever-intensifying brightness.

"Let good drive out evil." Endora brought her palms together, and the candles flared up another foot. She stood looking down at the witch who had caused her so much pain, and said calmly, "Obsidian Sammael Ashmedai, I arrest you in the name of—"

"Never!"

With a scream that sounded like the tortures of the damned, Ash raised both hands, pointed them at his face, and sent the last burst of magic he possessed directly at himself.

He was dead before his body stopped twitching.

"Goddess, what happened?" Marcus leaped forward, but it took only seconds to see there was no saving the witch who lay, smoke curling from his mouth, at their feet.

"I guess he didn't want to go through a trial by his peers."

Marcus removed the willow cage and rolled Ashmedai to his back. "To his way of thinking, he had no peers."

"Egotistical to the last."

Glenna padded over to sniff at Ashmedai. *He even smells evil.* She turned and moved to sit beside Marcus.

"He should have died hereafter," Mav paraphrased Shakespeare as he joined his friends.

"Was his life full of sound and fury, signifying nothing?" Endora asked, continuing the *Macbeth* motif. "Somehow, I don't believe that. It's far too simple."

Abruptly exhausted, she stared down at the dissipated body of a witch who had literally come within minutes of omnipotence, surprised to find her emotions mixed. Because of all the pain he'd caused her, she'd thought elation would accompany her triumph of gaining revenge on Ashmedai. But all she felt was relief, and a twinge of sadness.

Although they had intended to bring him to trial, this twisted, evil creature who preyed on the weak had been eliminated. There would be no second chance for corrupt officials to free him. Now, he would prey no more. That was the relief.

The sadness came from wondering what the sort of power Ashmedai possessed, and had sought to increase, would have done for the world had his intentions been good. She and Marcus would have been together for forty years instead of just now embarking on a life together. Josie would likely still be alive, and one hundred and one other witches would not have been mercilessly slaughtered. *No use looking back with regret*, she reminded herself.

"It's what we make of the future that's important," Marcus said, putting an arm around her shoulder and giving her a gentle squeeze.

What's that?

Glenna's acute hearing was all the warning they needed.

"Company." Marcus jerked his head toward the second floor. "Up there, guys." He scooped Glenna up and teleported. Endora did the same, while Mav threw Ashmedai's body over his shoulder before leaping from the top of the *Zohar* exhibit to a nearby monolith to the balcony.

"Good thinking, Mav." Marcus indicated a freestanding column. "Lay him down over there, out of sight."

They had little time to wait before two black-clad figures materialized near the place where Ashmedai's body had just lain. The two turned slowly in a circle, taking in the destruction all around them.

"The short little troll is Arthur Morass." Endora whispered for Mav's benefit. "I'm betting the tall guy is Mordecai Montrose, the Head Magistrate himself."

"He wasn't at your trial?" Marcus's low laugh was bitter. "He came to mine. Front and center. But the bastard didn't vouch for me and my mission." When Endora flashed him a questioning stare, he said, "Fortunately, the Magistrate who'd recruited me to go after Ash did."

"Lucky for me, too, since my sentence was totally predicated by yours."

Marcus stared down at the two magistrates. "These boys seem a bit confused. Should we enlighten them?" He started to stand up, but Endora grabbed his arm and kept him hidden.

"Think you can give me a few minutes, so I can leave the museum?" She saw him start to ask, and she filled him in. "I need to contact Cassie's mother. Medusa would want to be here for this, since she despises Morass for supporting Ashmedai."

"If she's got any friends who are current Tribunal members,

she should bring them. I'm sure they'd like to see this."

Endora nodded. "I'll check that out."

With that, she was gone.

Marcus turned to Mav. "Well, should we let them know we're here?"

"I would first like to observe their activities."

"That works." Marcus settled down to enjoy the show.

The two magistrates were even then closely examining the damage on the main level.

"Arthur, look at this." Montrose pointed to the crater Ash had blasted into the floor while trying to kill Endora. "This was done with magic."

"That's what I like about Montrose," Marcus murmured to Mav. "He's got an uncanny grasp of the obvious."

"All of this was done with magic." Morass looked around nervously. "It's after midnight. Where's Ashmedai?"

"Obsidian Ashmedai," Montrose called, staring hard into the gloom of the darkened exhibits. "Show yourself."

A snort of disgust burst from Marcus before he could stop it. "Our Head Magistrate is way too arrogant to understand that Ash would never answer to him."

"Had Ashmedai still been alive," Mav amended.

Marcus rolled his eyes. "You and Endora must have been separated at birth. You both have the same sick sense of humor."

"I have no siblings."

"Never mind, Mav." He turned his attention back to the magistrates. "Let's listen a little more before throwing a wet blanket on their planned celebration."

Likely, Morass would have preferred his voice to actually be steady when he said, "Ashmedai? It's Arthur Morass and Mordecai Montrose. We've come to congratulate you on your triumph."

"And set the terms for our collaboration. Come out."

"Oh, Monty, you'd have been the first magistrate Ash vaporized on his way to becoming a god." Marcus looked at Mav. "I think we can spoil the party now."

He started to tell Mav what he wanted but found himself fighting a sudden intense disgust for the plan he'd just devised.

"Is something wrong, Marcus?"

Ash is dead, and he was a monster, he told himself. *He doesn't deserve posthumous consideration of any kind.*

"Marcus?"

He took a deep breath. "When I give you the signal, I want you to toss Ashmedai's body down in front of our unwelcome guests. Okay?" At Mav's nod, Marcus rose a bit shakily and went to the balcony. "Wait for my cue."

The scene below hadn't changed much in the last minute. Both magistrates stood in the center of the floor, but now they were back to back, like the warriors of old who protected each other from enemies. Personally, Marcus wouldn't have wanted either of them at his back. They'd be far more likely to stab it than guard it.

He cleared his throat loudly to get their attention, then leaned both hands on the balcony rail. The grating sound it made when he touched it reminded him there wasn't much left in the building that was solid or completely whole. "Gentlemen, I'm afraid you've come at an awkward time."

Montrose snapped to attention. "Who are you? Where is Obsidian Ashmedai?"

Marcus sensed Endora's presence behind him. And she wasn't alone. Relief flooded him, as he realized he wouldn't have to desecrate Ash's body. *Tell Mav to put Ash's body down*, he silently told Endora. *I don't need him to carry out my original plan.*

She asked no questions, only moved to do what he'd asked. As she did so, Marcus sensed the others moving silently around the balcony to encircle the two magistrates below.

"Obsidian Ashmedai is dead," he stated harshly.

"Dead?" Morass's face clearly paled. "Who are you? What makes you say he's dead?"

"I say he's dead because I killed him."

With a little help from your friends, Glenna and Endora added.

Goes without saying.

Montrose was not so easily convinced. "Impossible!"

"Impossible?" Marcus baited. "Witches are mortal, are they not? And, since Ashmedai was a witch, he was also mortal."

"Who are you?" Montrose roared. "Show yourself!"

Why do so many witches shout? Glenna asked.

Just the males do, Endora answered mildly. *They get really cranky when they discover we females have stronger magic.*

We'll discuss that sexist statement later, Marcus said, turning to where Ash's body lay and, using a palms up gesture, raising it from the floor. He levitated it through the air, gently setting it down at Montrose's feet. "Satisfied, gentlemen?"

Morass gaped in abject terror. "Who could have done this?"

"This can't be!" Montrose raged. "We reinstated his powers before his birthday, even strengthened them, so he could destroy Endora Bast and Marcus Morion."

"And why did you need to destroy them," Marcus asked coldly.

"That bitch Endora Bast came to Ashmedai's circle," Montrose ranted. "The Tribunal had sent Morion in to infiltrate, but he was supposed to be the scapegoat for the murders."

"Why does everyone think I'm a bitch?" Endora groused.

"They don't know you well enough to love you like I do." Marcus flashed her a grin before he shouted to Montrose, "You still haven't said why Bast and Morion had to be destroyed."

"She and Morion are cosmic twins! Once we gave Ashmedai back his powers, they were the only ones who could kill him."

"And that's why the bastards kept us apart for forty years," Endora hissed. "I'd like to—"

Blinding white light suddenly wiped away all darkness in the building.

"And to what end did you give back his powers, Mordecai?"

Montrose spun toward the voice. "Millicent? What are you doing here?"

Millicent was the ancient witch who'd spoken for the Tribunal at Endora's meeting in New Orleans. Medusa stood to her immediate right, looking grimly resolute. Directly across from where she and Marcus stood, Endora was delighted to see Cassie. But this definitely wasn't the time to call out to her best friend. All seven of the witches who stood silently around the balcony were wearing formal black robes. Not a single one's expression even remotely conveyed humor.

"It is I who am asking the questions here, Mordecai." The old witch's tone could have frozen Hades over. "Answer me. To what end did you overrule a Tribunal mandate and commute a convicted witch's sentence?"

Montrose's jaw set. He locked his knees and stood straight as a T-square. "I stand mute."

"Arthur?" Millicent's tone warmed to slightly less glacial. "We know what you did. Don't make us torture the reasons out of the two of you."

Fourteen

Morass's personal courage was no match for a threat of such magnitude. He broke down in sobs. "Mordecai thought we could control him," he babbled.

"Shut up, you idiot!" Montrose raised his hand as if to strike Morass, but the blow never fell.

It was stopped by the spell cast by a younger male witch. He extended his hands to hold the magical restraints on Montrose.

Millicent's gaze was pitiless. "And by controlling him, do you mean to say you sought to control all of witchkind?"

"Yes." Morass collapsed on the floor, weeping like a heartbroken child.

"Arthur Morass and Mordecai Montrose, I arrest you on behalf of the Tribunal," Millicent said coldly. "The charges are treason, fraud, conspiracy, accessory to murder and intent to commit murder." She signaled to the witch casting the restraining spell and one other male. "Hold them. Arabella, summon the rest of the Tribunal. We'll meet here immediately to settle this."

As the tall, dark-haired witch nodded and left to do Millicent's bidding, the old witch turned to Medusa. "Well, this is certainly a mess."

"But one that's far less complicated with Obsidian Ashmedai dead."

The old witch looked down at the body. "I shudder to think of what would have become of us had he not been stopped." She looked up, then followed her friend's gaze to where Medusa's daughter was enthusiastically hugging Endora Bast. "And I know just who gets our thanks for that."

* * *

"Cassie! What are you doing here?" The moment Morass and Montrose had been taken into custody, Endora had literally flown across the atrium to her friend's side. "You look like you're ready to bring Troilus and Cressida into the world right now."

Cassie's eyes were filled to the brim. "I had to come, Endora. When Mom said you and Marcus were all right, well—"

Endora hugged her fiercely. "No tears, Cass." She turned to Marcus, beckoning him closer with the crook of her finger. "I want you to introduce you to someone."

Marcus stepped forward, suddenly aware that his clothes were dirty and ripped. Several cuts and scrapes were visible beneath the torn clothing, and his hair must have carried a pound of plaster dust. Wonderful first impression he was about to make.

Endora's smile nearly split her face. "Cassie, meet Marcus Morion, my soul-mate, my lover, and the witch least equipped for the sidekick role of any in history. Marcus, this is Cassandra Hathorne-Sandor, my best friend, my employer, and the witch who saved my life about forty years ago."

Whatever doubts Marcus may have had that Endora's best friend would accept him were erased when she raised her beautiful caramel-brown eyes to his and gave him an achingly sweet smile.

"You have no idea how happy I am to have the chance to meet you at all, given the trial you've just been through, Marcus," she said, grasping his hand. "Thank you for watching over Dora."

"It was certainly my pleasure."

"And it was the other way around," Endora cracked. "I watched over him."

As all of them laughed, Glenna butted her head against Endora's leg. *Hey, what about me?*

Endora bent down and gave the dog a good scratching behind the ears. "And this pathetic excuse for a canine is Glenna, also known as Wonder Dog." Endora turned her head sideways to grin up at Cassie. "She saved my assets a couple nights ago, so I've made her an honorary cat."

Glenna made a sound that closely mimicked a human snort. *As if I'd want to be some pussy. Cat.*

Cassie laughed and bent to shake the dog's paw. *Pleased to meet you, Miss Glenna. And thanks for helping out.*

Glenna cocked her head. *Actually, I like Endora. She gives me treats. So I forgive her for being feline.*

Very noble of you. Cassie looked up as Medusa approached, Millicent at her side. "Mom. Aunt Millicent."

With a nod of acknowledgment to Cassie, the elder witch strode up to Marcus and extended her hand. Her grip belied the years she claimed in the deep wrinkles of her face. "I'm Millicent Merlin." Releasing his hand, she shook Endora's with equal strength. "I speak for the Tribunal and all witches when I say we cannot properly thank you for all you have done here.

You have, quite literally, saved us all."

"I'd like to honestly say it was my pleasure," Marcus stated, smiling wryly. "But there was very little pleasant about it." He gave Endora a wink that said she was the pleasure he referred to.

"I can see that." With a flick of her hand, Millicent restored Marcus and Endora to their pre-fight condition.

"Wow, it feels good to be clean again," Endora stated. She examined her hands and arms. "And to not have all sorts of scrapes and scratches."

Millicent nodded. "It's the least I could do." Turning to Medusa, she added, "Would you consent to meet with the Tribunal tonight? I'd like your historical perspective on Obsidian Ashmedai. It will certainly help in our sentencing of Arthur and Mordecai."

"I would be honored." Medusa turned to Cassie and gave her a quick kiss on the cheek. "How do you feel, and how are Betty and Veronica doing?"

"We're all fine, Mom."

Next, Medusa gave Endora a quick kiss before she could squirm away. Extending her hand to Marcus, she said, "I'm Medusa Morlock, Cassandra's mother. I've heard quite a bit about you, Marcus."

Quickly assessing her, Marcus concluded Medusa would make a powerful friend. And an even more formidable enemy. He gave her a half bow. "And I've heard much of you, as well. I guess I should thank you for helping Endora." He saw from the corner of his eye that Endora was starting to squirm. "Things worked out very well."

"I was glad to offer my assistance. And glad Endora finally paid attention to my advice." Medusa turned to her daughter's familiar. "Dora, please watch over Cassandra while I'm with the Tribunal. And if Lucy and Ethel decide to come on the scene, interrupt the meeting and get me out of there. I refuse to miss the birth of my first grandchildren." She held up her hand to her daughter. "Not a word, Cassandra. You know you're too near your time to be out having these kinds of adventures."

"She almost ordered me to stay home," Cassie told Marcus and Endora. "But Mick stood up to her, bless his heart. Said I needed to be here with you."

"That's what happens when humans enter the picture," Medusa commented, a twinkle in her eyes. "That son-in-law of mine gives me no respect." She blew kisses at her daughter as she turned. "I must go. This meeting will likely take the rest of the night, so go somewhere comfortable."

"We'll take Cassie to the safe house," Endora called after Medusa. Then she turned to see a confused Marcus staring after Cassie's mother. "I thought you said Cassie's naming her children Troilus and Cressida."

Both Cassie and Endora laughed hysterically.

"Mick and I have been guarding the babies' names with our lives," Cassie finally managed to say when she caught her breath. "So, it's been a huge game among family and friends to try to catch me out. For some reason, everyone thinks if they say some outrageous name, I'm going to get upset and blurt out the ones we've decided on."

"So, I guess Salt and Pepper aren't among those choices?" he asked, straight-faced.

Cassie turned to Endora with a grin. "Now I know why you love this guy. Better keep him."

* * *

True to her promise to Medusa, Endora and Marcus took Cassie directly to the condo and settled her in Endora's bed for the rest of the night. Then, they set about repairing the damage Ash had done before the final confrontation in the museum. Working together, order had been restored in less than half an hour.

"Where's Mav?"

"Don't know." Marcus tested the hinges he'd just repaired, then closed the cupboard doors and stood up. "He took off as soon as Art and Mortie got arrested."

"Think he's all right?"

With a growl, he caged her between his arms and the counter where she had just finished mending the last broken dish, and kissed the top of her head. "He's fine. Probably out hunting." Nuzzling the side of her neck, he pressed himself along her back. When she turned to look over her shoulder at him, he kissed her thoroughly. "It's one-thirty in the morning, and I'm not at all tired."

Endora's smile was wicked as she turned and draped her arms around his neck. Rubbed up against him like the cat she was. "What do you want to do to kill time until Medusa gets here?"

"Well, we haven't made love in over eight hours. Why

don't we start there?"

"Race you to the bedroom."

She won, but only because he hit his head against the doorframe as he vaulted from the living area over the balcony into the bedroom. She laughed, kissed the bump on his head, then ripped off his clothes. Within minutes, he had other things to think about than a headache.

* * *

They were all up and around when Mav came in at nine the next morning.

Cassie immediately went on alert.

Friend, not foe, Endora told her silently. She rose from the sofa, grabbed Mav by the hand and dragged him over to where Cassie sat in the recliner. "Cassie, this is our friend and fellow Gang of Four member, Eripmav Alucard, Mav for short."

Both of Cassie's dark brows shot up to her hairline. "As in Dracula Vampire spelled backward?"

"My family were big fans of Bram Stoker," the vampire placidly replied.

"Mav, you made a joke!" Endora elbowed him in the ribs. "Listen to you, ya big galoot."

"Galoot?"

Marcus had just entered from the back hall, Glenna at his heels. "It's a term of endearment. But let me warn you, buddy. If you think you're going to steal my woman, you've got another think coming."

Endora snorted and shot him a disgusted look. "*Your* woman?"

"Me Tarzan, you Jane." Cassie made apelike sounds. "Typical male attitude."

"Marcus, I must speak with you in private," Mav said earnestly.

"Sure, no problem. Let's go in the office."

They headed for the tiny office located on the other side of the downstairs bathroom.

Once they were gone, Endora caught Cassie up on Mav's story. "He's a really great guy, Cass," she concluded. "I feel so sorry for him."

"He seems to be handling the situation fairly well."

Endora shrugged. "I've only known him for six days, so I can't tell whether that's true or not."

"You can only do for him what any friend can. Be there if

he needs you." Cassie smiled warmly. "Like you've always been for me."

"It goes both ways between us, of course." Suddenly restless, Endora brewed bat wing tea for herself and Cassie and brought the mugs to the living area.

Cassie studied her intently as she passed over the mug. "I know that look, Dora. What's on your mind?"

Even though Cassandra Hathorne was her best friend in the world, Endora still had trouble opening up completely to anyone. She supposed it was the feline aspect of her nature that made her reticent, but it bothered her more and more as she got older. She promised herself that, from that moment on, she'd try her hardest to express herself to those she loved.

"I've been thinking a lot since last night, Cass."

"You've had time to think?" She teased gently. "I thought Marcus kept you way too busy for anything cerebral."

Endora felt her face flame. Instantly, her defense mechanisms kicked into full protection mode. And her new resolve blew all the way to Hades. "Um. Never mind. It, ah, wasn't very important."

Instantly, Cassie's expression turned contrite. "Stop that right now. I shouldn't have teased you, and I'm sorry I did. Now, you do have something on your mind, so stop locking down and tell me what it is."

Endora sighed unhappily. This openness thing was so hard. "Dora."

"All right. I, uh, I thought that, since I was lucky enough to regain all my magic, I should use it to do good."

An encouraging nod preceded, "Excellent idea."

"But there's a problem. At least I perceive it as one."

When Endora added nothing more for a long minute, Cassie prompted with, "And that problem is?"

"I don't know exactly how to use all this magic." She sipped her tea just to give herself an excuse not to say anything.

"That's understandable. Having very little magic for so long, you've had little chance to practice your skills. But is that such a problem?"

"I guess not." She knew she was dying to ask, but the words caught halfway out of her throat. Closing her eyes, she focused as if casting a spell. Then she swallowed, took a deep breath, and blurted out, "Do you think Medusa would agree to tutor me until I got back up to speed? I mean, I'm not exactly sure how long that will take, or how many hours of the day I'd have to work with her. Or even how many days of the week. Would she even want to work with me? Maybe I'm just not good enough to warrant a witch of her stature tutoring me, but I'd try my hardest, and—"

"And, why don't you ask her?" Cassie finally managed to interrupt Endora's nervous babbling.

"Ask me what?" In her typically flamboyant manner, Medusa materialized in a puff of red smoke. She looked at her daughter and then at her familiar. "Ask me what, Endora?"

"I, well…" Suddenly tongue-tied, Endora lowered her head and wouldn't look up.

When Cassie started to explain, Medusa, shook her head, silencing her. Then she moved to sit next to Endora on the couch. "Millicent Merlin has been elected High Magistrate to take that worm Montrose's place."

"What happened to him and Morass?" Cassie asked.

Medusa's look turned grim. "Both are scheduled for execution at midnight tonight. I could attend if I wanted, but I think I'll pass. I suggested the Tribunal immediately institute some checks and balances go into immediate effect, and they were approved."

Endora, nearly choking on terror from worrying that Medusa wouldn't want to train her, seemed to be paralyzed, so she didn't raise her head to ask the question foremost in her mind.

Cassie asked a different one. "What checks and balances?"

"In order to prevent another Ashmedai fiasco, the Tribunal will rely on the majority of the witch population to remove incompetent or dangerously unbalanced Tribunal members."

"That makes sense," Cassie agreed.

"No handful of power-hungry magistrates will ever threaten us again."

Just then, Marcus and Mav entered from the office. Seeing Medusa, Marcus nodded politely. "Mav, come over here and meet Medusa Morlock."

Endora's head came up as Marcus and Mav approached. She smiled wanly at Marcus when he caught her eye.

"Medusa, I'd like you to meet a friend of mine without whom we never would have beaten Obsidian Ashmedai. This is Eripmav Alucard. Mav for short."

Medusa extended her hand. She didn't flinch when Mav's ice cold one pressed hers, palm to palm. "I'm pleased to meet you, Mav."

"And I, you, madam." Mav's tone was even more formal than usual. "Early this morning, I returned the Cauldron of Cerridwen. And I have just informed Marcus that I must leave."

His declaration shocked Endora more than she could say. "This very minute?"

"Yes."

"But why?"

Marcus headed off her protest. "We'll discuss this later, Endora." Throwing his arm around the vampire, he walked him to the door. "Let me know if you need anything, Mav. Anytime, day or night."

Mav clasped Marcus's hand in both of his. "You have been a good friend. I will miss you."

"Will you miss me, too?" Endora asked, jumping up to hurry to the door.

Mav turned to her as she stopped beside Marcus. "I will miss you most of all."

She stood on tiptoe to kiss him on his sallow cheek. "Stay safe, Mav."

"I will."

He was gone in seconds.

"Sorry for the drama. But this was something important that couldn't wait." Immediately, Marcus became the gracious host. "Can I get anyone anything? Medusa?"

"I'm fine. In fact, I'm not here just to pay a social call." Medusa adjusted her brightly-colored turban. "I've something to discuss with both of you. Is now all right?"

Endora and Marcus shared a look.

"Our calendar's open," she said.

"Fine." Medusa studied both of them. "You might want to sit down."

"Oh for goddess's sake, Mom," Cassie groaned. "Cut to the chase. The suspense is killing me."

Medusa smiled. "Anticipation is half the fun, Daughter."

"No it isn't," Endora muttered as she returned to her previous seat.

Marcus took the overstuffed chair opposite hers.

Medusa's smile was enigmatic. "In order to spare my daughter, I'll get right to the point. The Tribunal now has two open seats. Since the two of you have demonstrated courage, integrity, loyalty, and ingenuity, the magistrates have authorized me to approach you to fill those positions." When even her daughter's jaw dropped, Medusa hurried to reassure them. "This is just until the two current terms are up, and then you'd be up for review for the full fifty-year appointment. Arthur Morass had five more years to serve. Marcus, the Tribunal has requested that you fill that spot." She turned to Endora. "The remaining magistrates are hoping you'll finish Mordecai Montrose's remaining fifteen years."

Complete panic seized Endora. She wanted to run, to howl, to shape shift into a cat and never be human again. She jumped to her feet. "No. I...I can't."

Three gazes were immediately riveted to her face.

"And why not?" Medusa asked calmly. "What factors do you feel should eliminate you from contention?"

Endora squashed the urge to run her hands through her hair. "Well, for one, I don't have enough magic skills to qualify."

"It is the Tribunal's opinion that you could become Head Magistrate before you're seventy-five."

"Well, what do they know?" This was too much. She felt like her skin was going to crack open and her soul would pop right out and blow away. Anxiety had her starting to pace the living area.

"Why don't you ask Mom the question you were worrying about?" Endora stopped pacing toward the front windows and whirled to fix an icy glare on Cassie. It didn't faze Cassie in the least. "You said yourself you wanted Mom to tutor you."

"Stow it, Cass."

Despite being eight and a half months pregnant and sitting reclined in a chair, Cassandra Hathorne-Sandor would not be ordered to yield. "Stow it yourself, Dora. You know I'm right."

Bat shit. Yes, she was exactly right. That didn't mean Endora had to like it. Fortunately, feline practicality won out over pride. If she never asked, she'd never have a chance to get what she wanted. She hardly flinched when she looked the formidable Medusa Morlock in the eye and said, "Before you came here this morning, I was telling Cassie that I needed help with my magic. And I was wondering how busy you are, since I need a tutor."

Medusa's slow smile was brighter than a harvest moon. "What a coincidence. I just this morning received approval to be your mentor, Endora. Millicent has been asked to tutor Marcus." He jerked reflexively, surprise and delight on his face. "You'll like her, Marcus. Millicent is a fabulous teacher."

"Do we get any time to think about this?" Endora asked, still trying to comprehend that she could have what she'd wanted so badly. Medusa Morlock to help hone her magic.

"The Tribunal wants this deal done by noon tomorrow." Medusa studied first Marcus then Endora. "Should Cassie and I leave you two alone to discuss this?"

"I think it would be best," Marcus answered for them.

"I have to get back to Massachusetts, anyway." Cassie sighed. "Mick will be tearing his hair out if I'm gone much longer." She rose awkwardly from the chair and waddled over to Endora. Hugging her hard, she kissed her on the cheek. Then she did the same to Marcus. "Follow your heart, Dora. In this and all things. Only you know exactly what you need most. Marcus, take care of her, or you'll answer to me."

"I will, Cassie."

Medusa rose from the sofa to join her daughter. "I'll be back at noon tomorrow for your decisions."

Cassie and Medusa blinked out together.

Endora moved to the stairs and sat down on the bottom one. "Before we discuss what just went on, tell me about Mav."

Marcus sighed. "He's gone off to Europe, hoping to find a cure for his dyslexia."

"But if he finds a cure, that won't make him human, will it?"

Marcus walked over, sat on the stair beside Endora. "No, but at least he'll be able to have a normal vampire life."

"Goddess, what a choice." She leaned her head on his shoulder, and he wrapped his arm around her waist. "Did he say why he's all of a sudden decided to do this?"

"During the fight with Ash, when Mav's dyslexia short-circuited for a while, he realized he could act for good if he functioned like regular vampires do."

"That's really incredible. I hope he can figure out how to do that."

Marcus chuckled. "He could start the Vampire Justice League."

"I think he'd look pretty silly wearing tights, though. He's not too buff."

"You're so twisted." He kissed her hair. Then he gathered

her in his arms, resting his chin on the top of her head. "What do you think, babe? Should we take the jobs?"

"I'm scared spitless I'll screw up," she said without lifting her head to look at him.

He gave her a reassuring squeeze. "There's always a chance we'll make mistakes. But the Tribunal's made up of thirteen members, so we won't be alone in our decision making."

She had wanted to ask Medusa for help, and instead Medusa had approached her with an offer of aid. How could she throw away this chance? "Do you want to join the Tribunal?"

"Forty years ago, it was my only goal. Now my priorities have changed. But, still, I'd love to be in a position to do some good."

"Me too." She sighed. "I'm going to agree to the Tribunal's harebrained proposal."

Her heart lurched when she felt Marcus grow very tense. When he released her and took a step back, a somber expression in his gorgeous dark eyes, her heart started a mad gallop.

"Endora, I have a very important question to ask you."

When he left that hanging between them, her anxiety climbed. "Just spit it out."

He got down on one knee, took both her hands in his and said, "My alter-ego, Marco the Magnificent, has grown weary of his gypsy life. He wants a wife, a family, and no travel obligations. He wants to settle down forever with the one he loves more than his own life. Endora Bast, will you marry me?"

She yanked on his hands, trying to pull him upright. "Get up. Get up right now."

Laughing, he rose gracefully to his feet. "Was it something I said?"

"Don't ever do that to me again, Marcus," she scolded.

Now confusion marred his handsome features. "Do what again? Propose to you?"

"Get on your knees to beg."

His temper flared. "I wasn't begging, you nitwit. I was proposing!"

She started to argue, saw the angry disappointment in his eyes, and froze. Based on her reaction to his proposal, he thought her answer was no. Goddess, would she ever learn to say the right thing at the right time? "I know that. I mean, yes. Yes, I'll marry you."

With a war whoop that shook the pots and pans, Marcus scooped her up in his arms and spun her around the room. Then he kissed her until her eyes began to cross.

When he finally let her go, she found her knees rather weak and had to hold on to him to regain her balance. "I take it the answer pleases you."

"You please me, Head Magistrate in Training. You please me more than anything in the world."

"Was it worth the wait?"

"Only because I was waiting for you." He kissed her deeply. "It sort of works that way when someone owns your heart."

"And now we've got time to more fully explore that soul-mate thing we've got going on."

"Medusa's not due back here for about twenty-four hours." The leer Marcus gave Endora was purely wicked. "Let's start the exploration right now."

She laughed. "Lead on, Marco Polo."

"That's Marco the Magnificent to you."

She knew he'd prove that nickname in short order. And she couldn't stop grinning as he led her to the bedroom.

Epilogue

"They're beautiful, Cassie."

Endora stood in the bright, airy nursery of Cassie and Mick's ancient New England farm house and looked down at the tiny boy and girl nestled side by side in a large bassinet. Seven-week old Cassandra Endora Sandor and Mirek Marcus Sandor studied her solemnly.

"We're leaning toward keeping them." Cassie, sitting in the rocking chair near the window, adjusted her maternity top.

"Amazing how fast they came once your labor started."

"A miracle Mom and I made it back here in time. It would have been extremely messy to have not just one baby but two in the middle of a teleportation."

Endora snorted. "Fat chance of that happening without you breaking some sort of birthing speed record. About equivalent to the speed of light, in fact. Besides, Medusa would never have let anything bad happen. I think she could stop the sun if she really wanted to."

Cassie hadn't actually started labor during her trip home from the LoDo condominium. That just made for a good story. However, no sooner had she and Medusa materialized in Cassie's kitchen, but she went into labor. Twelve hours later, she had presented her husband with darling fraternal twins. And reasoning that when someone saves the universe they should at least have one child named after them, Mick and Cassie had scrapped their original choices and chosen to give their daughter Endora's name and their son Marcus's.

"And thanks so much for agreeing to host tonight's festivities. That was extremely generous of you, given the time of year and the new babies and all."

"What are friends for?" Cassie shrugged. "Besides, your being here works really well for me. I wouldn't miss this for anything. Now, I don't have to take the babies anywhere or arrange for a sitter. So, win-win."

"It's still a huge undertaking."

"Well, you only turn sixty once."

"That and a few other things." Endora's grin was wide.

"Bring Cass over first, would you?"

At her friend's request, Endora hesitated. She stared down at the bright eyes staring right back at her and felt her palms go sweaty.

"She won't break unless you drop her," Cassie said wryly.

Endora jumped back as if she'd been given an electrical shock. "Goddess, why'd you have to say that?"

"Because I *know* you won't drop her. So, lighten up." Cassie remained silent a moment while Endora fretted, then calmly said, "Honorary aunts have been picking up infants from time immemorial and bringing them to their mothers to be fed. Don't break the chain, Dora, or organ harvesters will submerge you in ice in your own bathtub and remove your kidneys."

Endora felt a shaky laugh rattle out of her chest. "Funny, Cass." But still she hesitated.

"Come on, Dora." Cassie's tone had shifted from coaxing to desperate. "My milk has dropped, and I've got to get on with this right now."

"Oh! I—" Clearing her mind of terror and replacing it with Cassie's baby-handling instructions, Endora reached into the bassinet. She slid her right hand under little Cass's head and her left hand all the way up from the baby's diaper-clad butt to her shoulders. Then she lifted the six-pound infant gently off the flannel sheet and held her to her chest. The baby raised her small fist and smacked Endora right on the chin.

"I think she likes me!" Grinning, Endora forgot her misgivings and moved without misstep to the rocker.

"Of course she likes you. You're her Aunt Endora." Cassie had no such reservations about handling infants, so the transfer from aunt to mom went smoothly, and soon Cass was happily getting her meal from her mother's breast. "All right, Rek's next."

While Cass had her father's exact coloring–the black hair and electric blue eyes of his Slovak heritage–Rek shared Cassie's features. His hair was a dark-chocolate brown, and his eyes caramel colored. Endora still had butterflies in her stomach when she picked him up, but they were no longer the size of 747's. They felt more along the lines of single engine twin-seaters.

Once Rek had joined his sister at breakfast, Endora pulled up the ottoman and sat next to her friend and soon to be former employer. She studied the room with its bright yellow walls and dark blue ceiling that boasted a galaxy of stars and a glowing full moon. She studied her beautiful friend, infants at her breasts. Endora didn't know if she herself was cut out to be a mother. But it was obvious Cassie was.

"You look wonderful together," she said quietly. "Like a magazine ad for the good life we all dream of."

Cassie's smile was as bright as the yellow paint on the walls. "It certainly feels like the good life." She shifted Rek so he could get more milk, then looked directly at Endora. "And it sounds like you're going to start enjoying the good life as well. It's about time."

"Do you think it was a good thing that I took the position with the Tribunal? It doesn't seem like it to me."

"Don't start with that 'I'm not worthy' stuff again," Cassie said firmly. "The consensus is that, even though your talent is raw right now, it's enormous, with almost unlimited potential. And Mom says you've already made amazing progress."

Endora shrugged. "Your mother's a good teacher."

"That's part of it. But word is, you've been working like a dog."

"Tough to do when you're a cat."

"Ha. Give yourself some credit, Endora. Why the lack of self-esteem all of a sudden? Lately, I haven't seen much of the cocky, mouthy business manager who's worked for me for forty years."

That brought Endora up short. She crossed her right leg over the left, grabbed her knee with both hands and leaned back, thinking hard. For the entire time she'd worked for Cassie, she'd maintained a façade of competent cockiness that had seen her through her darkest times and left no one the wiser. Now, when she had regained much of what she'd lost so long ago, that façade had almost completely collapsed. "I guess that was the persona and not the person," she said slowly. "I projected confidence, even arrogance, because I felt so insecure."

Endora didn't know how Cassie managed with both babies still suckling, but she gently touched Endora's knee. "Well, now you're on your way to getting real confidence."

"Actually, I am." It felt good to admit that was the truth. "I guess doubting myself is just more comfortable, since I've been doing it for so long."

"No more, though."

"Well...." She grinned when Cassie shot her a dark look. "No more."

Cassie looked up at Endora. "Here, take Cass and burp her. She's all done for now."

This time, Endora wasn't so hesitant. She took Cass from her mother, cradled the baby against her shoulder, then patted Cass's back until she belched like brats and beer fanatic. Then Endora slowly waltzed around the room, making low crooning sounds. The baby seemed to enjoy that, because soon she was asleep against her honorary aunt's neck. By the time Endora had made a second swing around the room, Cass's brother had finished his meal as well.

Cassie burped Rek and rearranged her undergarments just as the sound of hearty male laughter echoed down the hallway.

"Sounds like the guys are back." Cassie rocked her son against her shoulder. The sound of hearty male laughter echoed down the hallway.

"Sounds like the guys are back." Cassie burped Rek and rearranged her undergarments and maternity top. Then she rocked him against her shoulder.

"I'm amazed at how well Marcus and Mick get along." Endora continued to sway. "It was practically best friends at first sight."

"Well, considering Marcus is a huge M. S. Kazimer fan, why shouldn't they like each other?"

Mick Sandor had earned countless fans and huge sums of money as horror writer M. S. Kazimer, but he had left that success behind after the capture of a serial killer who patterned his crimes after Mick's books. It was during the hunt for that killer that Cassie had met and fallen in love with Mick. Since he felt the same way about her, a merger had quickly ensued.

Now he wrote children's books and was more than happy to put all of his dark stories behind him.

Suddenly, it grew quiet in the hall. Cassie rolled her eyes at Endora, then shifted her gaze to the door. A dark head with wisps of grey at the temples poked around the door frame.

"Hey, women," Mick said in a stage whisper. "What's shakin'?"

"George and Gracie are asleep," Cassie stage whispered right back. "So come on in and ravish us."

"Love to." Mick crossed the floor with quick yet silent strides and planted a long, intense kiss on his wife's lips.

She raised her hand to hold him there a moment longer, then released him, murmuring, "Pretty good for a warm-up."

Endora's jaw dropped. Was this what being a wife and mother did to normally self-controlled females? She glanced in Marcus's direction. His expression was wolfish, to say the least. As he started toward her, she brandished Cass like a shield. "Hey, no ravishing here, buddy. I'm on aunt duty."

He moved to wrap her loosely in his arms, the baby cuddled between them. "Not even as a birthday present?" he teased, eyes twinkling.

"You should be ashamed of yourself, Marcus Morion, acting that way in front of an infant." She scooted her niece up and looked into her eyes. "Don't listen to him, Cass. You're far too young to learn about the deceptive male of the species."

Marcus laughed and kissed Endora on the forehead. "That's all right. I'll have my wedding night later."

Feeling her face flame, she swatted him on the shoulder.

"And speaking of wedding nights." Cassie, using Mick's hand to lever herself up, rose from the rocker and laid Rek in the bassinet. "I've got something for you, Endora."

"You didn't need to get me anything, Cass. You're already doing way too much." She moved to carefully place Cass beside Rek and follow Cassie to the nursery closet.

"Of course I had to. I'm the matron of honor." Cassie reached up to the top shelf and brought down a fancy hat box that looked to be from the nineteenth century. "It's for the 'something old' part of your ensemble."

She opened the box to reveal a delicate silver shawl. Woven into the thin silver threads were stars, moons and suns. The effect was dazzling.

Endora found she couldn't speak above a whisper. "Isn't that Medusa's wedding shawl?"

"Yes. And, as you know, mine as well." Cassie lifted the beautiful garment out of the box and held it out to her friend. "Mom wants you to wear this."

Endora's eyes filled with uncharacteristic tears. "I'd be honored."

"Now, before I go all new-mom hormonal on all of you, let's leave the babies to sleep so we can get ready for tonight." Cassie hugged Endora close, released her, and left the nursery.

"When my wife speaks, people listen. If they don't, she turns them into toads." Grinning, Mick moved to give Endora a hug as well. Then he kissed her cheek before releasing her. "You're going to make a beautiful bride, Dora. I hope Marcus knows just what a lucky witch he is."

"Oh he does," Marcus said, smiling. "He does indeed." He crooked his arm to Endora and escorted her from the room.

Endora, feeling far more serious than she liked, looked up at Marcus as they moved down the hallway to the guest room they were using. "Think we're doing the right thing?"

He slowed to a stop. "Getting cold feet about the wedding?"

"No."

"So, what's on your mind?" He ran a hand lightly through the hair at her temple. "Want to elope?"

"Not a chance. We've got too many guests coming, and Cassie and Mick went to all the trouble to have it here." She clasped his waist, laid her head on his shoulder. "Were we right to join the Tribunal?"

He closed his eyes, a grin lighting his features. "Is that what you're worried about?"

She squeezed him closer. "I guess."

"Look at me, Endora." Grasping her chin, he gently levered her head up. "This is the right thing. The only thing we could do. We're warriors, love. And warriors need a cause. The Tribunal protects the greater good of all witchkind. And we're a part of that. All right?"

With a sigh, she replied, "All right."

He stared at her. "It can't be that simple. You've got something else on your mind."

Her smile had returned to its mischievous norm when she said, "I was just thinking that, by combining our sixtieth birthday party with our wedding, we're cheating ourselves out of lots of gifts."

He laughed. "Guess our future birthday bashes will be in the afternoon and anniversary celebrations in the evening. Two sets of invitations, with requests for presents in each."

"Good thinking. That suits my mercenary heart to a tee." She kissed him deeply. "But you really are the only present I want. Even though you're turning sixty."

"I'm a witch! I haven't even hit my prime." He pulled her closer still, let her feel his heartbeat, strong and steady, against her chest. Let the magic that pulsed between them surround them, flow from one to the other, bind them more closely than any vow could ever do. "Besides, you're right there with me."

"Always, and in every way."

Some Practical Magic
ISBN: 1-893896-37-4

"Kitchen Witch" Cassandra Hathorne doesn't know what she's getting herself into. To escape her mother's relentless matchmaking, Cassie jumps at the opportunity to go on a book tour headlined by blockbuster horror novelist M. S. Kazimer. Even though Mick's not one of her own kind, sparks fly between them. But he has a secret more disturbing than Cassie's being an actual witch. With a serial killer who's been copycatting the murders in M. S. Kazimer's books now stalking the tour, Cassie must choose between keeping Mick's love and protecting them all with her practical magic.

Writing as Laurie Carroll

A War of Hearts
ISBN: 1-893896-80-3

Sir Jeremy Blaine hopes to retire to a life of peace after fighting on foreign soil. But the lands promised Jeremy have been stolen, and he must fight for them. Healer Alicen Kent swore an oath at her dying mother's bedside to remain neutral in any conflict. But when Jeremy brings her the critically wounded rightful Duke of Tynan, Alicen is forced to harbor a central figure in the conflict ravaging her shire. Dedicated to her healing, Alicen wants no husband, but the amulet she wears has a spiritual mate—the dagger carried by Sir Jeremy. Kaitlyn O'Rourke's ghost guides her daughter's healing hand. But can she guide Alicen's heart?

Write to the Author

Laurie loves to hear from her readers. You can write to her at:

Laurie C. Kuna
PO Box 557
Ada, MI 49301

Printed in the United States
41747LVS00002B/313-333

9 781933 417769